DARK SURVIVOR ECHOES OF LOVE

THE CHILDREN OF THE GODS BOOK 21

I. T. LUCAS

CONTENTS

GRUD

*H*unched low, Grud crept from one shaded spot to the next while listening for signs of pursuit, or any sounds at all for that matter.

But other than the occasional vehicle traveling up or down the road bordering the industrial park, there was nothing. It was as if the entire area was deserted.

Except, he knew it wasn't true.

He was there, and so were the four immortals inside the facility he'd just escaped from—the woman, Dur, Shaveh, and Mordan.

There was also the driver of the car parked outside the building. Grud still hadn't heard the car door opening, nor had he heard the engine turning on, which meant that the driver was just sitting there.

Doing what?

Grud's best bet was that the guy was waiting for reinforcements, either human police or Guardians. There was always the possibility that the driver was talking on the phone or doing something else that had nothing to do with him or the other immortals inside the building. Except, Grud's gut knew better.

Experience had taught him that ignoring its warning signs was a bad idea. Besides, it was always better to err on the side of caution.

His general direction was north, where he could see the hill with the residential neighborhood. Getting there on foot would take him no more than an hour of brisk walking, but getting his hands on an escape vehicle would be preferable.

The faster he got out of the area, the better.

An opportunity presented itself as soon as he rounded the corner of the next warehouse over.

The gardener's truck pulling into a parking spot in front of the building's manicured front lawn was an old, beat-up clunker, but it was there, and Grud didn't get a bad vibe from its driver like he had from the other one.

Crouching even lower, Grud tightened his grip on the iron rod that had served as his escape tool and was now doing double duty as a weapon, and sprinted toward the truck. Opening the door, he yanked the driver out, and before the guy had a chance to open his mouth, brought the rod down on the back of his skull.

With no time to hide the unconscious human, Grud dragged him to a half-shaded spot under the low bushes bordering the grassy lawn. Quickly going through the guy's pockets, he found a phone and a wallet. Regrettably, the thing held only a few dollars and no credit cards.

Not a big deal, anyway he had no intention of keeping any of it. As soon as he got to the residential neighborhood, he was going to dump the truck together with the phone and the wallet and get himself something better.

Casting one last look at the human lying crumpled under the bushes, Grud climbed inside the cab, turned the ignition on, pulled the truck out of the driveway, and turned north toward the hill.

Except, a mile or so up the road he changed his mind and turned around.

If he left now without checking what was going on, he would always think that he'd missed an opportunity.

A quick drive by the facility should do.

If the car was still there, he would keep on driving and then come back later. But if it were gone, Grud could continue with his original plan, although he would probably need to make some adjustments.

He could get back inside the facility and listen from a safe distance to what Wonder and Dur were doing. As long as the woman had her Taser on, he couldn't get close enough to incapacitate her or kill Dur. But if he was lucky, the two had been done with the talking and had gotten busy fucking.

It was certainly worth a quick investigation, and the risk was low. Unless they'd already found out that he'd escaped. Then the risk was too high.

Fuck, the car was still there.

Grud kept on driving, made a U-turn at the nearest intersection, and headed north once again.

He hadn't expected the sense of loss that had twisted his gut in a tight knot. Up until then, he'd hung on to a small hope that the woman could still be his. But it seemed like this opportunity was lost to him forever.

Or maybe not. Should he turn around and make another pass through?

Searching for other possible explanations for why the car was still there, he remembered seeing the for sale sign outside the facility. Maybe the guy was a realtor taking a look at the property?

If that was the case, he would be gone soon, and Grud could go back.

The twisting in his gut was getting worse the further away from the woman he got, and eventually Grud pulled to the side of the road and killed the engine.

He needed to think.

It was hard to decide how long to wait before going back. Too soon and the realtor, if that's who he was, might still be there. Too long and Wonder would be done with Dur, return him to his cage, and discover that Grud was gone.

Fifteen long minutes was the most he managed to force himself to wait before turning the ignition on and once more turning around.

What he saw when he got there nearly made him shit his pants.

Five more cars were parked in front of the building, and Shaveh and Mordan were being led out in handcuffs.

Whether they were being taken away by the police or by Guardians, Grud would probably never know. He didn't even slow down.

If those were Guardians, Wonder was lost to him forever, and his best bet was to get out of there as fast as he could.

But what if those males were human policemen?

He was pretty sure Wonder had been using the place illegally. The police would arrest her as well.

Shaveh and Mordan might be too nervous to thrall the humans, but they would be allowed to make a phone call, and they would call their commander. A rescue team would arrive at the police station and free them. If Wonder got arrested too, they would take her as well.

No one was stupid enough to leave an immortal female behind.

But if the Brotherhood took her, she would no doubt become the property of Lord Navuh. Simple soldiers didn't get to fuck immortal or Dormant females.

Grud's only hope was that she'd managed to escape. If she

had, he could find her in the club she worked at. The name was printed on the T-shirts she always wore. And even if she quit that job, he could follow her trail.

The problem was that Shaveh and Mordan had seen those T-shirts too.

They would probably try to hide the humiliating fact that they'd been taken by a female, so there was a chance they wouldn't tell anyone about her. But they might go after her themselves.

And then there was Dur.

If he were captured with them, the son of a bitch would sing like a canary, making up a story of how he'd allowed himself to get caught on purpose to investigate her. And if he escaped with Wonder, he would claim her for himself.

Still, Dur could be taken out.

First things first, though. Grud needed to get away and lay low until he could figure out his next step.

ANANDUR

"Welcome to my home away from home." Anandur punched the numbers into the keypad and pushed the door open, peeking inside before pulling it all the way to let Wonder in.

Thank the Fates, the place was presentable. He was never again going to complain about the human cleaning service coming once a week and keeping the Guardians' apartments from looking like pigsties.

Walking inside, Wonder took a look around. "You have more than one place?"

"This used to be the clan's keep, but after everyone moved into the new village, most of it got rented out. We keep a few apartments for the Guardians who are on rotation here and are training in the basement."

Wonder didn't move from the entry. "Should I take my shoes off? Everything looks spotless."

"No need. We have a cleaning service." He took her by the elbow and led her to Magnus's bathroom. "This one is my roomie's, but since the service was here after we left for San Francisco, it's all nice and tidy. You can take a shower, and I'll bring you a T-shirt and a pair of sweatpants of mine." Having a good excuse for it, he allowed himself a thorough look-over. "It's good that you're so tall. My stuff is still going to be too big on you, but at least you're not going to drown in it."

Wonder blushed. "Yeah. I guess."

"What's the matter?" He bent his knees a little so he could look into her green eyes. "What's bothering you, lass?"

She shrugged. "I don't like reminders about my size. I know I'm big for a woman."

"What? Who told you such nonsense? You're perfect." He waved a hand over her body. "You're tall, not huge. And I happen to like women who don't need to crane their necks way up to look into my eyes." He flexed his pectorals, each one separately so they did a little dance. "Most women see only this. I know my muscles are awesome, but I have pretty eyes too." He pretended to pout.

Wonder couldn't help but chuckle. "And you're not shy either."

"Nope. I know that I'm gorgeous, and I own it," Anandur said in his best valley-girl impersonation while batting his eyelashes. "Now off with you, girlfriend." He snapped his fingers.

With one hand on his hip, he kept on snapping the fingers of the other. "Get in there and get cleaned up. I'm going to use the other bathroom, and when I'm done scrubbing the yuk off, I'm going to heat us up something yummy to eat." He didn't drop the act until he was done, wresting a few more smiles out of Wonder.

All he had as far as food selection were frozen dinners, which were as far from yummy as it got, but after surviving on rice and beans even those were a huge improvement. Besides, saying yummy went well with his valley-girl persona.

Damn, it felt good to slip into his old self again.

Making people smile was what Anandur liked doing best.

So yeah, he was an awesome fighter, but other Guardians were nearly as good, or better at one skill or another. However, there was no one better than him at spreading the cheer.

Except, entertaining would be much more enjoyable while he was all cleaned up and wearing freshly laundered clothes that fit.

Whistling a happy tune, Anandur walked into the bathroom, dropped the clothes he had on into the trash, and stepped into the shower. Cranking the temperature way up, he let the scorching water pelt him for a few moments before attacking the filth.

All throughout the soaping and scrubbing, shampooing and conditioning, he kept on whistling one cheerful tune after the other. At first, he thought that his good mood was about finally getting rid of the filth, but then he had an 'aha' moment. It had nothing to do with getting clean and everything to do with getting into his old role and following a familiar pattern, one that had been dearly missed.

Anandur had associated the unease he'd been feeling lately with all the recent changes the clan had undergone. But it wasn't about the move to the village, or about renting out Amanda and Kian's penthouses to humans, or even about all the new Guardians that had been added to the force.

None of that had been the real issue.

At the source of it was just one monumental change that had eclipsed all others.

Brundar didn't need him anymore.

Up until now, Anandur had refused to acknowledge the big chunk missing from his life because doing so would have implied, at least in his own mind, that he wasn't completely happy about his brother's good fortune, which was absurd. But the truth was that without having to take care of Brundar and ensuring that his brother was doing okay, Anandur felt lost.

Except, what did it mean?

Was he taking Wonder on as his new project?

Was she an honorary little sister to take Brundar's place?

The girl was so alone, and she needed a protector, maybe not in the physical sense, but in every other.

She had no one but him to look after her. It was the same as it had been with Brundar, and it felt damn good to be needed again.

After what had happened to Brundar as a boy, his brother had grown into a formidable warrior and didn't require Anandur's muscle for protection. But even though he would never admit it, Brundar had needed Anandur to keep him among the living in the metaphysical sense.

The dark abyss that constantly threatened to swallow Brundar up had never been far off. It had lurked in lonely moments of isolation and in the cold space that Brundar called the zone.

The only one standing between its destructive allure and Brundar's sanity had been Anandur, with his jokes and his smiles and the company of people who gravitated toward him because he was the clown who was cheering everyone up.

Anandur had made sure that Brundar was never alone with his demons for long enough to succumb to them.

But then Callie had taken Anandur's place and put him out of a job.

Except, it wasn't really the same with Wonder, not by a long shot.

As much as Anandur would have liked to believe that he was taking her under his wing as a little sister, he knew it for the big fat lie that it was.

Despite his best efforts, he couldn't stop thinking of her as a woman, albeit one who was much too young for someone like him.

The attraction between them was undeniable.

He might have been able to squash it down if it were only

him lusting after her, but her wanting him back made it mission impossible.

Damn, he needed to talk to someone about this. Someone who wouldn't think he was a dumb ass for believing that the girl was way too young to get involved with an immortal who was nearly a thousand years old.

To get a laugh out of people, Anandur was willing to put himself on the line and act the fool, but not about this.

Maybe he should talk to Vanessa.

The therapist should be able to give him advice. Unless the movies had it right, and all she would do was ask him how he felt about that. If that were all therapists did, then what was the point of going to see one?

He might just as well stand in front of the mirror and ask himself how he felt about things.

"Anandur?" Wonder asked from behind the bathroom's closed door. "Are you about done? I need the clothes you said you're going to let me borrow."

Crap, he'd been standing under the water and philoso-phizing instead of taking care of his girl.

"Look inside my closet," he called out. "Take whatever you want."

"Thank you!"

WONDER

"*That* was good." Wonder leaned back in her chair and rubbed her tummy. "I didn't realize how hungry I was."

Either she had been famished, or the frozen meals were much tastier than Anandur had given them credit for. She'd consumed three before finally sating her hunger, and Anandur was on his fifth. The portions were modest, probably meant for average-sized humans, and according to Anandur the entrees were basic.

One thing was for sure. His simple tastes in clothes and food didn't translate to his apartment. It wasn't just the generous size of the rooms and the beautifully appointed bathrooms that made the place look so fancy. The furniture and the rugs and the art on the wall seemed expensive, even to her untrained eye, and were coordinated to perfection.

Wonder had only seen such luxury in movies and magazines.

Maybe he held a more important position in the clan than he claimed? This didn't look like how she imagined a Guardian would live. According to Anandur, a Guardian was a cross between a policeman and a warrior, and in the movies she'd seen, law enforcers and soldiers lived much more modestly.

It wasn't something she could ask him about, though. It would sound as if she was accusing him of lying to her, which would be extremely rude. Most of the things he'd told her turned out to be true, and she was quite sure there was a logical explanation for the apartment as well.

For now, she would just watch and listen and try not to ask too many questions. People, even honest ones, tended to put a certain spin on things. Some did it out of modesty, not wanting to show off, while others did it for the exact opposite reason. The bottom line was that there was as much to be learned from watching and listening as from getting answers to questions. Maybe more.

Anandur finished chewing and wiped his mouth with a napkin. "You need plenty of fuel to repair massive damage like the injury you've sustained."

"It was only a knife wound. It's not like I needed to regrow a limb." She furrowed her brows. "Can we regrow limbs?"

"We can. But it takes a long time and hurts like hell." Anandur massaged his forearm as if reminded of an old injury.

"Did it ever happen to you?"

"Yeah. I had my hand cut off at the wrist. It was hell regrowing it."

As a phantom pain gripped her, Wonder cringed and cradled her own wrist. "How long ago was it?"

"Ages. I'm a very old immortal."

"How old is old?"

Anandur got up and started collecting the empty boxes from the frozen dinners they'd consumed. "Almost a millennium. I'm an old fart." He chuckled as he tossed everything into the trash.

"I never understood that phrase." Pushing her feet into her sneakers, Wonder leaned up and reached for a paper towel to wipe the table clean. "Farts can't be old. They dissipate as soon as they are released."

"That's true." Anandur nodded sagely as if it was a most important issue requiring further contemplation. "I need to check on this, but not now. People are waiting for us in the village."

Right. Wonder looked at her borrowed rolled-up sweatpants and oversized T-shirt. This was not how she wanted to meet the leader of the American branch of the clan and his wife. Regrettably, though, the only female Guardian whom she could've borrowed clothes from was currently on rotation in the village and not in the keep.

"I wish I was more presentable than this." She waved a hand over herself.

"Sorry, but that's the best I could do. I would've stopped by Walmart for you to buy new clothes, but I don't want to keep Kian waiting for too long. He didn't like it when I told him we needed to shower and eat first." Anandur grabbed his wallet and his car keys from the counter and headed for the door.

"No, of course not." It was better to show up in ill-fitting clothes than late.

Besides, she was comfortable wearing Anandur's things, and not just because everything was loose and soft, but because under the scent of the detergent they'd been laundered with, she could still smell his own unique scent and it was comforting to her.

Anandur had been different with her ever since they'd arrived at his apartment, no longer flirting or making suggestive remarks to make her blush. Instead, he was now treating her as if she were one of the guys.

Figures.

Wonder was used to that. People assumed that since she was a big woman she wasn't feminine, or that she wouldn't appreciate being treated like a girl.

Maybe things would've been different if she put more effort into looking girly, like wearing more makeup and putting on a nice dress or a skirt from time to time. Except, she didn't own any. It would've been frivolous to buy stuff that she had nowhere to wear. A bouncer with a side gig as a warehouse cleaner didn't need to dress up.

Which reminded her that she'd left both jobs suddenly and without giving notice. It wasn't fair to the people who were depending on her to show up and do the work. The problem was that Anandur had gotten rid of her cell phone, explaining she could be easily tracked by its signal, and he hadn't provided her with another one to replace it yet.

Stepping inside the elevator, she leaned against the mirrored wall. "What about Tony? I need to call him and let him know that I need to take a few days off."

"Already taken care of. Magnus called your boss and explained that you will be gone for a while."

"What did he tell him? I don't want to lose that job."

Anandur patted her arm. "Don't you worry about a thing. Magnus told Tony that you're in the witness protection program, and that it's not clear when you'll be coming back."

Shit on a stick. Tony wasn't going to wait for her. He would replace her with someone else. The idea of that door closing on her stressed her out even though she had a feeling that this part of her life was over. Having the option would've made her a bit less anxious. Without it, Wonder felt as if she were trapped.

"What about Shaveh and Mordan? Are they here yet?" Anandur had told her that they were being flown in by a different aircraft, but they should've arrived by now.

"I don't know. They are no longer your problem. You can forget about them."

Wonder crossed her arms over her chest. "I want to know what is going to happen to them."

"I'll tell you as soon as I know anything."

That sounded a lot like a brush-off, and she didn't appreciate it one bit. "You must have an idea of what is awaiting them."

"I do, and so do you. Interrogation and then stasis."

Yeah, he'd told her that, but she wanted to make sure he hadn't been trying to make light of what awaited her prisoners for her sake. Rightly or wrongly, Wonder felt responsible for the two.

"Are they going to be tortured?"

"Not likely. They don't know much, so why bother, right?"

"That's good to hear."

When the elevator stopped, Anandur held the door open for her. "After you, my lady."

"Thank you." She liked that he was treating her like a girl again. On second thought, though, it could've been a reflex and not something he was doing deliberately.

"No problem."

Anandur also opened the passenger door for her and waited until she was seated before closing it.

Wonder smiled. It seemed that her guy was a gentleman. It wasn't really a surprise but a confirmation of what she'd suspected before. Anandur had always been polite around her, and the way he'd done it had been so effortless that it seemed like it was second nature for him.

He isn't mine. Wonder sighed. *Way to get carried away.*

"Don't get scared when the windows turn opaque," he said as he fastened his seatbelt. "It will happen several minutes before we reach the village. For security reasons, its location needs to remain secret. The car is going to drive itself for the last few miles."

"That's cool."

"Technology rocks, right?" He backed out from his parking spot.

"Yeah, it does."

He'd probably meant the new inventions, but to her, all technology was awe-inspiring. Wonder was still learning the world around her and everything it had to offer.

For the next few minutes, they sat in silence, with Anandur searching for a station with the kind of music he wanted to listen to, and Wonder sneaking glances at his hawkish profile. When he didn't smile, Anandur looked formidable, even dangerous, but his warmth and his humor softened his harsh features. He was such a handsome man, and charming, and funny.

She missed his flirting.

Had he done it only as a persuasion tactic and had never been interested in her for real?

During the time they'd spent together in the facility, Anandur had seemed to be attracted to her. Heck, she'd seen proof of it despite his efforts to hide it. Unlike females, who could pretend to find a guy attractive, males couldn't do it convincingly. Some signs were impossible to fake.

Except, working at the club Wonder had seen enough couples hook up for only one night of pleasure to know that sexual attraction didn't mean he wanted a relationship with her.

Why not, though?

He obviously found her appearance appealing. Was it her personality that he didn't like?

Yeah, that was probably the reason.

He was funny, and she wasn't.

He was charming, and she was boring.

Add to that her being a killer, and it was no big surprise that Anandur wasn't interested in her romantically. He might have approved of her killing in self-defense, but that didn't mean he wanted someone like her as a girlfriend.

Ugh.

And if that wasn't enough, with one mighty pull on his arm,

she'd sent Anandur flying through the air landing him on his butt, and then she'd Tasered his brother.

Wonder had singlehandedly felled two trained Guardians.

That and the kill from before guaranteed her status as one of the dudes. Anandur thought of her as excellent Guardian material, and not a potential girlfriend.

All men wanted women they could feel strong next to. The good ones were protective and wanted to feel needed, the not so nice ones were bullies and wanted to be in control, but no guy wanted a woman who could kick his ass.

GRUD

*A*s Grud drove around the residential neighborhood looking for a good spot to dump the truck, he also had his eye out for a suitable patsy.

Old humans were the best for what he needed, especially those with weakening minds. They were the easiest to thrall. And if the mind manipulation caused them damage, some human aging brain disease would get blamed instead of anyone looking for a supernatural cause.

Not that the Brotherhood cared about such things. But Grud was on his own and wasn't sure how long he would need to hide in an old human's house. A grown child might call and notice their parent's mental ability dropping too quickly and come to investigate. But if the parent was already suffering from age-related brain disease, they would think nothing of it.

He spotted his victim from a mile away. The old human was walking a large dog. Or rather the dog was walking him, which meant that the human's house was close by. The way the guy was shuffling his feet, he couldn't have walked far. The dog was no problem either. Grud knew how to manipulate the animal's tiny brain too. They were easy. One terrifying image planted into its brain and even the largest dog would cower before him.

He parked and waited.

The good thing about driving the old clunker was that no one paid attention to a gardener's truck even if they'd never seen it drive through their neighborhood before. Gardeners came and went unnoticed the same way servants used to in rich people's houses.

It was such a shame he had to get rid of it.

Since Grud had made sure not to kill the guy he'd stolen the truck from, he wasn't worried about the human police chasing after him. A stolen vehicle was not a priority for them the way a murder investigation would have been.

Nevertheless, the gardener was going to report the truck missing, and the license plate number would be entered into the police database.

It was better not to take the risk of being spotted driving a stolen vehicle.

Grud didn't have to wait long for the old man to reach his house.

As the old man turned into the driveway, an equally old woman opened the front door. He waved at his wife and unhooked the leash from the dog's collar. Tail wagging, the dog trotted to the front door and pushed his head under the woman's hand for a pat.

The man stopped by the mailbox, took out a stack of papers, and then followed his dog.

Perfect.

Both old-timers seemed to be in functioning condition. The woman could cook for Grud, and the man could run errands. And after he showed the dog who was the boss, the animal would probably stay out of his way.

Lifting the gardener's phone from the passenger seat, Grud snapped a picture of the house so he could find it later.

Mortdh, he was such a fucking idiot.

He wasn't going to keep the gardener's phone and lead whoever was looking for the guy's vehicle right to the house he was going to appropriate.

First, he trashed the picture he'd taken and then scribbled the address on an old receipt he'd found in the glove compartment.

The real challenge would be to find the right place to get rid of the truck, the phone, and the gardener's wallet—somewhere that could hide the vehicle, but at the same time be walking distance away from the old couple's home.

After driving around the entire neighborhood twice, Grud realized that there was no such place. No supermarket to hide the truck among all the other vehicles, and no wooded area to hide it behind bushes.

On his third round, a 'for sale' sign caught his attention.

The house seemed vacant, and what's more, its garage was at the back of the property with a long driveway leading to it. He could park the truck in the backyard of the house so it would be hidden by the structure and not visible from the street. And if he were really lucky, the garage wouldn't be filled with stuff, and he could park it there.

Thank Mortdh, his luck held.

The garage door was unlocked. Grud lifted it with ease, drove the truck inside, and then pulled the door closed. Unless potential buyers wanted to inspect the separate structure, there was a good chance the vehicle wouldn't get discovered until the house was sold.

Getting rid of the smaller items was much easier. He smashed the phone with a rock, dug a small hole in the ground, and buried it there together with the wallet.

The last hurdle was to get to the old couple's home unnoticed. He still had no shoes and looked like a homeless vagabond. Luckily, the feature he hated most, his tightly curled hair, prevented his unkempt beard from reaching down to his chest. It hadn't got trimmed in months and was one messy tangle. His hair was in no better shape.

After he thralled the old couple and sent the woman to cook him a decent meal, he was going to take a long hot shower and trim that jungle. The best thing would have been to get rid of it all together, but Grud still hadn't made his final decision regarding the Brotherhood.

Just in case he needed to go back, it was better to at least leave some stubble. Mortdh's teachings specifically forbade shaving. Males were supposed to take pride in their manliness and not try to look like females. Showing up with a smooth-shaven face was almost as bad as showing up wearing a dress.

Grud brushed the dust off his clothes. Other than adopting the right attitude, it was all he could do about his appearance.

Instead of slinking along the shadows, he decided to jog to the old couple's house. Holding his head high and pumping his arms, he looked like any other human out for a run, only bare-foot and a little shaggy. Fortunately, there was no shortage of weird humans, especially in this area. He'd seen a bald male wearing red lipstick, and a homeless man holding the latest smartphone. A shaggy male running barefoot shouldn't raise anyone's eyebrows.

WONDER

"*I*t's beautiful out here," Wonder said as they walked out of the pavilion.

The entire trip to the village had seemed like a scene from a futuristic movie. First with Anandur's car taking over the driving and the windows going opaque, and then with the elevator ride up from the parking garage, which was located on the lowest level of the underground. Traversing through the ten levels hewn out from the insides of the mountain had taken mere seconds and terminated on the ground level of the village.

The glass pavilion the elevators spilled onto served as a lobby of sorts for the sprawling compound outside of it.

"That's the village square." Anandur pointed at a large open area that looked like a small park.

There were grassy patches surrounded by flowerbeds and bushes, walkways dotted with benches, and a large central pond and several smaller ones. There was even a playground for kids, but no one was swinging on the swings, or sliding down the slides, or building sand-castles in the sandbox.

Was it just her, or did a playground without kids look sad?

Maybe it was the wrong time of day for children to be out playing. Perhaps everyone had gone home to take a nap or something.

As they strolled down the central walkway, Anandur continued to point and explain. "The buildings around the square serve the community. They house offices, classrooms, meeting rooms, and the clinic. There is also the big assembly hall over there, and the movie theater is right next to it. On the other side of it is the gym. We have an Olympic-sized swimming pool, but it's located in one of the underground levels. We also have another gym down there for the exclusive use of the Guardians, and more classrooms for training."

It was a fantastic place for families. Except, there were none out and about. Other than the chirping of birds and the occasional rustle of leaves, there were no other sounds.

"Where is everyone? And where are all the kids?"

Anandur cast her a perplexed glance. "What kids?"

She waved her hand at the playground. "Is it too late or too early for children to be playing out there?"

Anandur shook his head. "As I told you before, immortals suffer from a very low fertility rate. At the moment, we have one baby and another one on the way. There are a few teenagers here and in the Scottish keep, and a couple of toddlers in the Alaskan sanctuary, but that's it."

It was so sad.

Maybe the clan should not have moved out of the high-rise. An urban environment was not as kid-friendly, and the absence of children had probably been less noticeable there.

Except, since this had always been the clan's reality, perhaps they were used to the quiet and it didn't bother them.

Wonder, on the other hand, was accustomed to the sounds of children. Small feet scuttling through the shelter's corridors, excited voices talking loudly in several languages, and even the occasional screaming or crying. To her, those were the sounds of life, of vitality.

All of that was missing from this little slice of paradise the clan had built.

"What about the adults? Where is everyone?"

"Many are at work, and the others are at their homes."

"Where are we meeting your boss?"

"At his place. Syssi came home early from the university so she could welcome you as soon as you arrived." Anandur scratched his beard. "Amanda, who is Kian's sister and Syssi's boss at the lab, is going to be there too. Everyone is eager to meet the new immortal. In fact, there might be a bunch of people there so get ready for that."

"Great." Wonder looked at her rolled up sweatpants and her cheap sneakers. "And this is how everyone is going to meet me. Talk about lousy first impressions."

Anandur wrapped his arm around her shoulders, the first sign of affection since he'd brought her to his apartment. "You have nothing to worry about. Everyone knows you've been injured. You've captured three Doomers and me. And you nailed Brundar with a Taser. That is what everyone is going to be talking about. Not what you have on."

"Great. That's even worse."

Anandur stopped and turned to look at her. "What's that supposed to mean?"

"Nothing." She looked away. "Let's go."

"I promise that no one is going to be mad at you because of that. You're going to get a hero's welcome."

"Yeah, okay." He wouldn't understand so there was no point in explaining.

Except, the tight press of Anandur's lips was a sure sign he was not going to let it go. "We'll talk about it later."

"Fine." She had no intention of doing so. Hopefully, by the

time this welcoming party was over, he would have forgotten all about it.

"That's their house." He pointed.

It looked exactly like all the others. "I was expecting a fancy mansion."

"Nah. They live almost as simply as the rest of us. The only luxury they've splurged on was a larger backyard with its own lap pool. Kian likes to swim. He says it calms him down." Anandur chuckled. "Ask any clan member, and they'd agree. Whatever can do that is worth every penny. They would've gladly donated to the effort if it were necessary."

As Anandur prepared to take the steps up to the front porch, the door was flung open, and a dainty blond woman ran out, followed by a tall, stunningly beautiful brunette. The second woman was about Wonder's height, but slimmer and built more delicately.

A pang of envy darted through Wonder's heart.

She had no doubt that the woman had never been considered one of the guys. Despite her impressive stature and boyish haircut, she was the epitome of feminine poise and elegance.

The blond halted in front of Wonder and lifted a pair of wide eyes at her. "Wonder," she gasped, "I can't believe it." She then shook her head as if to dispel a pesky memory or thought and pulled Wonder into her arms. "I'm so glad you're all right. I'm Syssi." She let go only to transfer her to the brunette. "Meet my sister-in-law, Amanda."

"Hello, gorgeous." Amanda hugged Wonder briefly before letting go and giving her a thorough once-over. "The things I'm going to do with you," she murmured.

She was probably referring to Wonder's attire. But whatever the big boss's sister had meant, Wonder was going to do her best to stay away from the intimidating woman.

"I was so worried about you." Syssi wrapped her arms

25

around Anandur's neck, forcing him to bend almost in half. "Don't ever do that to me again."

"I'll try." He chuckled.

Her arm wrapped around Anandur's middle, Kian's wife leaned into him as if he were her long-lost brother and wiped tears from her cheeks with her other hand.

It was nice to see how much his boss's wife loved Anandur, but Wonder would've preferred a little less touching. It also reinforced her suspicion that Anandur was more important to the clan than he'd let her believe.

Was he closely related to Kian? A direct cousin maybe?

"Let's move this party inside." Amanda cast a quick glance around before leading Wonder through the front door. "Once the news leaks out that Anandur is back and that we have a new immortal in our midst, everyone will want to come over and greet you guys. I know I'm selfish, but I would like the chance to get to know you first."

As a man got up from an armchair and advanced toward her, Wonder didn't have to be told who he was. Kian's face was as harsh and as unwelcoming as it was blindingly beautiful. If not for Amanda's arm around her, she would've taken a step back.

"So this is the girl who kidnapped one of my best Guardians and Tasered the other." He offered her his hand.

Shit on a stick, he looked mad. Well, she would be too if some random person overpowered her best warriors.

"I'm sorry. When I abducted Anandur, I thought he was trying to kill a woman. And later, when I realized I'd been mistaken and released him, I didn't know it was his brother on the stairs. All I wanted was to protect Anandur."

Finally, the guy cracked a smile. "We have ourselves a real Wonder Woman here. Welcome to my clan, Wonder."

She released a relieved breath. "Thank you."

"Please, take a seat." He pointed at the couch.

"Not yet," Amanda said. "I'm sure Wonder would appreciate a change of wardrobe first."

Oh, so that was what she'd meant before. A change of clothes didn't sound that ominous.

Kian cast Wonder a quick look-over, one that was so far from interested that it was almost insulting, and raised a brow. "What's wrong with what she's wearing?"

"Where do I begin?" Amanda rolled her eyes. "It would take too long. Just sit tight and wait for five minutes. Can you do that?"

Kian shook his head. "I know better than to argue with you. Take your time. I need to talk with Anandur first anyway."

"Smart man." Amanda tightened her arm around Wonder's middle and started walking. "Syssi, are you coming?" She looked over her shoulder.

"But of course." The blond smiled and followed.

Amanda opened the door to one of the bedrooms. "Let me explain, in case you're wondering what this is all about. Anandur texted Kri, who is a Guardian and a tall girl like you, that you need to borrow some clothes. Kri couldn't do it because she is on assignment elsewhere, so she texted me, telling me that you need an outfit or two and that you're about my size. That was very smart of her, since I always have things I need to get rid of to make room for new ones. Especially here. The closets in my new house are tiny. That's my only complaint about the place."

She leaned to whisper in Wonder's ear. "The architect made a big mistake with the size of the walk-in closets. I need to convert one of the bedrooms so I can bring at least part of my wardrobe. Anyway, I brought you plenty of things to tide you over until you get your own stuff."

"That's very nice of you." And it was very nice of Anandur too. And Kri, who'd apparently decided Amanda would do a better job than her. Or maybe the Guardian really was out on an assignment.

"Think nothing of it. I love doing stuff like that. Right, Syssi?"

The blond sat on the bed. "If you let her, she will do your makeup and hair and dress you up like a harlot."

Amanda huffed. "I love you, darling, but you're such a prude." She put her hands on her hips. "Syssi thinks that a skirt reaching her mid-thigh makes her look like a hooker."

Wonder didn't know what to say, so she remained quiet.

Despite being much friendlier and outgoing, Amanda was just as overwhelming and as intimidating as her brother. The woman was stunning, and stylish, and exuded enviable confidence.

"Not very talkative, are you, Wonder?" Amanda waved a hand. "That's okay. Let's get you dressed, and you'll feel much better."

She lifted a folded pair of pants and a T-shirt off the dresser. "I brought you a bra too, but I'm afraid it's not going to fit." She glanced at Wonder's chest and chuckled. "You're built more like the original Wonder Woman. Lynda Carter was at least a double D."

Wonder had no idea what Amanda was talking about, but she could answer her about the bra. "I don't wear them. What are they good for anyway?"

Syssi started laughing. "Indeed. It's not like we need to worry about sagging."

"Yeah, but what about sticking out?" Amanda put a hand on her hip. "I'm not modest, but I don't want my nips to point the way when I'm cold or horny."

The other woman laughed again. "There is that. What do you think, Wonder?"

This whole conversation was strange, but it was also kind of fun. Wonder had never had girlfriends to chat with about bras and stuff like that. Not since she'd awoken from her coma, and whatever was before seemed to be lost forever.

"I wear dark T-shirts. That way I can get away with the occasional poking"

Syssi nodded. "A frugal girl. I like it."

"The T-shirt I brought you is dark purple. I hope that's good enough."

"I'm sure it is." Wonder took the items from Amanda and headed for the adjoining bathroom.

"Wait. I have brand new panties for you as well." Amanda handed her something that looked like a triangle with strings.

"Those are panties?" Wonder let the thing dangle from her fingers.

"It's a thong, darling."

"Oh." She'd heard girls talking about them, and she'd seem some of the popular styles in advertisements, but she had no intention of wearing them. They looked painful.

6

ANANDUR

*K*ian walked over to the bar. "Can I get you a drink? I know it's a little early in the day for that, but after what you've been through I assume you can use one."

"You know me well." Anandur joined Kian at the bar and watched him pour Black Label into two glasses. It wasn't Kian's usual fancy fare, but it was what Anandur liked.

"Sláinte!" Kian said as they clinked glasses. "Let's go outside. I want to smoke." Which in Kian speak was code for 'let's talk in private.'

Since moving in, Kian had added several features to his backyard, the most prominent being a noisy bubbling fountain. The thing was annoying as hell, but it provided protection from nosy neighbors. Not that he had anything to fear from Amanda and Dalhu on one side or Brundar and Callie on the other, but still, sometimes a guy wanted to play footsie with his wife in his own backyard without being overheard.

"Tell me about Wonder," Kian said as he sat on the outdoor sofa and reached for the pack of cigarettes on the coffee table.

"There isn't much to tell. She woke up from a coma about

nine months ago and can't remember anything from before. Even her name is one she adopted without even knowing what it meant. Some kid pointed at her on the street and said 'Wonder Woman,' and that was it."

"I can see why." Kian pulled out a cigarette. "Mostly it's the height and the dark coloring, I don't think their facial features are similar at all. Wonder's eyes are different. Very unique color."

Mesmerizing was a better description.

"What else?" Kian asked.

"She woke up in Egypt, so we have to assume she is from that part of the world. After getting attacked by a group of thugs and killing one of them in self-defense, she ran away and hid onboard a cargo ship that also took passengers. When she got to San Francisco, she was granted refugee status."

Kian lit his cigarette and took a puff. "Can you explain how a civilian female managed to take down three Doomers and two Guardians?"

"She must've been trained, but she doesn't remember it. But that's not all. Wonder is incredibly strong, much stronger than any other immortal female including Kri. She's probably stronger than most immortal males."

"Hmm, why do you think that is?"

Anandur shrugged. "I guess that is her special gift."

"Interesting. I've never heard of physical strength being a special talent. Is it possible that she's biologically a male, or maybe a hybrid? It sometimes happens in humans."

Anandur felt his cheeks getting hot. He hadn't blushed since he was a teenager, but Kian's suggestions were making him furious.

"If you're asking whether I checked her equipment, the answer is no. The girl could not be older than nineteen or twenty, and I'm not a pedophile."

Kian waved a dismissive hand. "Don't get your panties in a

wad. I'm just thinking out loud. And a twenty-year-old is not a child. Maturity level aside, a seventeen-year-old is kosher."

"Maybe for another teenager, but not for someone my age." Anandur took a long swig from his drink.

"We can have Bridget take a look at her anatomy."

It had been a very long time since Anandur had felt like punching Kian in the face, but he was a hair's breadth away from doing it now. "Over my dead body. I promised Wonder a sanctuary, not an interrogation that includes medical probing. The girl is probably still a virgin."

By the sly smile on Kian's face, Anandur had fallen straight into the trap he'd set up for him. "You like her, you dirty old man."

Damn. He should've known better than to let Kian goad him.

Anandur took another swig from his drink. "What's not to like? She would make an awesome Guardian."

"And that's the only reason." Kian took another puff from his cigarette. "Her beauty has nothing to do with it."

Finishing the last of his Chivas, Anandur pushed up to his feet. "Mind if I take a refill?"

"Go ahead. Refill mine too." Kian handed Anandur his empty glass.

Still seething, Anandur walked inside and headed for the bar. From down the hallway, he could hear Amanda talking and Wonder and Syssi laughing, which helped calm his anger. The girl needed to laugh more. It was good for her.

As he refilled the two glasses, Anandur felt his belly rumble again. The five frozen dinners he'd consumed were no more than an appetizer for him. He still didn't have the half a cow and mountain of mashed potatoes he'd promised himself when he got free. Regrettably, the only thing he could get at Kian's were veggie burgers, which tasted like crap.

How could the guy live on that shit? Didn't he have taste buds?

Whatever. To each his own. Anandur opened each one of the bar's cabinets until he found a bag of pretzels. It would have to do for now.

Later, Wonder and he were going to eat a proper dinner at Callie and Brundar's.

Bag under his arm and a glass in each hand, he returned to the backyard.

"Here." He handed Kian his drink. "Do you want some pretzels?"

"No, thank you. Aren't you going to your brother's house for dinner later?

"We are. But don't worry about it. I'm so damn hungry I'm going to wolf down everything Callie makes."

Kian arched a brow. "Do I look worried to you? I know how much you can eat. After you're done with dinner, bring Wonder back here. Syssi will get her settled in one of the houses. Unless you want her to room with you and Magnus?"

Right, as if he needed temptation right under his nose.

"No. Magnus and I switch between the keep and the village every two weeks, and she would be all alone in the house. It's better for her to room with other girls who are permanently here."

"I agree."

Anandur scratched his head. "But I think it would be better if I were around. I'm the only one she knows. Is it okay if I don't finish my rotation at the keep and stay in the village for a while?"

"Good idea. I'll have Bhathian take over your trainees, and you can take back your post as my bodyguard."

"Thanks."

The smirk on Kian's face portended another taunt. "Can't stay away from the girl, eh?"

"Let's get one thing straight," Anandur said. "There is nothing going on between Wonder and me, and I don't want to hear any comments about it. Can you please not follow in your sister's footsteps? One yenta per keep is plenty."

Kian took a swig, put his glass down on the table, and pinned Anandur with his intense stare. "I'm very grateful for my sister's unsolicited meddling. Thanks to her, I found my true-love mate, and my life has been changed infinitely for the better."

7

MAGNUS

"*M*ister Finder of Lost Things." Magnus offered his hand. "Thank you for coming and bringing along your three lovely associates. I'm Magnus."

"Jeff." The guy transferred the dog leashes to his other hand and shook what was offered. "What happened to Brad?"

"There was a change of plans. I took over for him. I hope you don't mind."

"No, of course not. I was just under the impression that we were looking for Brad's missing partner. I thought he would like to be here in person."

"Yes, he would. But unfortunately, he was called elsewhere." Magnus smirked. "Just between you and me, though, I'm a much nicer fellow."

"I'm sure," Jeff said. "Different location, too. We were supposed to meet at the club where Brad's partner had last been seen." He took a look around the largely deserted industrial park. "Are you sure you don't want to start there?"

"We received a new tip." There was no reason to tell Jeff that the missing person had changed as well. As far as the guy was concerned, they were still looking for Brad's missing partner.

One of the three Golden Retrievers took a fancy to Magnus, pushing his head under his hand and wagging his tail furiously.

"What a cheerful doggie smile you have." Magnus crouched and scratched the dog behind his ears. "What's your name, buddy?"

"Ralph," Jeff said. "This one is Ross, and that one is Reese." He pointed at the dogs as he said their names.

Magnus patted the other two as well, but they seemed only mildly interested, while Ralph looked like he was ready to go home with him.

"Do you have an article of clothing of the missing person?" Jeff asked.

"Yes, I do." Magnus pulled out one of the Doomer's T-shirts from a plastic bag.

After a short sniffing session, the dogs put their noses to the ground and started searching.

Following Jeff, Magnus asked, "Does it take long to train a dog to do that?"

"It does, and not every dog is good at it. I like to work with Golden Retrievers because they are just great dogs, but Rottweilers are good too. But even within the same breed, there are differences in attitude and aptitude."

The dogs were well trained, not running or pulling on the leashes as Magnus had expected them to. They led him and Jeff behind the building and sniffed at the grass.

"The screen of that window is torn." Jeff pointed.

"I noticed."

That must've been Grud's escape route. They'd mistakenly assumed that he'd walked out the front door.

Regrettably, the handyman Onegus had hired to fix the hole in the cage room was long gone, and it would be hell to find another one on a short notice. Maybe they would just leave the screen as it was.

The tear wasn't as incriminating as the hole. Any random thief or vandal could've cut the screen to try to get into the vacant building and check if there was anything worth stealing. But a hole made in a concrete block wall was a different story. The only reason for anyone to make it was if he'd been imprisoned in the cage. Except, the cages were meant for apes and hadn't been used for that purpose in decades.

With the screen, Wonder might get in trouble for "forgetting" to turn on the alarm, but no one could prosecute her for it. The worst that could happen was her losing the cleaning job that she was not coming back to anyway. In contrast, the hole could've opened a whole can of worms.

The dogs kept going, sniffing a path that was anything but direct.

Grud must've still been in the building when Liam had parked outside, or maybe even when Brundar and Magnus had gotten there. That was why he hadn't used the front door and why he'd zigged and zagged from wall to bush to tree and then to another wall.

Either way, he'd been long gone by the time the rest of the Guardians had arrived and started searching for him. Even on foot, by that time he'd probably been halfway up the road leading to the residential area on the hill.

The Guardians were searching both sides of that road, going from one warehouse to another, and from one workshop to the next, but given the numerous potential hiding places in each of those buildings, it was quite a futile search without dogs.

Other than the industrial park they were in, there were four more along the road, two of more or less the same size, and two that were bigger and had mixed-use commercial and industrial facilities. And unlike this park, which seemed to have been vacated for some reason, maybe for repurposing, the others enjoyed full occupancy.

Talk about a needle in a haystack.

Magnus had high hopes for the Finder of Lost Things and his dogs. If Jeff could locate the escaped Doomer, all of them could finally go home.

Home. When had the village become one?

Magnus had thought it would take a long time to adjust to a new place and a different culture, but apparently being surrounded by family both here and in Scotland meant that he now had two homes.

Cool.

"Easy, boys," Jeff said as the dogs started pulling on the leashes. "Not so fast."

"What's got them excited?" Magnus asked.

"We will soon find out."

The dogs stopped next to another warehouse and started sniffing the grass again.

Maybe Grud had been hiding right there the entire time? If he had, the guy was much smarter than Magnus had given him credit for. Assuming the Doomer would want to distance himself from the facility as fast as he could, no one had thought to search the nearby buildings.

"Should we go inside?" Jeff asked. "Could your friend be in there?"

"Let's give it a try." Magnus pulled on the door handle, half expecting it to be locked, but the thing opened into a simple reception room. Even more surprising was finding a living, breathing receptionist, and a pretty one at that.

"Oh, good. Are you here to search for the guy who knocked out the poor gardener?" she asked.

Magnus put his hand on Jeff's arm to shush him. "Can you tell us what happened? We weren't given many details."

"Some thug knocked Jorge out with a blow to the back of

his head." She pointed to hers. "And robbed him. He took his wallet and his phone and stole his truck. I wanted to call an ambulance for him, but he begged me not to." She leaned over her desk. "I think Jorge is illegal. His wife came and picked him up. I'm so glad he decided to report it. I don't think the police care if he is an illegal immigrant, right?"

"They don't," Jeff said. "Their job is to catch criminals, not to chase after illegals. Did your gardener see the face of the robber?"

She frowned. "He didn't say. The poor man was too distraught, and frankly so was I. All I could think of was getting Jorge medical help."

"Jeff," Magnus said to catch the guy's attention.

"Yes?"

Magnus looked into his eyes and pushed a small thrall. "You should take the dogs out."

Luckily, the guy's brain was easy to manipulate. "Yes, I should take the dogs out."

When Jeff left, Magnus turned to the receptionist and flashed his most charming smile. "Do you happen to have Jorge's number? I would like to ask him a few questions."

She narrowed her eyes. "He is not going to get in trouble, is he? I don't want him to get deported."

"Don't worry, that's not my jurisdiction, and I couldn't care less. I just want to find his truck for him. Its loss means no income for Jorge and his family. I doubt he has insurance, and even if he does, it will take time until he gets the money to buy a new one. And what about his equipment? He needs that truck and his work tools back right away."

After that speech, no thrall was necessary.

The girl nodded solemnly. "He gave me his wife's number to call. I still have it." She picked up a post-it note but didn't hand it to Magnus right away. "Let me copy it for you. I want to organize a fundraiser for Jorge. If everyone who works here and our other locations pitches in, we might collect enough to help him replace his tools."

"That's a wonderful idea."

"I'm also adding our number with my extension. I'm Megan, by the way." She scribbled both numbers. "Call me if you find the truck. It will make me feel much better knowing that Jorge has it back."

Magnus took the note and tucked it inside his jacket's inner pocket. "I will."

8

WONDER

*I*n the guest bathroom, Wonder checked herself in the mirror after putting on the things Amanda had brought for her. It was nothing fancy, just a pair of black leggings that were quite comfortable, and a purple T-shirt that was a little tight across the chest but other than that looked great.

In fact, she had never looked better, and that was without doing anything with her hair or even the benefit of eyeliner. Her black pencil was inside the purse that she'd left at the facility. Magnus was supposed to bring it with the rest of her things, but she would have to wait for him to catch Grud first because he wasn't coming back until that was done.

Oh well, there was no rush. Amanda had supplied her with a whole wardrobe. There were about twice as many items in that suitcase than in Wonder's closet back at the shelter.

Not only that, but everything was of such high quality that she would not have even known where to look for things like that, let alone afford to buy them. The cut of the simple garments and the feel of the fabrics were amazing.

The only reason she didn't recognize the designers' names was probably because they were known only to the rich and famous.

In contrast, her cheap sneakers looked even worse.

But that wasn't her biggest problem. The thong panties Amanda had given her were a pain in the butt. Literally.

Why would anyone voluntarily submit to such torture?

At first, she hadn't planned on wearing them, but after putting on the leggings she realized that Anandur's boxer shorts were too bulky to wear under the tight-fitting pants.

They were so much more comfortable, though.

Wonder turned around and looked over her shoulder at her butt.

Shit on a stick. Without proper panties there was nothing to cover the separation line between her ass cheeks. It was on full display for everyone to see.

That wouldn't do.

Syssi had been right about Amanda. There was a very wide gap between what Kian's sister considered appropriate and what a decent woman felt comfortable in.

Then again, what was considered decent or indecent was subjective. Wonder didn't wear bras. Maybe that was indecent too?

Kicking off her sneakers, she pulled down the leggings and the thong, put on the boxer shorts, and then spent a couple of minutes trying to pull the leggings over them without them getting all bunched up.

The first opportunity she got, she was going to buy a couple of bras and two or three packages of normal panties, instead of waiting for Magnus to bring her things over.

Ugh. He was going to pack her underwear. How awkward. For some reason, she hadn't thought of that before. Maybe she should tell him to skip it? She could replace all of her panties for as little as twenty bucks.

But calling Magnus and telling him that would be just as awkward if not worse.

"Are you okay in there?" Syssi asked.

"Yeah. I'll be right out."

Wonder pushed her feet into the sneakers and opened the door. "How do I look?"

Amanda put a hand on her hip. "Why are you wearing boxer shorts under the leggings?"

Syssi giggled. "Because she doesn't think floss should go you know where. Right, Wonder?"

It took a moment for Syssi's meaning to sink in, and when it did, Wonder felt her ears heat up. "I've never worn a thong before. It's very uncomfortable."

Amanda waved a hand. "Nonsense. You get used to it. If you don't want unseemly panty lines, that's the only way to go. Besides, it makes you feel sexy all day long." She waggled her brows.

The heat spread from Wonder's ears down to her cheeks. "I don't want to feel like that all day. It's distracting."

Laughing, Syssi took her elbow. "Amanda is special. Let's leave it at that."

"Hold on!" Kian's sister caught Wonder's other elbow. "I want to do something about your hair."

Wonder patted her thick braid, making sure all the strands were still tightly woven together. "What's wrong with my hair?"

"Nothing, darling. But it will look so much better freed from that braid."

Not wanting to offend Amanda, who as Kian's sister was no doubt someone important, Wonder forced a smile. "Maybe some other time. I don't want to keep Mister Kian waiting for too long."

Amanda sighed, "It's just Kian, without the Mister. But you're right. We don't want to upset the grouchy goat."

Thank the gods.

"Hey!" Syssi pretended offense as she led Wonder out. "Don't call my husband names."

"I'm not. I'm calling my brother names." Amanda followed behind them.

"Told you. She is special," Syssi whispered loudly.

"I'm right behind you."

"I know."

It seemed like the sisters-in-law were good friends, and their easy banter was fun except when Wonder was the target of it.

Would they accept her as a friend too?

It would be nice. She was starting to warm to Amanda. The woman was still intimidating, but a little less so, and she meant well. Wonder didn't even mind Amanda's proposed makeover as long as she got to hang out with the two of them again.

As they stepped outside, Anandur got up, but Wonder didn't think he did it for her. It was probably out of respect for Syssi and Amanda.

"Do you feel better now?" he asked.

"Much. Thank you."

"You look nice."

Wonder couldn't help but glance down at her ugly sneakers. "Thank you."

"Come, sit over here, Wonder." Kian waved her to the chair across from him.

"Does anyone want a cappuccino?" Syssi asked.

"I do." Amanda raised a finger.

"Wonder, what about you?"

It felt incredibly awkward to be served by the boss's wife. But Wonder was thirsty, and besides, refusing might offend Syssi. "I would love some, thank you."

"Awesome." Syssi clapped her hands.

All along, Wonder could feel Kian's intense eyes on her.

"Anandur tells me you don't remember anything about your life before the coma," he said.

"That's correct."

"No recollection whatsoever?"

"None, sir."

He grimaced, apparently not liking the honorific. "But you did know that you're an immortal?"

"Yes."

"How?"

She shrugged. "It was like knowing that I'm a female. It was a fact. Later, I started doubting it, trying to explain my fast healing as just an anomaly. But when I found Grud, I knew right away that he was an immortal too. The same happened with Mordan and Shaveh and then Anandur."

"How did you know that they were immortal?"

Wonder rubbed her hand over the back of her head. "I got that prickling sensation, as if all the small hairs back there stood up."

Kian and Anandur exchanged glances, with Kian's expression saying 'I told you so,' and Anandur's turning sour.

"That's an odd reaction for an immortal female." Kian lifted a pack of cigarettes off the coffee table and pulled one out. "The prickling sensation you're describing is something immortal males feel when they encounter another immortal male they don't know. It's a warning mechanism. But I've never heard of a female getting the same reaction."

Wonder's face flushed with heat. As if she needed more proof that she was a freak. Not only was she strong like a male, she also had the same instincts. Next thing she knew she would start growing facial hair.

"Your fangs do not elongate, do they, darling?" Amanda asked.

Wonder shook her head.

Amanda crossed her arms over her chest. "Bummer. I always wanted to have real fangs like the guys."

Someone kill me now.

"Wonder is a natural born warrior," Syssi came to her defense. "That's why she was gifted with special abilities that are usually reserved only for males. Right, Wonder?"

"I don't want to be a warrior."

"Why not? I think it's awesome that you're a formidable fighter. And you chose Wonder Woman as your name. That can't be a coincidence."

Wonder lifted her eyes to Syssi, who other than Anandur seemed to be the nicest of the bunch. "But it was a coincidence. I had no idea what Wonder meant. It just sounded nice, and the kids who thought I was her were smiling, so I thought it was a good name."

"What would you like to do?" Kian asked.

Picking at the end of her braid, Wonder twisted the strands around her fingers. "I don't know yet. I don't have any education, so there isn't much I can do other than manual labor or security. But that's not what I want to do for the rest of my life."

Kian nodded. "Perfectly understandable. But if you could get an education, what would you like to study?"

"I don't know enough to even know that. Right now all I can think of is a teacher. I like kids. But you don't have any here. Could I teach human kids?"

"One day there will be." Syssi's voice quivered a little. "Callie, Brundar's mate, is studying to become a teacher. You can ask her about it."

"I didn't even go to high school."

"Not a problem," Amanda said. "We can put you in a home-schooling program, and you'll breeze through it."

"That's a great idea," Syssi said. "I'll get right on it tomorrow. You can get a GED. It's a high-school equivalency certificate."

"What do I need to do to get it?"

"Study and then pass the test," Amanda said. "No biggie."

9

ANANDUR

"Callie, as always, it was awesome." Anandur leaned to kiss her cheek.

She smiled up at him. "Are you finally full?"

"Yes. Thank you for making my dream a reality."

"If all it takes to make you happy is grilling a few steaks, then you're an easy guy to please. Right, Wonder?"

After the stressful time Wonder had had at Kian's, she was finally unwinding, mainly thanks to Callie. The girl knew how to put people at ease. Which was the opposite effect Kian had.

Still, Anandur had to admit that Kian had made an effort to throttle down his intensity and smile at Wonder from time to time.

"I'm just glad you're not mad at me for Tasering your boyfriend. I was afraid that you were going to put something in my food."

The fact that Wonder was joking was an excellent indicator that she was starting to get comfortable around his family. The girl didn't have anyone, and Anandur was more than happy to share his with her.

Callie waggled her finger. "I will never tamper with food.

But that doesn't mean I won't use some of my sharp knives. So beware." She winked.

Brundar wrapped his arm around Callie's shoulders. "My girl is a killer cook and extremely handy with the knives."

Anandur wasn't sure Wonder would understand his brother's dry humor. Those who knew Brundar would get that he was joking, but his toneless delivery might confuse others.

Fortunately, it seemed Wonder got it.

She smiled. "That she is. Thank you. I don't remember ever eating so well."

"You're welcome to come join us any day. Our door is always open, and I always cook way too much food. In fact, just to make it official, you are both invited to dinner tomorrow."

Anandur pulled the door open. "We'll see. I have to check my assignments first."

"Are you guys sure you can't stay for dessert?"

Wonder cast Anandur a sidelong glance.

He shook his head. "Maybe next time. Syssi is waiting for us to come back so she can take Wonder to her new place. I don't want to keep her waiting."

"Okay, that's an excuse I can't argue with," Callie said. "But make sure you can come tomorrow at the same time and bring Wonder with you."

"I'll do my best."

"Good night, you guys." She pulled Wonder in for a quick hug and then hugged Anandur.

Brundar only nodded.

"You too." Wonder waved as they went down the steps.

"Did you have fun?" Anandur asked.

"Yes. Callie is so nice. And Brundar is not as scary with her around."

Anandur chuckled. "You can say that again."

"What now?"

"Syssi is going to introduce you to your new roomies." She'd texted him during dinner. Apparently, Gertrude and Hildegard had a spare bedroom in their house and were eager to take in Wonder as a third roommate.

"Are you sure they are okay with me staying with them?"

"Everyone other than the couples, which aren't that many, is sharing housing in the village. They've got a three-bedroom house, so naturally they were expecting another roommate. They are very excited about you joining them."

"Are they nice?"

"You'll have to find out for yourself. But don't worry. You're a celebrity. They are going to love having you."

She cringed. "Are you sure? I was the bad guy in this story."

He stopped and put his hands on her shoulders. "Don't do that. You took down three Doomers and by doing so saved at least three women, probably more. You're a hero. Own it."

"You're right, but what about taking you down? Everyone has been worried sick about you. Callie said it was like a graveyard here. People weren't smiling and were moping around."

"Well, what can I say? I'm dearly loved. But I'm back safe, and all is well except for my pride. I don't think I'll ever live down being taken by a civilian female. My life is going to be hell."

She smiled. "I doubt it. People love you and are scared of Brundar. They wouldn't dare."

He wrapped his arm around her shoulders again, which she seemed to enjoy, and kept walking toward Syssi and Kian's place. "You've got it figured out pretty quick."

"It's not hard to do. It's quite obvious."

"Hi, guys." Syssi came out of her house, hefting a huge suitcase.

"What's that?" Anandur asked and rushed to take it from her.

"Amanda collected more things for Wonder. You know what she's like."

"Very generous," Wonder said.

Syssi chuckled. "Yes, that too. You don't need to shop for clothes for about five years. And as far as torture panties go, don't worry. I found a new five-pack I didn't open yet of comfy cotton panties for sensible girls. Regrettably, though, I didn't have any new bras."

Wonder looked a little uncomfortable. "I'm so grateful for all that you're doing for me."

Syssi waved a hand. "Think nothing of it."

"Which house is it?" Anandur asked.

"The first one after this turn." She pointed before turning to Wonder. "You'll be rooming with Hildegard and Gertrude who are both nurses. Hildegard works full time in the clinic, and Gertrude only when she's needed. She grows herbs the rest of the time."

"That's an interesting hobby," Wonder said.

"It's more than a hobby for her. She supplies several high-end restaurants and makes good money off it."

"Callie uses Gertrude's herbs in her cooking," Anandur said. "She says they make everything taste better, and I agree."

"Here we are." Syssi walked up to the front door and knocked.

Hildegard opened up. "Hello, Wonder. I'm so glad you agreed to share the house with us. We are so excited."

From behind her, Gertrude nodded. "You have no idea how refreshing it is to have someone new around who hasn't heard all of our stories yet."

"Thank you for having me," Wonder said.

Less than fifteen minutes later, Gertrude and Hildegard had Wonder settled in her bedroom and shooed Syssi and Anandur out.

"The girl needs to get some rest," Gertrude said. "I can't believe you dragged her around the entire village on social calls. After the injury she sustained, you should have insisted on her taking it easy. Go home, Anandur. You can come back and see her tomorrow." She practically shoved him out the door.

"I'll stop by tomorrow morning," he called out from the front porch.

"Good night, Anandur." Wonder waved before disappearing down the hallway.

"She is going to be okay." Syssi threaded her arm through his. "She is in good hands."

"I know."

It was just so damn hard to say goodbye to her. Spending the entire day with Wonder had felt so natural, it was as if they belonged together, and without her, he felt like part of him was missing.

Stop that. It's nonsense. He was getting carried away on the wings of his romantic soul.

"Remember the dream I told you about?" Syssi said.

"What about it?" He hadn't thought about it in weeks.

"Wonder is the girl I saw in the dream with you."

Anandur felt as if Syssi had punched him in the gut with a battering ram. "Are you sure? Because Wonder never cried on my shoulder or off it. She is a tough cookie."

"I can't be completely certain because I didn't see her eyes in the dream, or her entire face. I just saw her profile, her hair, and her build. But everything that I did see matched. I'm ninety-nine percent sure it was her."

10

WONDER

The sounds that greeted Wonder upon waking were very different than those she was used to. The shelter's hustle and bustle started early in the morning and didn't quiet down until late at night. Loud conversations in the adjacent rooms and hallways were the norm, and in the background, there was a constant buzz of cars zipping by along the nearby highway.

In contrast, the village's peaceful morning was filled with the pleasant chirping of birds and the soothing rustle of leaves. Through the open window, the sight that greeted her wasn't of other block-like buildings but of tree branches swaying in the gentle breeze, their green leaves blinking on and off as they reflected the morning sun.

Compared to the city, life in the village seemed serene.

Having a room of her own was also something she could get used to. It was almost like having a little apartment. There was a big bed with crisp sheets, an armchair with a side table, a private bathroom for her exclusive use, and a walk-in closet that was still empty because she'd been too tired to unpack the suitcase full of clothes Amanda had gifted her.

Her new roommates were awesome too.

So far, everyone had been super nice to her. Even Kian had made an effort to make her feel welcome.

When Anandur had told her she would find a new home with his people, Wonder hadn't believed him, thinking he was exaggerating, and that there was no way things were going to be as fantastic as he'd made them out to be. But after less than a day, Wonder actually thought that he'd under-promised and not overpromised.

Last night, Gertrude had made her tea with some herb that was supposed to speed up recovery and restore energy, but Wonder doubted it had done her any good.

After saying goodnight to her roommates, she'd crawled into bed, snuggled under the soft comforter, hugged the over-stuffed down-filled pillow, and had fallen asleep in seconds. But even though she had the best night's sleep ever, she still felt tired, exhausted really.

The fatigue wasn't the result of her injury, though, or even the stressful events of the past few days. It was the accumulation of everything that had happened to her since waking up from her coma.

For the first time that she could remember, Wonder felt utterly safe, which for some reason manifested in her feeling tired from all the restless days and nights that had come before.

Her life up to that point had been a constant struggle on multiple fronts.

At first, it had been all about basic survival. She'd scavenged and stolen, living in constant fear of getting caught. Then she'd had to fight off attackers and run away. And while all that had been going on, she had been learning about the world she was living in like a newborn baby.

In time, things would have probably normalized for her if not for the Doomers she'd captured. But fate had different ideas, putting the right person in the right place, at the right moment to stop them from killing the women they'd lured into Wonder's back alley.

Who else could've done what she had?

Human men would've gotten either thralled or killed as collateral damage, and it wasn't as if immortal Guardians were routinely patrolling the alleys behind clubs ready to intervene.

Wonder didn't regret her actions, not even for a moment.

They had been necessary. She was strong enough physically and mentally to stop the murders and then carry the burden of holding three dangerous immortals locked up.

Still, it felt awesome to leave all of that behind her. Now she could have a normal life, or whatever these immortals considered as normal.

"Wonder, honey." Gertrude opened the door a crack. "Anandur is here for you."

Her heart did a little happy backflip. "Tell him I'll be ready in five minutes."

"Okay." Gertrude closed the door.

Wonder couldn't wait to thank Anandur for bringing her to his people and to apologize for doubting him.

Perhaps capturing the Doomers had been more lucky than unlucky. If not for them, she would've never suspected Anandur and captured him as well. Wonder would have missed out on the best opportunity life had given her since waking up from the coma. He was the reason she was here, finally ready to start living and not just surviving.

In fact, it seemed as if everything that had happened to her so far hadn't been accidental. Every eventful occurrence was another milestone in her journey to find a home with her people.

Could it be that her coma and loss of memory were also part of some grand plan fate had for her?

Nah, she was taking it too far. The bottom line, though, was that she'd been very fortunate and she should be thankful for that.

After a quick visit to the bathroom to take care of the morning necessities, Wonder opened the suitcase and pulled out the first two items on top of the pile. Amanda had done a commendable job with the packing. Everything looked as if it had been professionally cleaned and folded. On second thought, though, Kian's sister probably had servants to do stuff like that for her.

Yeah, something like that would probably be Wonder's job. Did they have a central laundry facility in the village? Or did everyone launder their own clothes? There was still so much she didn't know.

Hopefully, Anandur could spare her a little time before he had to go to work.

After pulling on a pair of stretchy jeans, Wonder put on a loose peasant blouse that was absolutely gorgeous but then took it off and searched the suitcase for a camisole. The fabric was so thin it was practically sheer, and she wasn't wearing a bra.

Thankfully, she found a simple black undershirt that went well with the colorful blouse. With that done, all that remained was to braid her hair and put shoes on. Regrettably, there were none in the suitcase, and she had to make do with her dreadful sneakers.

Even a pair of simple flip-flops would have looked so much better with the beautiful outfit.

"Good morning," Anandur greeted her with a beaming smile. "How was your first night in the village?"

"Awesome." She smiled back, doing her damnedest not to grin like a fool because he was there. "Good morning to you too. Did you sleep well?"

"Not really." He took her elbow. "Come on, let me buy you coffee."

"Wait. I need to tell the girls I'm leaving." She pulled her arm away and looked around. "Where did they go?"

Anandur took her elbow again. "Gertrude is out in the garden and Hildegard is at the clinic."

"Hold on. I need to bring my purse."

Amanda had included a very nice one in the suitcase she'd packed for her.

Wonder didn't have anything other than a debit card and a few bucks to put in it, but it would look great with the outfit, and she felt like looking girly for a change.

The money she'd had in her pocket when Brundar had nailed her with the knife was all she had available right now, but it should be enough to buy a cup of coffee. She also had her debit card, but the question was whether she could use it here. A village of immortals that was hidden from the world of humans probably functioned differently than San Francisco. Maybe they even had their own currency here?

"You don't need a purse unless you have a lipstick or a comb you want to bring with you. We are only going to the village café."

"I don't even own a lipstick. But is the coffee free at the café?"

"For you it is." He pulled her out the door. "I'm taking you out for breakfast."

"Okay."

The money she had might have been enough for coffee but not for a full meal. Besides, it almost sounded like he was taking her out on a date. Wasn't it customary for the guy to pay? In the movies, the men always picked up the bill for dinner, so she assumed it was the way things were done on a date.

Except, Wonder doubted it had been Anandur's intention. He was all business-like, still friendly, but not at all flirtatious.

"A word of warning. There are always people hanging around the café. Are you okay to socialize?"

She looked up at him. "I'm not shy around people. I'm not overly friendly either, but everyone I've met until now was really nice. Even Kian was okay after the first couple of minutes. He is kind of intense, but he seems like a good person."

"One of the best." Anandur chuckled. "I love him, but that doesn't mean I never feel like punching his too pretty puss. He can be a smug bastard sometimes and opinionated as hell, but then being the son of a goddess will do that to a guy."

That's right. Kian and Amanda were the goddess's children. No wonder they were gorgeous.

"Is that why they are so perfect? I mean Kian and Amanda. Because they are direct descendants of the goddess?"

"Yep." Anandur stopped and turned to face her. "Wait a minute. So I'm not perfect?" He put a hand over his heart. "I'm deeply wounded that you think Kian is more handsome than me." He sniffled for good measure.

Wonder slapped his bulging bicep. "You're such a clown."

He sniffled again, put his finger on his lips and looked up to the clouds as if holding back tears. "And now I'm also a clown. How can you be so cruel?"

Was it all one big joke to him? Or was there some truth under all the clowning around?

"You're very handsome too. Just in a different way. You're more rugged and manly. Kian is almost too pretty. You know what I mean?"

The big grin splitting his face was proof that he'd been fishing for just that. "You think I'm manly?"

Was this the right time to ask him how closely related he was to Kian? And why everyone treated him like a celebrity?

"Very." She took his elbow and kept on walking.

"Even though you kicked my ass twice?"

Damn. Did he have to bring that up?

"If it were him instead of you, I'm sure I could've kicked Kian's ass too."

Anandur laughed. "I would've paid good money to see that."

"What does it make me, though? Less feminine? Overly masculine?"

"On the contrary. It makes you a one of a kind Wonder Woman, the heroine every little girl wants to be when she grows up."

She cast him a sidelong glance. "What about the little boys?"

"They want to marry her, of course."

11

ANANDUR

*W*onder shook her head, but Anandur caught the smile she was trying to stifle.

Mission accomplished.

Every time he managed to make her laugh or even just smile felt like a triumph. In fairytales knights slew dragons for their fair maidens, in real life they made them laugh.

The quest was almost as difficult and required unique skills only a few brave knights possessed, but in his opinion, it was way more beneficial to the fair maiden. After all, there wasn't much she could do with a dragon's carcass, but everyone could use a good laugh.

Casting him a suspicious glance, Wonder asked, "Why are you smirking?"

"Just stupid thoughts bouncing around in my head."

She grimaced. "I bet."

"What is that supposed to mean?"

"Oh, I don't know, maybe something about little boys wanting to marry girls who can kick their asses?"

"Ah." For some reason, Wonder was sensitive about her unique gifts, thinking they made her less feminine.

He had no problem sharing his musings with her and setting the record straight. "Not at all. I was thinking how in fairytales knights slew dragons for their fair maidens, and how that wasn't as big of a deal as making the maidens laugh. I consider myself a better knight because my jokes bring real value, true?"

She looked at him as if he had a screw loose, but that was nothing new. He got that reaction often.

"Hmm, so if you had a choice between impressing a maiden with your incredible fighting skills or a good joke, you would've chosen the joke?"

"Of course." He threaded his arm through hers. "Dudettes are usually much less bloodthirsty than dudes. They don't want to see gory displays of blood and guts. They might need reassurances that their guys can protect them if needed, but without actually watching them tear each other apart, or slaughter some poor dragon who's minding his own business."

Wonder laughed and leaned her head against his bicep.

Surprisingly, that small sign of affection flooded him with a potent mix of endorphins and testosterone. The result was intense desire and the need to protect and to possess.

Fates, why did she have such a profound effect on him?

He wasn't a young boy who got excited by a girl's slightest touch. But then, he hadn't been with a woman since Rosie or whatever her name was, and that didn't even count because Wonder had ruined it just by being there.

So yeah, he was abnormally horny, but unfortunately only for one female. One who was way too young for him and emotionally fragile.

A virgin child, that was what she was, and he would keep telling himself that until his body got the message and aligned itself with his brain.

"I agree," Wonder said. "I accept you as my knight, Sir Anandur, and I expect many gifts of jokes and funny stories."

"You got it, Lady Wonder."

Had that been Wonder's attempt at flirting? Or just her response to his silliness?

Except, it didn't matter if she was flirting.

As the mature adult, it was Anandur's responsibility to steer her away from that and into something more appropriate, like a young immortal male closer to her age.

Except, the only two available were Vlad and Gordon, and neither was suitable for Wonder. Vlad was a good kid, but she could snap him like a twig, and Gordon had the maturity level of a four-year-old.

Then there was Julian and several other young immortals who were somewhat appropriate for a girl of her age. But again, he couldn't imagine her enjoying the company of any of them.

And it wasn't because the thought made him jealous.

Well, there was that too, but it wasn't about him. Wonder needed a big guy who wouldn't be intimidated by her physical strength, someone good-natured who would patiently answer all of her questions...

Yeah. He was describing himself.

Damn.

"Anandur!" Carol yelled and ran toward them.

He barely had time to let go of Wonder before getting toppled by the small torpedo coming at him full speed.

"I heard you were back. You have no idea how worried everyone was." She cast an accusing glance at Wonder. "Is that her? Is she the one I need to beat up for abducting you?"

It was funny coming from the tiny blond. Carol was feisty, but Wonder could probably hold her off with one finger.

"Just joking." She winked. "Nice to meet a fellow fighter." She offered her hand. "I'm Carol."

"Nice to meet you too." Wonder didn't sound convincing at all. "I'm Wonder." She shook Carol's hand.

"I know. It's such a cool name. I should've thought of it." She threaded her arm through Wonder's. "Come, breakfast is on me."

Casting Anandur a beseeching glance, Wonder asked, "Didn't you offer to buy me breakfast?"

"I did, but Carol runs the café. If she wants to give you a freebie, who am I to argue, eh?"

Wonder looked at Carol, her eyes taking in the small, curvy woman. "I thought you said you're a fighter."

"I am. I teach beginner self-defense classes. Naturally, those are not for you. You need an advanced one."

Dragging Wonder with her, she waved at her customers. "Everyone! A round of applause for Anandur and Wonder!"

For the next half an hour or so, Wonder and he had to repeat their story over and over again. While he sang Wonder's praises, exaggerating for the sake of making the story more interesting, she blushed and stuttered every time someone commented about her kidnapping one of the clan's toughest fighters.

"Okay, guys." Carol clapped her hands. "Party time is over. Wonder and Anandur want to eat their breakfast in peace."

Amazingly, people listened.

Despite her diminutive size and her less than stellar reputation, Carol had a commanding personality.

Evidently Wonder was impressed too, watching with wide eyes as everyone returned to their tables. "Wow. Thank you. I was afraid we would spend the entire morning like this."

"Pfft." Carol waved a dismissive hand, then pulled out two stools from under the counter. "Sit!"

"Yes, ma'am." Anandur waited for Wonder to take a seat before straddling the other stool.

"Cappuccinos?"

"Yes, please," Wonder said.

"Coming right up."

"She is a bossy one," Wonder whispered as Carol turned the coffee grinder on.

"Carol is a character. That's for sure. She has the heart of a lioness inside that soft body of hers."

Wonder nodded. "I got that vibe from her. She must be a fierce fighter."

"You're a good judge of character, I'll give you that. Carol is an excellent sharpshooter, but she has a problem with an actual hunt. Give her a target, and she hits the bull's-eye, but she won't shoot at an animal."

"Why does it surprise you? I can totally understand that. The fact that she can kill doesn't mean that she wants to."

He nodded. "I agree. But if she ever wants to go on a mission, I need to know that she can do what needs to be done."

Wonder shook her head. "I have a feeling she would. If she is anything like me, that is. I would never harm an innocent just for practice. But I know I could do it to defend others, or even myself, but especially others."

WONDER

*O*nder finished eating her sandwich, emptied her cappuccino cup, and wiped her mouth with a napkin.

"What now?"

Anandur shifted on the stool. "Do you want a pastry?"

Why did she have a feeling that he was stalling? Maybe he was not in the mood to start his workday?

Or did he want a few more moments with her?

She certainly wanted more time with him. Anandur was fun to be with, perhaps because he didn't take anything seriously, himself included. His sunny attitude was the perfect antidote to her serious one.

"I'm full, thank you." But if he wanted to take her out again, she was all for it. "Do you get breaks? Can we meet for lunch?"

"I'll see what I can do. It depends on Kian's plans for today." Anandur scratched his beard. "I'm going to take you to see Bridget, the clan's doctor. Well, she was until Julian came back, that's her son who is also a doctor. But he is away at some conference. Kian thinks it's a good idea for her to check you out and make sure your injury is healing all right. Maybe she can also find out why you can't remember anything."

"Sounds good to me."

Anandur scratched the back of his head. "He also wants Vanessa to talk to you. She is a therapist who specializes in trauma."

For some reason, he seemed very uncomfortable with Kian's commands.

Wonder put a hand on his thigh. "It's okay. I don't mind. In fact, I would love to talk to them. I'm open to anything that might help restore my memories or at least explain why I lost them."

Anandur expelled a relieved breath. "I'm glad you have no problem with that. I was afraid you wouldn't want to talk to strangers and answer a bunch of intrusive questions, especially not on your first day here. But the boss insisted."

"I have nothing to hide." Wonder rose to her feet and picked up her paper plate and cup. "What do I do with these?"

"I'll take them to the trash."

"Wait." Wonder wiped the table with a paper napkin and added it to the pile.

Observing Carol running around and fulfilling orders, she realized that the blond had no one helping her and was doing everything herself. The least Wonder could do was wipe the table clean.

"Thanks for breakfast." She waved at Carol.

"Come back for lunch. But I'm afraid the selection here is the same for breakfast, lunch and dinner. Sandwiches and more sandwiches and pastries."

"It was very good."

"Come on," Anandur said. "The clinic is right over there." He pointed at a one-story building recessed a little from the rest of the communal facilities surrounding the village square.

As they entered, a woman with a wild head of hair that was

even redder than Anandur's beckoned them into her office. "Come right in."

"Wonder, this is Bridget, the doctor. Bridget, this is Wonder."

The doctor offered Wonder her hand. "A pleasure to meet you."

"Same here." The doctor's small hand had a surprisingly firm grip.

"I'll leave you two to talk," Anandur said. "Can you find your way back to the house?"

"Of course. But I don't have a key."

"There is no need. No one locks their doors in the village." He leaned in and gave her a quick peck on the cheek. "I'll see if I can get a break for lunch and come check up on you."

He was so confusing. One moment he was kissing her, even if only on her cheek, and the next he was sounding like a parent saying goodbye to a kid who was afraid to be left alone with a stranger.

It was embarrassing.

Wonder rolled her eyes and waved a dismissive hand. "Don't worry about me. I'll be fine."

Still, he didn't move from his spot.

"Go already. I want to talk to Bridget in private." She gave him a slight push.

"I'll see you later." Anandur pivoted on his heel and walked out without looking back.

Wonder sighed. Pretending to be just friends was going to be tough. It was easier when he was keeping his distance, but then he did things like giving her a kiss or taking her hand, which implied intimacy.

"Take a seat, Wonder," Bridget said. "Tell me about your coma."

"All I can tell you is what happened after I woke up. I have no memory of how it happened or of the life I had before it. I don't even know my real name. I chose Wonder because it sounded nice."

The doctor smiled. "I heard the story. You have no idea how fast rumors spread over here. I was told you woke up in Egypt."

"Yes."

"Was it in a hospital?"

"No. It was on a construction site. Someone must have dumped me there without checking whether I had a pulse. They probably thought I was dead."

Bridget narrowed her eyes. "Were you very thin when you woke up?"

"How did you know? I was skeletal."

"Your body must've gone into stasis. A severe injury might do that to an immortal, and after several weeks in that state a bare minimum of the original musculature remains."

"I see. Anandur told me what stasis was, but I didn't make the connection."

Over the next several hours, the doctor asked many more questions, took a lot of blood samples, and put Wonder inside a weird machine that scanned her brain and another one that scanned her heart.

"There is nothing wrong with you physically, Wonder," she declared after all the tests were done. "If you suffered head trauma, your body repaired itself beautifully. There is no sign of anything. Your heart is perfectly mended as well. You're healing very fast even for an immortal."

"What does it mean? Are there different kinds of immortals?"

Bridget put her tablet down and steepled her fingers. "The theory is that the closer you are to the source, the stronger you are as far as your special immortal capabilities. This is especially true in the case of healing. Your mother must have been a very old immortal. Someone whose blood wasn't diluted by generations of humans."

"Maybe I'm a very old immortal myself?" Wonder would have loved nothing more than to stick it to Anandur and tell him that she was older than him.

Bridget shook her head. "You're a very young immortal. I estimate that you are between eighteen and twenty-one years old."

Disappointing. "Are you sure?"

Bridget nodded. "I'm very sure."

Well, if she was indeed so young, then there was no shame in asking the question that had been bothering her for a while. "Is there any way to know if I was ever intimate with a male?" She bit on her lower lip. "I don't remember anything, and I would like to know."

Bridget smiled. "That's perfectly understandable. I can check if your hymen is still intact, but that's not conclusive proof. Some girls don't have them, and still others tear it other than via intercourse. But in any case, I will have to perform an internal exam, which means that I will have to put my fingers inside your vagina. Are you okay with that?"

Wonder blushed profusely. Not because of the internal exam Bridget had suggested, but because the doctor assumed she was so utterly ignorant that an explanation was needed.

"I know what a gynecological exam is. I never had one, but I know what to expect." Between television and YouTube, one could learn anything.

"Good. So is it a yes?"

Wonder nodded. "I want to know."

13

GRUD

"Vera!" Grud hollered as he entered the house. "Is the food ready?" The smell was great. The old woman was an excellent cook.

"It's almost done, dear. Don't you want to wait for your Uncle Harold? We can all eat together when he comes back. It's so nice to have lunch as a family."

"Fifteen minutes. If he is not back by then, I want my food on the table."

"Yes, dear."

Grud plopped on the couch, leaned back, propped his feet on the coffee table, and clicked the remote to change the channel from the boring cooking show the woman had been watching. He needed to check the local news.

It was only his second day at Vera and Harold's house, and already the novelty of the arrangement that had seemed so sweet was starting to wear off.

The woman was fussing over him as if he were her real nephew, which was what he'd thralled the old couple to believe, but it was annoying as hell.

There were advantages of course, like Vera cooking all of

her signature dishes for the beloved nephew, and old Harold running around and buying everything Grud was asking for.

Yesterday, he'd sent the old guy to the mall to buy him clothes, shoes, a new phone, and a wallet, which Harold had also kindly filled with cash.

Grud had even considered having them buy him a new car, but their bank account didn't have enough money in it. Not a problem; when he left, he was going to take Vera's car, same as he'd done an hour ago.

With his curiosity getting the better of him, Grud had driven to the facility and had gone to investigate.

He'd been careful, parking Vera's car next to another building that had several cars in its parking lot, and then strolling casually to the facility he'd spent the last several months at.

It had been very low risk.

Even if Wonder had been there and seen him, she would not have recognized him. With most of his beard gone, the neat haircut Vera had given him, and the new clothing Harold had bought for him, Grud could barely recognize himself.

But just as he'd expected, the building was vacant.

The front door had been locked, but apparently no one had checked the office he'd escaped through. The window had been still open, and the screen had remained torn. Grud had gotten in the same way he'd gotten out.

What he hadn't expected was to find the hole he'd made in the wall all patched up as if it were never there. The mattresses and blankets and spare clothing were all gone too, as was his stack of books.

Someone had taken great care to erase all evidence of anyone other than the apes ever being locked in those cages.

Why would anyone go to all that trouble?

Not the human police, that was for sure. They would've wanted the evidence to stay intact.

Whoever had done it must've wanted to protect Wonder and cover up her criminal activity. Using the facility without permission was no doubt a punishable offense even in the West, where the laws were lax and civilians were allowed way too many personal freedoms.

Humans weren't meant to be free. Mortdh's teachings said that it wasn't good for them. They'd been created to be slaves to their betters and needed a firm hand to guide them.

But if not the police, then who could've done it?

Grud had been watching her for months and collecting the little bits of information she'd let slip. Wonder didn't have friends, human or immortal.

Maybe it wasn't about Wonder at all?

Maybe it was about Dur?

What if Dur had overpowered Wonder, taken her phone, and called his people?

As a spy, Dur probably belonged to a secret division of the Brotherhood, and the men Grud had seen leading Shaveh and Mordan out had been from that unit.

That could explain the cover-up job, but it didn't explain why Shaveh and Mordan had been taken away in handcuffs. Although it did explain why they hadn't tried to get free.

"Gary, honey." Vera pushed the kitchen door open. "Harold is back with the things you asked for. Would you like me to set the table?"

Grud waved her off. He really hated all these cutesy names she called him. He was a warrior, not 'dear' and not 'honey.'

"I said I was hungry."

But in case someone came to visit the old humans, he had to keep up the nephew named Gary charade. A few more days of repeated thralling and the couple would not remember their own names, let alone the invented nephew's. By then he would probably be gone.

Vera smiled. "It will be ready in a minute."

After the woman's interruption, it took him a few moments to gather his thoughts again.

Why would the Brotherhood arrest Shaveh and Mordan?

Getting caught by a female was humiliating, but it wasn't a crime.

The other possibility was that Dur wasn't a Brother at all. He might have been a clansman, and those who'd arrested Shaveh and Mordan had been Guardians who came to rescue him.

The spy story might have been a clever cover to hide who he really was while he pretended to be one of them. That would also explain why he'd seemed odd for a member of the Brotherhood.

The guy was too polite and too charming, behaving like a human male who was practiced in wooing females rather than just taking what he wanted from them.

Still, if he were a Guardian, the bastard was a very convincing liar.

Grud shook his head. All that thinking was starting to give him a headache. He had a hard time combining all the possible threads into something that made sense.

If Dur was a clansman, and those who'd arrested Shaveh and Mordan were Guardians, they would have taken Wonder with them. Why would they care if the evidence of her trespassing was discovered?

Fuck. Thinking in circles wasn't going to solve the puzzle for him. Besides, his rumbling stomach was too distracting for him to think clearly.

Maybe once he was full, the answers would come.

14

MAGNUS

*a*fter driving around the neighborhood nearest the facility for over an hour, Liam parked the car, opened his box of mints, and popped one into his mouth. "You should get the guy with the dogs again."

"Dogs can't track someone in a vehicle." Magnus leaned his head against the headrest.

Earlier that morning, he'd had one of the Guardians call Jorge's wife with some bullshit story about insurance. The guy spoke fluent Spanish, which had been instrumental in getting her to cooperate.

With a detailed description of the truck and the license plate number, Magnus had been sure they would find it parked somewhere in that neighborhood, but apparently he'd been wrong.

"Not true. I read about a dog that tracked an abducted child over forty miles away. The child had been driven in a van."

Magnus cast Liam a sidelong glance. "Don't believe everything you read in the newspapers. And even if that were true, Jeff's dogs can't do it."

"Did you ask?"

"I didn't have to. They sniffed around the place the gardener was found and then stopped."

Liam rubbed his jaw. "If I were that Doomer, I would've dumped that truck at the first opportunity and got another car."

"I had William check on it. No cars were reported stolen in a twenty-mile radius from the facility."

"None would be reported if he thralled the owner." Liam popped two more mints into his mouth.

"Are you hungry? Or is it some kind of a nervous tick?"

"I think better when I chew on something."

"How about we pick up a burger instead of you popping those mints like they are candy?"

"I'm all for it."

As Liam turned the ignition on, Magnus pulled out his phone and rang William again.

"Sorry, mate, but we can't find that truck for you. It's an old model, and it has no LoJack."

Magnus switched the phone to his other ear. "What about the phone? I'm pretty sure the Doomer dumped it in the same place he left the truck."

"That would have been a stupid move. He probably destroyed it and then dumped it somewhere else."

"Not necessarily. We are talking about a Doomer here. They are not taught to think independently. They follow orders."

"If you can get me the phone number and the login information we can track it to its last location."

"I'll have Vince call the wife and ask."

"Let me know when you have it." William disconnected the call.

"Are you okay with a drive-through?" Liam asked.

Magnus glanced at his freshly pressed slacks. If he got them stained, they'd be ruined. "I prefer to sit at a table if you don't mind."

"As you wish. I'll try to find something."

After texting Vince, Magnus put the phone back in his pocket. "I still think the Doomer is hiding somewhere in this neighborhood. He could've thralled a resident to let him use the garage."

"As I said before, those dogs could come in useful. We can split up, you, Jeff, and me, each one with a dog, and comb the neighborhood."

"Maybe. I don't know if Jeff or his dogs will like your idea."

"Found it!" Liam said as he spotted an In-N-Out.

"I told you that I wanted a decent place with a table to eat on."

"They have seating inside. I just love those burgers."

It wouldn't have been Magnus's first choice, or his fiftieth, but when partnering with another Guardian compromises had to be made.

"I thralled Jeff to forget the details from yesterday. I don't think he would've wanted to assist in finding my supposed partner after learning he'd robbed a gardener. If I want him to bring his dogs tomorrow, I will have to drive to his place, wait for him to come back home, and thrall him again to agree. The guy is booked for weeks in advance."

"I don't see a problem with that." Liam got out of the car and waited for Magnus to join him.

"I guess it's not a big deal. Two consecutive thralls are not going to cause damage, provided they're done right." The guy had been easy to thrall, which was an advantage. The lesser force needed for entry, the more precise the thralling could be.

Liam pulled the hamburger joint's door open. "Maybe the hacker will find the truck by the phone's last recorded location, and there will be no need for the dogs."

"I hope so."

15

ANANDUR

*R*egrettably, lunch with Wonder wasn't happening. Kian had an appointment in the city and needed both him and Brundar to accompany him.

Letting her know he wouldn't be picking her up, though, was complicated by the fact that he had no way of communicating with her. He'd smashed her cellphone and hadn't supplied her with a new one yet.

But he had Bridget's.

"What's up?" he asked as she picked up. "Are you done with Wonder?"

"I am. She is with Vanessa now."

"Do you know how long it will take?"

"They've just started. I assume several hours."

"Can you do me a favor and tell her that I can't make it to lunch? And also make sure she is fed?" He wanted to suggest paying her back for Wonder's lunch, but Bridget would've been insulted.

The doctor chuckled. "Don't worry, we won't let your girl starve. Vanessa is taking good care of her."

Damn busybodies. "She is not my girl, she is my friend, and I feel responsible for her. That's all."

"Right. Anyway, check with Vanessa in a couple of hours."

"I will. Thanks."

"No problem."

He switched the phone to his other ear. "By the way, did you find anything?"

"Doctor-patient confidentiality, Anandur. You'll have to wait for Wonder to tell you."

He'd expected as much. "I will."

His next phone call was to William.

"What can I do for you, Anandur?"

"Can you hook Wonder up with a new phone?"

"Sure thing."

"When will it be ready?"

"You can pick one up in five minutes."

"I can't. I'm in the city with Kian. I'll come over when I'm back."

"See you then."

THE FIRST THING Anandur had done once he returned to the village was to stop by William's.

"Thanks for the phone." He tucked the box under his arm.

"You're welcome. Tell Wonder where she can find me if she needs help with it. I put the instructions up on our site, but there is nothing better than one-on-one demonstration, especially for someone who is new to our systems."

"I'm sure she'll be able to figure it out on her own." William's disappointed expression prompted him to add, "I guess it might get a bit confusing, though. I'll tell her to come see you if she needs a more in-depth tutorial."

William grinned. "That would be great. I want to meet the girl who defeated the undefeatable duo."

"Yeah, about that. I suggest you don't mention it to her. She's touchy about it."

"Why?"

Anandur shrugged. "The day I understand all the strange intricacies of the female psyche, will be the day I solve the secret of life."

"I hear you. Isn't there a Nobel Prize waiting for the first male to crack the code?"

"If there isn't, there should be. It might be the most important discovery of all times." With those parting words, Anandur walked out of the lab and headed for the clinic.

Hopefully they were done, because Callie was waiting for them with dinner.

A smile spread over his face as he found Wonder sitting on a bench outside the clinic. Her eyes closed and her face tilted up to absorb the last rays of the setting sun, she looked so serene.

Beautiful.

Taking a moment to absorb her beauty, he stared at her relaxed, youthful face, trailed over the thick braid resting over one plump breast, and finished at her long legs that were stretched out in front of her.

Fates, the girl was an impossible to resist temptation.

Right.

He shook his head. Little sister—that was how he should think about her, a young girl who needed his help to start her life. Lusting after Wonder was not cool.

"Hey, sleepyhead, wake up." He nudged her sneakered foot with his boot. "I have something for you."

As Wonder opened her eyes, the vivid jade color took his breath away. "You got me a present?"

"A new phone."

"Thank you. I had to ask Vanessa to let me use hers. I called the maintenance service to let them know that I won't be cleaning the warehouses until further notice."

He sat on the bench next to her, but not too close. "How did it go?"

"Oh, I said I had a family emergency and that I didn't know when I'd be able to come back to work."

"I meant with Vanessa and Bridget."

A blush skittered across Wonder's cheeks, disappearing as soon as it had appeared. "It was interesting. Bridget says there is nothing wrong with me physically. Vanessa asked me about a thousand questions before declaring me sound of mind."

"Did she remember to feed you?"

"They were both very nice. Vanessa took me to the café for lunch." She cast him an accusing glance. "I didn't have any money on me and had to let her cover the bill. It was very embarrassing. When is Magnus coming back with my stuff?"

"Shit, I should have left you some money. I was sure I could grab a quick lunch with you, but Kian needed me, and I had no way of letting you know other than calling Bridget. Did she tell you I called?"

"Yes, she did. That's why I'm sitting here instead of going home. I was waiting for you."

He pulled out a bunch of twenties and handed them to her. "Here, this should cover you until Magnus returns."

After a moment's hesitation, she took the money. "I'll pay you back when I get my purse. By the way, does Carol accept cards? I had my debit card in my jeans pocket when you took me away from the facility, but I didn't see anyone using credit or debit at the café."

"We don't use them here. Not yet. William is working on it."

"Who is William?"

"He is our tech guy. If you need any help with the new phone, he is your guy. I'll show you where he works. I'll also get you the clan-issued charge card for the vending machines."

"Thanks."

Anandur glanced at his watch. "We have about half an hour before dinner at Callie and Brundar's. Do you want to take a walk?"

"I would love to."

As she pushed to her feet and stretched, the buttons on Amanda's too small blouse nearly popped open.

"Are you coming?" she asked.

Gazing at those buttons and hoping they'd give, he'd remained seated.

"Yeah." Anandur forced his eyes away from her breasts to look into her captivating eyes. "So what else did Vanessa have to say?" he asked as they started walking.

Wonder tucked her hands into the back pockets of her jeans. "She says I'm anxious because I don't know who I am and that's natural. There isn't much she can do for me since she can't hypnotize me or thrall me. The only way for me to regain my memories is to expose myself to as many experiences and as much information as I can, hoping that something will trigger them. She's going to prepare for me a tablet with audio books that are summaries of the originals so I can learn as fast as I can."

"What about the high school equivalency?"

Wonder shrugged. "I think I'll wait with that. For now, I want to feel like a normal person my age. I still have huge gaps in general knowledge, and I don't have a full command of the language yet. I want to focus on that for a while. Vanessa said that reading a lot would help with that. Mrs. Rashid said the same thing."

Anandur rubbed the back of his neck. "Speaking of age. Did either of them figure out how old you are?" *Please let it be twenty-five and older.*

Not that it really mattered. Wonder's innocence and inexperience were what they were, regardless of her actual biological age.

"Bridget thinks I'm as young as you said I am." She avoided his eyes, looking ahead into the distance. "She said I could be between eighteen and twenty-one."

He could live with twenty-one, barely, but it was better than eighteen.

"The thing is, in some ways I feel much older than that, and in others younger. I don't think it matters much, though." She cast him a sidelong glance from under her long lashes.

Anandur shook his head. "The reason it matters is that a young person can be easily influenced and manipulated by someone older and more experienced. It creates an unfair advantage. In your case, it's even worse. You know less about the world than the average twelve-year-old."

Turning toward him, Wonder's jade eyes blazed with indignation.

She humphed. "That's the worst bunch of nonsense I've heard in a while. I might not know much about anything, but do I seem to you like someone who is easily manipulated? Was it easy for you to convince me of your innocence? Were my three prisoners successful in influencing my decisions?"

He had to admit that she made a good argument. "Two points for Wonder. You win this round." He lifted two fingers in the sign of victory.

She humphed again. "I would say that I won every round so far. Maybe not easily, but still, a win is a win."

Her spirited reaction was interesting. This was not the cool-headed, soft-spoken girl he'd gotten to know. When riled, Wonder found her voice and then some.

Good for her.

Perhaps he should needle her more often. Wonder always looked beautiful to him, but while miffed she was magnificent.

16

WONDER

"*T*hank you for inviting me again." Wonder followed Callie to the dining room table. "Can I help bring stuff from the kitchen?"

"There is nothing to bring. Sit, eat, and enjoy. Brundar did the cooking this time." Callie sat down. "All I did were the mashed potatoes." She lifted the lid off a large glass dish. "The asparagus." She repeated the reveal with a smaller dish. "This one is for us girls. Anandur thinks that anything green is bad for him, and Brundar is not a fan of veggies either."

As he glanced at his girlfriend, Brundar's harshly beautiful features softened, the warmth in his expression taking Wonder aback. The change was startling in a guy that most of the time looked like a beautiful but ominous statue.

"I'll go check on the steaks." Brundar slid open the glass doors leading to the backyard.

As the room filled with the smell of grilled steaks, Anandur closed his eyes and inhaled. "I love the smell of dead animals on the grill."

"You make it sound so gross." Callie lifted the lids off the two remaining dishes, one with corncobs and another with a small mixed-greens salad. "This one is also just for us girls." She winked at Wonder.

Anandur unfurled a napkin and put it over his lap. "You're spoiling me, Callie. Steaks and mashed potatoes for two days in a row is a real treat."

She leaned toward him and kissed his cheek. "I think you deserve a little pampering after surviving captivity on rice and beans."

Wonder felt heat creep up her cheeks. "I couldn't afford more than that. Immortals eat a lot, and I was trying to save up for a rent deposit, so I could leave the shelter. Do you know how expensive rent is in San Francisco? Even with roommates?"

"Oh, sweetie, no one is accusing you of anything. You did what you had to do, that's all."

"Speaking of money," Anandur cut Callie's apologies short. "Earlier, I got a text from Kian. He approved an allowance for you."

When had that happened? Anandur hadn't mentioned it when he loaned her the money. He must've gotten a text after that. The guy was constantly getting texts and replying to them. Though most of the time it seemed like he was trading jokes. Either that or his work was funny enough to make him laugh, and she doubted that was the case.

"It's not much, only twelve hundred a month, but given that your living expenses are covered, I think it should be enough. And when you decide what and where you want to study, the clan will naturally pay for the tuition as well."

Wonder was rendered speechless by such generosity. She'd expected the allowance to be a couple of hundred, not a dozen. It was too much, and it made her uncomfortable. She wasn't a charity case. "I appreciate the offer, I really do, and I might take Kian up on the offer to pay for tuition, but only as a loan." She lifted her hand to stop Anandur's protests. "I'm an able-bodied woman, not a child. I will work for my spending money."

Brundar entered the room holding a platter of steaks, and slid the glass door closed behind him. "If you join the Guardian training program, you will get paid a salary that's quite decent while you're in it. When you graduate, the pay will triple."

Wonder wished people would stop suggesting it. She'd made it pretty obvious that it wasn't a career path she was interested in, and yet they kept pushing.

"Guardians make good money," Callie said. "The housing is provided by the clan, and they get a month's paid vacation a year, a pretty sweet deal. Not that Brundar is taking advantage of the paid vacation part. I'm still trying to teach him how to take it easy and just chill for a while."

Well, that explained Anandur's luxurious apartment at the keep and the fancily appointed houses in the village. The living expenses were covered by the clan. A member didn't need to be rich to get a nice place to live.

It was cool, but it also meant that Anandur wasn't someone important after all.

Well, that wasn't true. It seemed like everyone in the clan knew and loved him. That made him important enough.

Getting behind Callie, Brundar removed a steak from the platter and placed it on her plate. "I can't take off while all these Guardians need retraining. When they are combat-ready, we can go on a vacation."

"And when is that going to happen?"

"Soon." He put a steak on Wonder's plate. "Another one?"

"No, thank you. Maybe later."

"Given my brother's appetite, I doubt there will be any left over. But suit yourself." He put four steaks on Anandur's plate and took two for himself.

"Dig in, everyone," Callie said.

Anandur rubbed his hands before picking up his utensils. "Don't mind if I do."

Brundar popped the cap of a beer bottle and handed it to his brother, and then opened another one for himself. "I'm not offering you any since you said you don't drink alcohol."

"I don't," Wonder said. "I don't like the taste."

Callie handed her a cold coke can. "I noticed that you like these."

"I do, thanks."

"Cheers!" Brundar clinked bottles with Anandur and then with Callie and Wonder's coke cans.

"To family and good friends," Anandur said.

Family and friends.

That sounded awesome. Maybe one day she would find hers. And if not, maybe the clan could be her adopted family. Everyone she'd met so far was super nice.

"So, how about it, Wonder? Do you want to join the force?" Brundar asked. "With those killer reflexes of yours, you're a natural. I wouldn't be surprised if you completed the training in record time."

Wonder finished chewing a piece of steak and wiped her mouth with a napkin. "Thank you. But I would rather do something that doesn't involve fighting."

"That's a shame. I wish there were another job I could offer you, but I'm afraid there isn't much to do in the village."

"I'm sure there is." Wonder cut off another piece of the juicy steak.

Anandur waved his fork at her. "You're not going to clean houses or offices if that's what you're thinking."

"There is nothing wrong with cleaning. It's good, honest work. But that's not what I had in mind."

He arched a brow. "What else is there?"

"Carol needs help in the coffee shop. Maybe she would consider hiring me? I don't know how to make cappuccinos, but it shouldn't be too difficult to learn, and I can manage sandwiches just fine."

Callie clapped her hands. "That's an awesome idea! Carol keeps complaining about having to work two jobs. I'm sure she would love to have you."

Anandur nodded. "It could be really good for you too. If you work at the café, you'll eventually get to meet everyone. I'll talk to Carol and Jackson tomorrow."

Wonder released the breath she'd been holding while waiting for Anandur's response. She knew Carol wouldn't object to having some help around the café. Anandur had been the only possible obstacle to her plan. Except, who was that guy Anandur had mentioned?

"Who's Jackson?"

"He is the guy who is actually supposed to run the place. Carol is supposed to be helping him, not working full time," Anandur said. "But he has two other cafés to manage until he trains his replacement."

Shit on a stick. That meant that she could only have that job temporarily.

Still, it was better than nothing.

"How long until he takes over?"

Anandur put his fork down. "Not anytime soon. There are some complications that are preventing him from moving into the village. But that's a story for another day."

17

RUTH

*W*ith music blasting from a portable speaker, Ruth chopped vegetables for her famous minestrone soup, while swaying her hips to the beat and singing along.

The good news of Anandur's safe return had lifted a heavy weight off her chest.

She felt years younger and happier.

When he'd gone missing, the entire village had been submerged in a dark cloud. Maybe Ruth had noticed it more because she didn't live there and only visited when Sylvia and Roni invited her over. The one time she'd been over during his abduction, the place looked and felt like zombie town, with everyone walking around a little hunched over, their eyes downcast.

Ruth suspected that it hadn't been just worry about Anandur, whom everyone including her loved, but a general sense of dread. At least that was how she'd felt.

If a fearsome warrior like the huge Guardian could have been taken, then no one was safe.

She was still trying to wrap her head around the fact that Anandur hadn't been taken by Doomers, thank the merciful

Fates, but by a lone immortal girl who thought he was a Doomer out to harm a human female. Ruth couldn't wait to meet Wonder, who according to the rumors was aptly named after Wonder Woman. Not only was she a powerful warrior, but she also looked a lot like the actress who played her.

The arrival of the new immortal female was also cause for celebration. The guys were probably going crazy trying to woo her.

Ruth smiled. It would be fun to watch them try. Maybe she could ask Carol to switch places with her for a few days. In the near future, the village café, which was the central hub of the place, was going to be much more interesting than Fernando's.

As the front doorbell rang, Ruth lowered the volume on the speaker and rushed to open the door for Nick.

"You look like you're in a good mood." Moving the cake box to the side, Nick leaned to give her a quick peck on the lips. "I should put the tiramisu in the fridge."

She opened the door wide. "I feel silly about sending you to buy a cake when I manage a coffee shop."

"Yeah, but Vlad only bakes pastries." Nick shook his head. "A Goth baker. Kudos for the nonconformity."

"Vlad is a sweetheart. He only looks odd until you get to know him. He is really a nice kid."

Crap, she'd sounded like a mother.

But apparently the remark went over Nick's head. He opened the fridge and moved things around to make room for the cake. "Is Vlad his real name? Because I'm sure he chose it to go with the whole Dracula theme he has going on."

The real story wasn't one Ruth could tell Nick. Vlad's mother had named him after the infamous immortal who'd gone raving mad and had to be put down. Strange woman. Who names her child after a crazed murderer?

"Maybe you got it in reverse, and he adopted the Goth look to match the name."

Nick pulled her into his arms and lifted her up. "I think that's enough talk about Vlad."

"What are you doing?"

"Time for a proper kiss." He carried her to the living room and sat on the couch with her on his lap. "But first, tell me what's the good mood all about?"

Ruth smirked and put her cheek on his chest. Nick probably thought it was because of the great sex they'd had.

Hey, maybe it was.

To be frank, the heavy weight she'd been carrying around for years had been lifted the night she and Nick had discovered that they were perfectly matched in bed. It had been better than good. It had been amazing.

Except, until Anandur had been found she couldn't allow herself to feel happy. As long as he'd been missing and his fate had been unknown, it hadn't felt right to rejoice.

She couldn't tell Nick about the Guardian, but she could tell him exactly what he wanted to hear and it would be the honest truth.

"It's about you and me. We are good together."

His arms tightened around her. "Yes, we are."

Lifting her head, Ruth looked into Nick's smiling eyes. "After dinner, we could watch another movie." She winked.

"Oh, no, I created a monster!" Nick laughed. "What do you have in mind?"

"Does that actor have more movies like that one?"

Nick pretended to frown. "It's the big schlong, isn't it? Because he sure as fuck ain't a pretty boy."

"It's not the schlong." She shrugged. "I love his voice. I'll probably get excited just from hearing him talk."

"Is it when he talks like this?" Nick deepened his voice in a failed attempt to mimic the actor.

"No, silly. And it's not just the voice. It's his attitude." It was hard to put into words what she found so sexy about a guy she would not have given a second glance on the street. He had a certain quality about him that was rare. "I think it's his intensity. When he looks at the actress, you can tell he wants her. It's not an act. He is lusting after her for real."

Nick rolled his eyes. "Well, duh. She is hot, and he's not."

A man wouldn't understand. Heck, Ruth wasn't sure other women would. It wasn't as if she talked about the subject with anyone. Besides, people rarely told the truth. Not because they were liars, but because sometimes it was embarrassing to admit to certain yearnings.

And yet, despite her shyness and her reluctance to discuss personal issues with anyone, she didn't want to withhold things from Nick more than was absolutely necessary. Already, there were too many secrets she was forced to keep.

He was a goofball, but he wouldn't make fun of her or ridicule her desires, not even inside his own head. It was okay to share things with Nick.

Ruth felt safe with him.

Not that she could be absolutely sure. The one time she'd been tempted to take a peek inside his head, she couldn't.

At first, it had taken her by surprise, and she rationalized it as guilt over the intrusion preventing her from seeing anything. After all, she had no such problems with the other humans in the café. Not that she did that often, or searched for things that were none of her business.

Ruth only took the occasional peek to reassure herself that people liked her and didn't think of her as a weirdo.

But then she'd encountered another human into whose mind she couldn't peek, and then another.

Some humans erected instinctive protective shields around their minds, which made sense, but Nick wasn't the type. He wasn't suspicious, or timid, or reclusive.

The opposite was true.

Nick had no filter, and because of that some might have thought that he wasn't smart.

But he was highly intelligent, which was the other reason some human minds were tough to penetrate. His powerful brain probably made him more resistant to thralling, or maybe even an immune, which could pose one heck of a problem.

Until that was determined, Ruth needed to be careful about what she revealed to Nick. If it turned out that he wasn't a Dormant, there would be no way to erase his memories.

Except, with her meager thralling abilities, she might not have been good enough to penetrate his mind, but someone more talented might succeed where she'd failed.

In the meantime, though, she couldn't share with him what she was, or even who he possibly was, but she could share with him what turned her on. Not that it was going to be easy. But this was as good of an opportunity to start as any, and Ruth was sick of being a mouse.

Besides, with her head tucked under Nick's chin and her cheek resting on his chest, he couldn't see her flaming cheeks.

"He is also kind of commanding, but without being aggressive. I think the combination is hot."

18

NICK

*N*ick rubbed his tummy. "That tiramisu was over the top." He should've stopped after the linguine.

Ruth forked a little piece and put it in her mouth. "I have the perfect remedy for that."

"Sex?" That was all he could think of during dinner.

Hell, he was a fairly intelligent guy, and usually he had a lot to talk about, but not this evening. Ruth's comments from before had been taking up all his not too shabby bandwidth.

"Strong, black coffee," Ruth said. "I'll make us some."

Typically, Nick would've offered to help, but he needed a few quiet moments to think. "I'll do the dishes later if you don't mind. I have to digest first."

"Take your time."

Commanding, but not aggressive. What the hell did it mean?

He needed to pay better attention to tonight's movie. Apparently, girls noticed things that guys ignored. Who the fuck cared about a voice? The dude could've been the best-known newscaster in the world, and Nick would not have noticed anything special about him.

Aside from her throaty moans, he couldn't care less about

the actress's voice either. Maybe guys were more visual, and women were more auditory?

Well, duh. All guys saw in a porn flick were tits and asses. No one paid attention to what the actors said to each other.

Who cared?

Evidently, women did. They actually cared about the story. He'd read somewhere that women read four times as many fiction books as men.

Aha!

Suddenly it all clicked into place.

To Ruthie, the story was more important than what was happening on the screen. That was why she'd gotten so turned on the other night.

Well, that and the actor's voice.

Damn, he had to find another good movie with the same ugly actor who apparently sounded sexier than he looked.

Go figure.

Nick pushed his chair back, got up and walked over to the coffee table where Ruth had left her laptop. He should've realized why it was there the moment he'd gotten in.

"Do you want to drink your coffee on the couch?" Ruth asked.

"Yes, please. I want to find us a good movie to watch."

Ruth's cheeks were flaming red, but she pretended to be all cool. "Here you go." She handed him the small cup. "It's very hot, so give it a minute or two to cool down."

He took the cup and put it down on the table. "Aren't you going to sit with me?"

"I'll clean up while you search."

Crap. He'd promised to do that. "I'll help." Nick started to push to his feet, but Ruth put a hand on his shoulder.

"I don't need help to clear the table. Find us a movie."

Talk about a commanding tone. "Yes, ma'am." He sat back.

After a long search, he finally found what he was looking

for. Turning the volume down almost all the way, he let the movie run for a few moments to make sure he remembered it correctly. He'd seen so many porn flicks that it was hard to remember what happened in which, especially since he hadn't been paying much attention to the stories.

The only reason he knew girls liked them best were the comments they'd left.

"Why did you start without me?" Ruth sat next to him on the couch. "I want to see it from the beginning."

"I don't remember what the movie is about, but I think it's in the same series about the professor and his students."

Ruth arched a brow. "There was a series? I thought those were full-length independent movies."

"They are. But if one was a hit, it made sense to continue with the theme."

"I see." Ruth took a small sip of her coffee. "You didn't drink yours."

He'd forgotten all about it. "Let me cue the movie to the beginning first."

When the titles started, Nick lifted his cup, leaned back, and wrapped his arm around Ruth's shoulders.

A student wearing a traditional schoolgirl outfit, including a plaid skirt, knee-high white socks, a tie and a jacket, walked into the professor's office with a leather satchel slung over her shoulder. He'd fast-forwarded that part before, skipping over the uniform. Was the movie about high-school girls this time?

That was bad. The actress was obviously not a teenager, but Ruth might have a problem with that.

"Does it bother you that she is supposed to be a high-school girl and that he is her teacher?"

Ruth tilted her head. "Did they employ underage girls in the porn industry back then?"

"No, of course not. And this one is probably in her mid-twenties, which means that she is fifty-something now." He grimaced.

"What's wrong with a fifty-year-old?" Ruth sounded offended for some reason.

Women were strange. "Nothing, as long as she looks good. So are you okay with the movie or not?"

Ruth waved a hand. "I think I've already proven that I'm not a prude. This is a schoolgirl fantasy that is reenacted by adults."

"That's true." He put his hand on her knee and slowly slid it upwards, stopping on her inner thigh. "Did you ever have a crush on a teacher?"

She smirked. "Once. He was a very young substitute who happened to have a great voice too."

Again with the voice. "Was he handsome or ugly like this dude?"

She shrugged. "He wasn't ugly, but he wasn't handsome either. He was skinny and tall and had terrible posture."

"So it was all about the voice."

"Yes."

This was ridiculous. Maybe instead of losing weight and developing muscles, he should've taken voice-coaching lessons.

Well, it was never too late. He could still do that.

On the screen, the actor assumed the pose he had in the other movie, leaning against his desk and crossing his arms over his chest. "You've been late submitting your homework assignments every day this week, Kimberly. Is everything all right? Do you need help with anything?"

Kimberly chewed on her bottom lip, lowered her gaze to her ballet flats, and shifted from foot to foot. "Um, maybe?"

"Is it a yes or a no?" the professor said in a stern tone.

"I get easily distracted," the student whispered. "I want to do my homework, but I have all these thoughts going through my head, and before I know it, I've been daydreaming for an hour, sometimes two."

"And what are you daydreaming about?"

She lifted her eyes and smiled coyly. "You, professor. I daydream about you."

"Is that so?" The actor's voice dropped an octave.

"Yes, it is. I can't stop thinking about your hands." She glanced at them and licked her lips. "I imagine them all over my body."

"Tsk, tsk, Kimberly. You know it's wrong to have naughty thoughts like that about your teacher."

"I do. Are you going to punish me, professor? Like you punished Heather?" She looked at him from under her lowered lashes.

As Ruth's lips parted and her breathing became faster and shallower, Nick contemplated his next move. Skirts were very convenient for snogging, but it was too early for more than just resting his palm close to Ruth's heated center.

"Aha, I see. You're craving the same correction Heather got."

"Yes."

"Very well." The professor pushed away from the desk. "Sit on the couch."

"Yes, sir."

The guy took his jacket off, draped it over the back of his chair, and then started rolling up his sleeves, revealing very hairy forearms.

How Ruth could find the dude sexy was beyond Nick. The guy was hairy like a monkey. Even his knuckles were hairy.

Yuk.

The actress playing Kimberly was hot, but in a slutty way. Well, duh, what did he expect from a porn star? To look virtuous?

The whole scene was ridiculous. What was the professor going to do? Spank the girl?

Smirking, Nick glanced at Ruth.

Apparently, his Ruthie found the scene arousing, which

once again proved that women were not only strange but loony. Her eyes glued to the laptop's screen, she licked her lips and squirmed a little.

Well, well, it seemed like his shy girlfriend had some naughty fantasies. She must've read those Fifty Shades books that had been all the craze a while back.

Could he fulfill them without laughing his ass off, though?

19

RUTH

*T*his was hot.

Ruth hadn't read the Fifty Shades books or seen the movies that Sylvia and her friends had been going on and on about.

The whole idea had seemed absurd to her.

The romances she liked to read were sweet, and sometimes funny, and some of them had sex scenes that had caused her to blush, but she stayed away from anything that resembled those Fifty Shades books. Or worse.

Out of curiosity, she'd once downloaded a free book from the dark romance genre. The two chapters she'd read had given her nightmares for weeks.

What woman in her right mind wanted that?

It was crazy what some people found arousing. And yet, watching the scene on the screen unfolding, she was turned on.

It didn't mean that she wanted to reenact it with Nick, though. She would die from embarrassment before suggesting such a thing. But she could watch and enjoy.

The professor sat next to his student and took her hand, kissing the back of it. "Tell me, Kimberly. Are you a virgin?"

"Yes, sir, I am. I'm a good girl."

The professor tapped his finger on her pouty lips. "A good girl wouldn't be sitting here on this leather couch, goading her teacher to give her what she needs. But that's okay, sweetheart, naughty girls are my favorite." He placed her palm over his bulging erection.

"Oh, professor, you're so big."

Nick chuckled. "Here comes the big schlong."

Way to spoil the mood. Ruth slapped his thigh. "Stop it."

"Sorry."

The professor cupped the back of Kimberly's head, holding her in place as he kissed her.

Ruth felt a pang of disappointment. After all that sleeve rolling, he wasn't going to spank her?

"You're such a sweet girl, Kim. I don't feel right about taking your virginity."

"Please, professor, I need you to. I can't concentrate on anything else, and my grades are dropping."

He leaned back. "Well, we can't have that, can we? But first there is the issue of your late assignments and your lack of discipline. If after your punishment you still want to proceed, I will grant you your wish."

"Thank you, professor."

Ruth was giddy with excitement. There was going to be a spanking scene after all.

The professor tugged on the girl's wrist and pulled her over his lap.

"Last chance to change your mind, Kimberly."

The actress pushed her bottom up. "I want this."

From under her lashes, Ruth glanced at Nick to see if he was getting as excited as she was. The scent of his arousal was strong, but that could've been her proximity and not what was going on in the movie.

He had a slight smirk on his face, and she wasn't sure whether it was because he was embarrassed watching the scene or because he found it silly.

Probably the latter.

She'd better play it cool and not let him know how much this was arousing her.

Except, Nick was more attuned to her than she'd realized.

The hand he had on her thigh started a slow glide toward her heated center. When the tip of his finger touched her soaked panties, Nick sucked in a breath. A moment later he pushed the gusset aside and brushed his finger over her wet folds.

With a moan, Ruth let her head fall back on his arm and closed her eyes.

As Nick leaned and took her lips in a ravenous kiss, his finger slid inside her wet sheath. Thrusting his tongue into her mouth, he penetrated her with another finger.

Over the sound of her own throaty moans, Ruth heard the unmistakable slap and opened her eyes, but it was hard to see with Nick's head blocking the way.

A dilemma. Should she cut the kiss short to watch the hot scene? Or should she forget the movie and concentrate on the sensations bombarding her body?

Could she do both?

Nick let go of her mouth and glanced at the screen. "I see that you want to watch, baby." He gave her a slight push and helped her lie down on the couch. "You can keep on watching while I get busy doing other things." He pulled her panties down.

"Okay," she whispered.

As Ruth tilted her head to look, her breath left her in a whoosh.

Fates, why did she find the scene so erotic?

The girl's white panties were down around her thighs, and her round bottom was on full display, getting smacked by the professor's big hand.

The girl was wiggling all over, but not because she was trying to get away. He was caressing her perfectly shaped bottom more than he was smacking it, and when he did it was very lightly.

It was a game, not a punishment, and it was hot.

While she watched, Nick pulled down her skirt, leaving her bottom half bare, and then pushed her shirt and bra up instead of bothering with the clasp.

For some reason, being exposed like that was more erotic than being completely naked. It was naughty and lewd and it made her feel sexy.

"God, you're beautiful." He leaned down and took one nipple between his lips, sucking on it gently while thumbing the other.

As she kept watching, Nick put his hands on her knees and parted them, then dipped his head between them.

Tensing for a moment, Ruth wasn't sure whether she was ready for that, but when Nick delivered a soft kiss to her lower lips, she was a goner. He could do whatever he pleased with her.

Except, Nick wasn't the kind of guy who took anything for granted. Lifting his head, he looked at her and waited until she nodded.

"Thank you," he mouthed, then grinned and licked his lips before lowering his head between her spread thighs again.

Feeling loved and cared for, she put a hand on his head and caressed him. "I love you, Nicki."

He looked up. "Keep watching, baby. I want you to come all over my tongue."

A week ago she would've felt scandalized by his words, now they only aroused her more.

Nick was turning her into a wanton woman.

Or was it her doing?

It seemed that all she'd needed to release her inner wanton-ness was to feel safe and loved.

20

ANANDUR

*a*s Anandur spotted Jackson's blond head behind the counter, he grinned and waved. "Jackson, buddy, I'm glad to catch you here so early in the morning. I need to talk to you."

"Give me a minute." The guy finished frothing milk for a cappuccino, filled the small paper cup, and handed it to Ingrid. "Anything else? Can I offer you a pastry with that? They are freshly baked."

The boy was a born salesman.

"I had my eye on that Danish." She pointed. "Can you heat it up for me?"

"Sure. Let me pop it in the toaster oven."

Anandur pulled out a stool and sat down. "As long as you're at it, heat up one more for me."

Jackson smirked. "I knew you wouldn't want to talk on an empty stomach."

"How did you know I didn't have breakfast yet?"

"Is Magnus back?"

"No."

"That's how. Unless he makes it for you, you never eat at home."

Astounding observational skills. "True. Listen, I wanted to ask you if you still need someone to help around here."

"Why, do you have anyone in mind?"

"In fact, I do."

As the toaster oven beeped, Jackson grabbed a pair of tongs, pulled out the steaming Danishes, and put them on two plates. "One for you." He handed a plate to Ingrid. "And one for you." He put the other one in front of Anandur. "Do you want coffee with that?"

"A simple drip will do. Small, black."

Jackson lifted the carafe and filled a small paper cup. "Here you go. So, who is it?"

"You must've heard about Wonder, right?"

The boy's lips twisted in a smirk. "The girl who kicked both your and Brundar's asses? Yeah, I did."

Anandur pointed a finger at him. "Wipe that smirk off your face, boy, before I wipe it for you." He went for a stern expression and failed.

It was hard to pretend anger while watching Jackson's face contort in an effort to keep his lips from smiling.

"Yes, sir," Jackson croaked, his belly shaking with suppressed laughter.

"Anyway. She needs a job, and she thought she could help Carol out."

"Is she going to scare off my customers? I heard she is huge."

Apparently, the clan rumor machine worked just as well in the village as it had in the keep, blowing things out of proportion and turning every molehill into a mountain. Or in this case a gorgeous young woman into an ogress.

"She isn't huge. She is about Kri's size, and she is a beautiful young girl with a sweet and gentle personality."

Unless someone pissed her off, but he wasn't going to mention that. "She had very good reasons for what she did to Brundar and me."

Jackson lifted a brow. "You have a thing for her, don't you?" It wasn't a question.

"No, I don't. She is still a baby immortal, like you. I'm just helping her get settled."

"A baby, really?" Jackson's blue eyes blazed like Wonder's had last night.

It was ridiculous how the young took offense to being called young.

"Do I seem like a baby to you? I'm a mated male, and I run my own business."

Anandur lifted his hands in the universal sign for peace. "Don't get your panties in a wad. You're an awesome guy, Jackson, and I didn't mean to belittle you in any way. It's just that to an old fart like me you're a baby and so is Wonder. I can't think of her as anything other than a little sister."

He heard Carol snicker behind him. "Liar, liar, pants on fire." She sauntered over and pulled out a stool for herself.

"Whatever. Can Wonder work here or not?"

"Of course she can work here." Carol waved a hand. "Starting today. Mister Jackson the Great is only here for a couple of hours before heading back to his business empire."

Jackson flicked her with the corner of a dish towel. "That's no way to talk to your boss."

"Ouch! This is workplace abuse!" She turned to Anandur. "Guardian, arrest that man."

"Sorry, but I need him to hire my friend."

She threw her hands in the air. "Old boys' cliques. That's what it is."

Jackson smirked. "He is an old boy. Supposedly, I'm a baby."

Carol chuckled. "Baby boss. I like it. I think I'll start calling you that."

He pointed a finger at her. "I can always replace you with more vending machines. The keep's old café is running well and turning a good profit without any employees. I can do the same here."

Anandur grimaced. "Well is a relative term. You're not there at the end of the day to see how messy the tables are. The Guardians are pigs. They leave crumbs and spills behind. It's good that Kian allows the cleaning service to take care of the place at night."

"Why didn't anyone tell me?"

"And what would you do? Come over twice a day to wipe the tables?"

"You should hang up a sign," Carol said. "It should say self-serve also means self-clean."

Anandur stuffed the rest of his Danish in his mouth, washed it down with the remainder of the coffee, and rose to his feet. "I'm going to get Wonder. Which one of you is going to interview her, and what's the starting pay?"

"She is hired," Carol said. "No need for an interview. I like her."

"And the pay?" Anandur looked at Jackson.

"Same as what the waitresses at Fernando's are getting. Fifteen an hour plus tips."

"Sounds good." He pulled out his wallet and put a twenty on the counter. "Keep the change. I need to start leaving more generous tips."

21

WONDER

"The coffee part is simple," Carol said. "You just press this button here, and it grinds and does everything else automatically." She demonstrated. "The frothing requires some skill."

"Got it." Wonder watched Carol froth the milk and pour it into the cup. "Can I try?"

"Go ahead."

Everything was happening so fast. She had a new place to live, a new job, and was making new friends. It was everything Anandur had promised her and more.

With every passing moment, the idea of going back to her old life was becoming less and less appealing. There was nothing for her in San Francisco. She missed Tony and Natasha, but only a little, and she didn't miss her jobs or the shelter at all.

"Is that good?" She showed Carol the contents of her pitcher.

"Needs a little more foam. Give it one more minute and move it up and down the wand." She demonstrated with a chuckle. "Gently, like you would the other kind."

Wonder raised a brow. "Is the hand movement different for soymilk?"

Carol's eyes widened, and she slapped a hand over her mouth. "Don't tell me you're a virgin."

Mortified, Wonder glanced around. Thankfully, the morning rush was over, and the café was deserted save for one guy sitting with a newspaper at the furthest table. "Shh, don't talk so loudly."

"I'm sorry," Carol whispered. "Not that it's anything to be ashamed of. I just thought that you and Anandur had something going on. I was sure he was full of shit when he said he thinks of you as a little sister." She gave Wonder a once-over. "Because, honey, there is nothing little about you."

Wonder grimaced. Obviously, Carol hadn't meant to offend her, but to Wonder the remarks had felt more like barbs than compliments. She didn't like it when people commented on her size, and she hated Anandur's stupid attitude toward her.

Little sister? Really?

Ugh, what a frustrating male. Carol was right. Anandur was full of shit.

Over the few hours she'd spent working at the café, Wonder had had more guys come on to her than in the entire nine months she'd been awake, all of them handsome immortal males who found her attractive despite her size.

It had been a nice boost to her ego, that was for sure. The problem was that she hadn't felt a thing toward any of them.

There was only one guy she was interested in, and he was acting incredibly stupid.

Little sister indeed. Anandur should tell it to his manhood. That part of him didn't think of her as little or a sister.

"What's the matter?" Carol looked at her with worried eyes. "Did I say something wrong?"

Wonder glanced at the pitcher of milk. The foam was ruined. Cringing, she emptied it in the sink. "People judge me by my looks. I don't like being called big." She wasn't going to mention her virgin status, or Anandur's weird ideas of propriety.

None of the other guys who'd flirted with her thought she was too young.

"Why the hell not?" Carol put her hands on her hips. "I would love to be as tall as you." She waved a hand over Wonder's body. "You can wear whatever and look great. You know how hard it is for me to find flattering clothes? Everything is either too long, or too tight in the wrong places."

"Yeah, but you can wear heels and dresses and look feminine. I always have to wear flats, which I don't think look good with skirts, so I'm always in pants."

She looked down at her sneakers. "And those are the only shoes I have here. Magnus is going to collect my stuff and bring it when he returns. I'm okay as far as clothes go because Amanda gave me a bunch of her old discards, not that they are really used. Some still have the price tags attached." Wonder rolled her eyes. "Talk about pricy. But anyway, I don't even have flip-flops. How does anyone shop for things here? Is there a store somewhere?"

"Do you have a phone?" Carol asked. "I mean a clan issue one that works here."

Wonder pulled it from the back pocket of her jeans. "I do. And?"

"Come on." Carol took her hand. "Let Auntie Carol show you how it's done." She led her to a table.

It was funny for Carol to call herself auntie when she looked only a few years older than Wonder. Although as far as Wonder knew, she could be as old as Anandur. Living among humans, Wonder had got used to thinking of age in human terms.

"Have you ever shopped online?"

Wonder shook her head.

"What size shoe are you?"

"A nine."

Carol typed a few words on the screen and then handed the phone to Wonder. "Here you go. Go crazy, girl. Do you have a credit card?"

"I have a debit card."

"Works too. When you find a shoe you like add it to the shopping cart. You see that little icon up there?"

Wonder nodded.

"You can always edit the shopping cart before checking out. So just put in there anything you like. When you're done, show me, and I'll input the keep's address. All the deliveries go there, and every evening one of the Guardians brings them over here and puts them in the office building's lobby. You can collect your packages from there."

"Wow, that's awesome. But what if the shoes don't fit?"

"Easy. You send them back." Carol pointed at the top of the screen. "See that? Free shipping and free returns."

22

GRUD

"*D*o you want more eggs, dear?" Vera asked.

Grud handed her his plate. "More hash browns and sausages too."

Regrettably, it was time to say goodbye to home-cooked meals and to having two personal servants at his disposal.

Yesterday evening, he'd gone to the club Wonder worked security at. When he couldn't find her, he'd asked the barman about her.

"A vacation," the guy had said while looking Grud over suspiciously.

After that, he'd sat down, ordered a drink, and thralled the waitress who'd delivered it.

"Witness protection," the woman had said, adding that it was a secret and that Wonder's life might be in danger.

With the barman still eyeing him suspiciously, Grud couldn't have kept her talking for too long, so he'd ordered another drink, and then another, and each time had probed a little further.

"Here you go, dear." Vera put a heaping plate in front of him, then waited.

"Thank you," he growled at her. It was better to say the words and get rid of the old crone rather than suffer her annoying presence.

"You're welcome."

Crap, she'd ruined his concentration. Grud forked a sausage and stuffed it in his mouth.

The waitress had told him about two police detectives who had been asking everyone at the club questions about their redheaded friend. They'd also questioned Wonder.

Had they been Dur's buddies from his spy unit?

Was that how they'd found the facility? By following Wonder?

Grud doubted she'd caved under questioning. That female was too tough for that.

Over the last drink, he'd also discovered that the redhead, aka Dur, and his partner had come to the club before, asking about suspicious characters.

Like who?

Who had Dur and his partner been looking for?

Was it part of their spying activity?

Had Dur been working undercover as a police detective?

None of that made any sense.

The bottom line was that Wonder was gone and he wasn't going to find her because none of her coworkers knew where she was.

Which meant that there was no reason for him to stay away from the Brotherhood. Grud was smart enough to realize that he was in over his head and that he wasn't good at detective work.

It was better to stick to what he knew, which was taking orders and doing what he was told. There were worse fates than that. At least in the Brotherhood, he was part of something. Being on his own in a world full of humans wasn't how he wanted to spend his immortal life.

If he had the female, it would've been a different story. But that wasn't going to happen.

The question was what to tell his commanding officer when he called. It was best to stay as close to the truth as possible. He just had to come up with a good excuse for why he hadn't reported immediately and had waited until the third day after his escape.

Gommed would demand to know what had taken him so long.

"Are you done, dear?" Vera looked at his empty plate. "Do you want anything more?"

"That will be all." He wiped his mouth with a napkin and dropped it on the dining room table. "Where is Harold?"

"He is in the kitchen. Do you want me to call him for you?"

He waved a hand. "Harold! Get in here!"

It took the old man a couple of minutes to get up and shuffle his feet to the dining room.

"Sit down!" Grud pointed to a chair. "You too." He pointed at Vera.

When the two humans were seated, Grud got up and put his hands on the table. "Look into my eyes," he said, imbuing his voice with command. "Forget that you ever saw me. I was never here. You are going to sit here and not get up until the clock over there shows ten o'clock. Nod if you understand."

The couple nodded like zombies. A little drool started running down Harold's mouth.

It was the old man's fault. If he weren't such a tough cookie, Grud would not have used such brute force to manipulate his brain. The guy had probably suffered permanent brain damage.

Grud collected his new wallet, which now contained several thousand dollars and the couple's credit cards, his new twelve-hundred dollar phone and Vera's car keys, and headed out.

It wasn't until he'd driven all the way to the city that he stopped at a supermarket parking lot and pulled out his phone.

"Yes?" His commander answered after several rings.

"It's Grud, Sir."

23

MAGNUS

"*I* don't like the idea of splitting up," Jeff said.

Magnus scratched Ralph behind the ear. "This one likes me. He'll have no problem going with me. We can cover more ground faster if we split up."

Jeff cast a glance at Liam who was talking to Reese as if she was a girl he was asking on a date.

"Who is this pretty girl?"

Reese sniffed Liam's hand suspiciously.

"I'm a good guy. I promise. If you behave, I'll take you out to lunch. Do you like burgers?"

Reese's ears perked up as if she understood him.

"Ah, that's my girl. We are going to have so much fun together. Do you like In-N-Out? Because I do. Best burgers ever."

Jeff shook his head. "I guess your friend is okay too."

That was a relief. Magnus didn't want to thrall the guy again. He felt bad enough about forcing Jeff to cancel the appointment he had scheduled, so he could come and help them search for the Doomer.

But the bigger picture was that a Doomer on the loose had

the potential to cause much more damage than Jeff's disappointed clients would incur.

It wasn't as if they were looking for a missing child, although to them it might have felt like that. People got very attached to their pets. Hopefully, he wouldn't need Jeff's help for the entire day, and the guy could still help Mr. and Mrs. Faber find their missing pooch.

"What about them?" Jeff glanced at the four additional Guardians.

"Insurance. The guy we are looking for is dangerous. He might get aggressive. I didn't tell you that before, but my missing partner is an ex-commando suffering from a resurgence of post-traumatic stress disorder. He might think that he is still in the war zone." The story was a last minute inspiration to explain the inconsistencies without messing with Jeff's brain again.

The guy frowned. "You should've told me that."

"Don't worry. He will never get near you. Once we find his location, you and the dogs can go inside your van and wait a safe distance away. We will handle it from there."

"Why do I need to wait, then?"

"In case he is no longer there, and we need to keep on searching." Magnus made a sad face. "I have to find him before he does something that would have him put away for a long time. It's not right for a war hero to end up in a mental institution."

The patriotic speech achieved the desired result.

"Yeah, okay."

"Good." Magnus clapped Jeff on the back. "Let's get going, gentlemen. We fan out from here."

The hacker had found the last location the phone had transmitted information from, and just as Magnus had thought, it was right next to the truck.

The Doomer was cleverer than he had given him credit for.

Parking the truck inside the garage of a vacant home for sale proved that he was resourceful. The stupid part was dumping the phone right next to it. Except, the Doomer probably had no idea that smashing the phone would not erase its location history that was stored in the cloud.

Frankly, Magnus hadn't known that either.

Still, the guy hadn't been inside the vacant house, which meant that he was hiding in someone's home. Hopefully, he'd only thralled the occupants and hadn't killed them.

Doomers didn't have much respect for human life.

"Let's go, Ralph," Magnus told his new friend after stopping for a short pee break.

Seven minutes into the walk his phone rang with Liam's number on the screen.

"I found the house." He rattled out the address.

"I'm on my way. Don't do anything until I get there."

24

LOSHAM

*O*ut in his backyard, reclining comfortably on a chaise lounge, Losham unfolded the morning newspaper and prepared to read the headlines when Rami rushed out from the house looking all excited.

"Gommed called." His assistant sounded breathless as if it had been Lord Navuh and not the commander of a small unit.

"Yes, Rami. And what news did he have to share to make you so happy?"

"Grud escaped captivity. Gommed asks if you would like to question the warrior personally."

Well, that was certainly exciting news. To date, no member of the Brotherhood had ever managed to escape the clan's captivity once captured. That was why it had always been assumed that whoever had gone missing was dead, executed by the Guardians.

Losham put the newspaper down and straightened up. "Of course I want to question him. But we need to make sure he is not being followed and that there are no bugs on him or his vehicle. I find it hard to believe that he managed to escape from Guardians."

"Maybe he was held by humans? It could have been one of the gangs we put out of business."

"You forget that he was captured before we took over the drug distribution."

"Is it possible he was detained by the police?"

"He would have been allowed a phone call."

"True."

Losham smoothed his palm over his beard. "Did Gommed give you any details?"

"Only that Grud called saying that he'd escaped and asking to come home. He called from an unsecured line, and Gommed said that he preferred to wait with the questions for when they were face to face in a secure location."

"Good thinking. Gommed is not stupid. Tell him to double and triple check that Grud is not wired or followed and only then bring him to the warehouse."

"Yes, sir."

"We will go there when Grud arrives. Tell Gommed to call you when he has him in the office." Losham didn't like to spend any more time at the warehouse than absolutely necessary, but that was where all the meetings were being held.

The apartment building, which served as the men's lodging, was a short distance away from it, but the place had no facilities available for conducting meetings or anything else. The decrepit building's only redeeming quality was its low price.

Losham was perfectly happy with the arrangement.

The budget that had been allotted for office space had gone toward the purchase of the house he and Rami lived in.

Gommed's wasn't the only cell currently operating in the Bay Area, there were several, and Losham liked to keep them as separate from each other as possible.

He conducted most of his work from home and traveled to the various locations when meetings with the commanders couldn't be avoided.

Naturally, none of them had been given his house address, so if any of them ever got caught, they couldn't tell where he lived.

Losham loved the place too much to risk compromising its location.

Rami came back holding his phone. "Gommed is meeting Grud at a supermarket parking lot first to make sure he isn't followed and to check him and his car for bugs. After that, he is bringing him to the apartment building for a more thorough search."

"Good plan."

If the location of the apartment building got compromised, it wouldn't be a big loss. The warehouse, on the other hand, was full of expensive equipment and even more expensive stockpiles of drugs. Not to mention the humans working on the assembly line, who after being subjected to repeated thralling were nearly brain dead.

"When does he think he'll be done with all that?"

"He says forty-five minutes to an hour tops."

"Very well. We will leave in an hour."

Rami bowed. "Yes, sir."

It was a forty-minute drive, but Losham wanted to finish reading his newspaper and have another cup of coffee before heading out. Grud could wait.

25

MAGNUS

"My car was stolen," Vera lamented.

Her husband sat on a rocking recliner, staring at the wall with a vacant look in his eyes.

The good news was that the dogs had found the house Grud had been hiding in. The bad news was that the guy was gone and he wasn't coming back. Thralling the couple to forget he'd ever been there was a sure sign that he was done with the place.

The Doomer had done a hatchet job with the couple's brains, but Harold had it much worse. The old man had probably tried to resist.

Magnus was afraid the damage was irreversible. "Is there any money missing from your bank accounts?"

Vera looked at Harold. "Honey, could you check with the bank? I don't know how to do it."

The guy didn't respond.

"Oh, my, I'm afraid his Alzheimer's has taken a turn for the worse."

That was bad. "Are you sure you can't check the bank, Vera?"

"I can call. I don't know how to use the computer."

"Please do so. I have a feeling that the same man who stole your car has also taken money from your account. I need to know how much is missing."

"How come I don't remember anything?"

"He is a talented hypnotist. Harold is probably still under the influence of it. That's why he isn't responding."

Vera hefted herself off the couch. "I better go check. I need to find the last bank statement to see how much we had in there. Harold takes care of all the financial stuff." She cast her husband a worried glance.

"What are we going to do about them?" Liam said after Vera had gone to call the bank.

"First of all, we are going to replenish their accounts. That's the least we can do. I don't know what can be done about him."

"Maybe Vanessa can help?" Liam sounded hopeful.

"She has enough on her hands as it is. I can't have her come all the way over here."

Vera came back with tears in her eyes. "There is nothing left. Thank God he couldn't touch the annuity. We would have been left with only social security, and that's not enough to pay the bills."

Magnus got up and patted her arm. "Our department will pay you back every missing penny. How much was in there?"

"Over the past two days, Harold withdrew almost twelve thousand dollars."

Thank the Fates it wasn't a huge amount. "We will send you a check to cover it."

"That's so kind of you. I didn't know the fraud department took such good care of senior citizens."

"It's a special case. What is the year and model of your car?"

"It's a brand new Honda Civic. We leased it. That's why I'm less worried about the car than the money missing from our accounts. The insurance will pay for it."

Thank the merciful Fates the car was new. That meant that it could be easily located.

"Do you have the lease papers? I want to jot down the information."

"Yes, I do."

As soon as they left the couple's home, Magnus texted William the information and then called him. "The Doomer stole a car. I texted you the license plate number and the VIN."

"I got it."

"Call me when you find it."

"Give me five minutes."

"You're the best."

"I know."

The other four Guardians were waiting for them down the street, while Jeff and the dogs were inside the guy's van a little farther away.

Magnus was glad he'd told Jeff to stay.

The hunt wasn't over yet.

26

WONDER

"The café is closed," Carol said. "You can use the vending machines."

The latest batch of guys who wanted to meet the new girl had shown up after Wonder and Carol had been done with the cleaning.

It had been like that the entire day, guys coming to check her out and introducing themselves.

Wonder felt like a monkey in a zoo.

"Hi, I'm Ruben," one of the four introduced himself.

"Nice to meet you. I'm Wonder." She smiled thinly as she shook his hand.

The other three took turns shaking her hand and telling her their names, but there was no way she was going to remember them. She'd met so many.

"Shoo." Carol waved her hands at them. "Wonder and I need to get going. You can come back tomorrow."

After the four mumbled something about stopping for lunch the next day and left without getting anything from the vending machines, Wonder released a relieved breath.

It had been a long day, and it wasn't over yet because Carol wanted her to accompany her to the training center, which meant meeting more people and smiling politely while pretending she didn't get the hints or see the covetous looks.

But that was also where Anandur was, and she wanted to see him. Heck, she needed to.

"Come on. I have ten minutes to get to the center and change clothes." Carol glanced at her watch. "My class starts at six."

The blond walked as briskly as her short legs allowed, which meant a leisurely stroll for Wonder. "You said that you're teaching a beginner self-defense class, right?"

"Aha."

"Do you take advance training classes yourself?"

Carol was in decent shape, but in Wonder's opinion not good enough for a fitness instructor.

"Yeah, I do because Brundar makes me. I'm a sharpshooter. I don't need to know how to fight hand-to-hand."

"Brundar is your instructor?"

"Kind of. He is more like the one in charge of my training regimen. With the new Guardians, there is a lot of shuffling around going on. Everyone is busy with retraining the guys and making them combat-ready for this century, so I had to take on the beginners' classes because we are short on people. I was a trainee myself not too long ago."

Wonder followed Carol into the pavilion. "Maybe that is something I could do? I mean after I get some training?"

"I thought you said you didn't like violence." Carol pressed the button for the elevator.

"I don't. But teaching self-defense is not the same as actual fighting, is it? I can think of it as dance moves with a purpose."

Carol laughed. "That's an interesting way to look at it." They stepped into the elevator. "Fifth floor," Carol said, and the elevator lurched down.

"I've never been in a voice-activated elevator."

"Yeah, not one of William's brightest ideas. It gives the Scots hell. It can't understand their accents. It's good that there are also buttons."

They exited into a wide, well-illuminated corridor lined with doors.

"Do you want to participate in my class?" Carol asked as they entered a locker room.

"Sure, I can start with that." She watched Carol change into a workout outfit. "I'm not dressed for it, though."

Carol put her work clothes inside the locker and closed the door, but there was no lock, probably because there was no need for one.

"You can just watch today. Maybe check out some of the other classes." She smirked. "Anandur's is right next to mine, you know. You can take a peek."

Wonder avoided Carol's smiling eyes. "He is training Guardians. I'm sure his class is too advanced for me."

"You can still take a look. Unfortunately, all these hunks are my cousins, so I can't enjoy watching them, but you can." She winked.

"I think I'll start with watching you and your students. I'm curious to see what shape ordinary immortals are in."

Carol laughed. "Prepare to be disappointed. They are a bunch of couch potatoes who get winded after twenty minutes. Not that I was any better a few months ago. But at least I worked at it. Most of the civilians come to the classes to socialize. Very few make an effort to get in shape."

The blond didn't look like someone who belonged in a gym, let alone as a self-defense instructor and a sniper. She was too small and cute and soft for it, evoking feelings of protectiveness even in Wonder.

Males probably went crazy over her.

Then again, Wonder knew all about appearances and how deceptive they could be. Carol could have a heart of a tigress trapped in her small body, while Wonder had a gazelle's trapped in a powerful one.

"What prompted you to take up training?" she asked as they entered Carol's classroom.

For a split moment, Carol's cheerful demeanor was replaced by an expression that was almost vicious. "It was when I realized that charm alone can't get me out of every kind of trouble. Sometimes the only choice is to fight."

"I guess." The thugs who'd attacked Wonder in Alexandria were a good example of that. If not for her strength and natural fighting skills, things would have ended much differently for her.

Imagining it, she felt a shiver run down her spine.

Carol patted her arm. "No need to get upset. My motto is to leave the crap in the past and focus on the future."

"Yeah." Wonder sighed. "You're right."

Carol turned to her students and clapped her hands. "Line up, people."

The six females and four males arranged themselves around a sparring mat.

"This is Wonder, for those of you who haven't met her yet, and she is only going to watch today. So don't embarrass me." She winked and smiled.

A few words of greetings were exchanged, and then the lesson began.

Leaning against the wall with her arms crossed over her chest, Wonder pretended to pay attention to the class for a few minutes, but all she could think about was that instead of watching a bunch of out of shape beginners fumble around the training mat, she could be watching Anandur.

A trained Guardian teaching other Guardians would no doubt be magnificent. And not any Guardian, but Anandur, with his hulking, muscular body, and his charm.

Would he act all tough with his trainees? Or would he stay true to his character and joke around with them?

Wonder was itching to find out.

Right, as if that was the only thing she was curious about and not the sight of all those magnificent muscles of his in action.

27

MAGNUS

*a*s soon as he arrived at the location of Vera's car, Magnus pulled out his phone. "Vera, I just wanted to tell you that we found your car and it's perfectly fine. No damage whatsoever."

"Oh thank goodness. Where is it?"

"Somewhere downtown. I'll have one of my guys drive it back to your house."

"Don't you need to collect evidence? I watch crime shows all of the time and the detectives check for fingerprints and other things like that."

Magnus chuckled. Already, Vera sounded much less distraught. "This is a simple fraud and theft investigation. Not a murder scene." And thank the merciful Fates for that.

"Yes, of course. You have to excuse an old woman."

"I have to go, Vera. I'll call you later."

"Good luck on catching the thief."

"Thank you. I'll do my best." He disconnected the call.

"Drive to the parking lot of that hardware store we've just passed," he told Liam. "I'm going to text everyone to meet us there."

There was a good chance Grud was going to lead them to a Doomer nest, and Magnus wasn't taking any chances.

"Yes, boss."

As they waited for the Guardians and Jeff to arrive, Magnus texted Onegus with the update.

Do not engage. Just scope the area. It's vital for the Doomers not to realize that their location is compromised.

Magnus was disappointed, but the chief was right to exercise caution.

As much as he would have wanted to storm the Doomers' hideout with the Guardians he had with him, Magnus had to agree with the chief that it would've been irresponsible. A raid required extensive reconnaissance and a well-prepared plan. Besides, the Guardians were not combat-ready yet, not for modern warfare, and not in the middle of a densely-populated city.

Liam parked at the far end of the hardware store's parking lot. A few minutes later Jeff's van pulled up next to them, and some of the other Guardians he'd summoned were starting to arrive as well.

Magnus got out of the car and signaled for Jeff to lower the window. Unfortunately, he had to thrall the guy again. Seeing so many burly men arrive was no doubt going to freak him out. The guy had signed up for a simple search job, not for a war.

"Everything is okay. I called in more buddies from my old commando unit to help find our friend. They are all good men. You have nothing to worry about."

Jeff nodded.

When all the Guardians were accounted for, Magnus signaled for them to gather around. "I'm going with Jeff and the dogs. I want you to fan out and watch our backs. Don't get too close and make sure to keep some distance from each other. Onegus wants us to check things out, not to storm the place. It's crucial that we don't alert the Doomers to our presence."

He waited until the men dispersed before opening the van's door and letting the dogs out. Surprisingly, the animals had been fine with the small group of immortals that had searched the neighborhood, but they might have gotten agitated around a larger one. Too many predators in one place were sure to scare the dogs.

As Jeff got out of the van, his responses were markedly slower. He was starting to show the effects of the repeated thralling.

Hopefully, it would pass. Magnus had been careful to use as little as possible, but the guy was very susceptible.

"Can you keep the dogs from barking? I don't want our guy to notice us. I want it to look like we are just two guys walking our dogs."

"They won't bark unless they feel threatened."

"Then let's go."

ANANDUR

*E*ven though Anandur was sparring with his back to the door, he felt the moment Wonder entered his training room.

It wasn't her scent, since the place was saturated with the smell of fifteen sweaty Guardians, and it wasn't even the sound of the door opening and closing. He could just sense her presence.

Unfortunately, his momentary loss of concentration was all that Gilbert needed to get out of Anandur's arm lock and flip him down on the mat.

The class erupted in cheers.

Damn each and every one of them.

Lying on his back with his trainees hooting and hollering because the undefeated champion had gone down so easily was not how Anandur wanted Wonder to see him.

This was the first time she was watching him in action, and instead of him impressing her with his skills and his strength and his speed, she'd seen him lose to a trainee.

Gilbert was going down.

Unleashing his full strength, Anandur dislodged the guy's

grip on him, wrapped his legs around his middle, and flipped them both over.

One punch and it was lights out for Gilbert.

The room went quiet. Anandur had never before finished off an opponent in a training session.

Damn. He hadn't meant to punch so hard.

"Come on, Gilbert." He lightly slapped the guy's uninjured cheek. "One little punch and you go down like a rookie? Get up!"

Gilbert groaned. "You call that a light punch?"

Thank the merciful Fates it hadn't been a knockout. Anandur got to his knees and offered the guy a hand up.

"Sorry, buddy. I got a little carried away."

Rubbing his jaw, Gilbert cast a glance at Wonder. "That's why pretty lassies shouldn't come to watch matches."

A few of the Guardians murmured in agreement.

"I don't know about that," Vernon said. "Wonder can come watch me spar any time." He took off his training shirt, tossed it to the floor, and flexed his pecs to the great joy of his fellow idiots who started another cheer.

Anandur jumped to his feet and helped Gilbert all the way up. "You okay, buddy?"

Gilbert moved his jaw from side to side. "Nothing's broken."

"Good." Anandur clapped him on the back, then turned and walked over to where Wonder was leaning against the wall.

"What are you doing here?"

For a moment, she just stared at his bare chest, then lifted her chin and looked into his eyes. "Why? Is there a problem with me being here?"

Crap. He hadn't meant to sound so harsh. "No, of course not." He scratched his beard. "I'm just surprised to see you here. I thought you'd go home after a long day at the café. How was it? Did you enjoy it?"

Wonder glanced behind him at the Guardians who were

standing around, watching and listening to the exchange as if it was the best show in town.

"Don't you have a class to teach?"

Anandur turned and looked at the bunch of immature old farts. "Vernon, take over for me, will ya?"

"Sure. Whatever you say, boss." Vernon sauntered to the middle of the mat puffing his chest out like a gorilla.

Apparently, one pretty face was all it took to transform centuries-old Guardians into adolescent boys. Him included.

He grabbed the shirt he'd discarded before and pulled it on. "Let me find you an intermediate class." He put his hand on the small of Wonder's back and led her out. "Kri teaches one, and most of her students are females." He cast a glare over his shoulder at the smirking Guardians. "It's a much more mature crowd."

"Kri is the female Guardian you were talking about, right?"

"Yes. And she is a relatively young immortal too. I think the two of you can become good friends."

Wonder rolled her eyes. "Why, is it because she is also tall? Or because you still think I should join the Guardian training program?"

Well, yeah, they had those traits in common. Why would she take offense at that?

His friends were mostly other Guardians, not guys from the accounting department, and for a good reason. What the hell would he talk with an accountant about?

Not much, unless the guy was interested in war stories or battle strategies. Anandur could talk about movies and maybe gossip a little, but that would cover about thirty minutes.

True, it was overgeneralizing and casting people into preconceived molds, but most of the time that wasn't such a bad approach. It simplified life.

"I don't know, Wonder. If you hit it off with Kri, it's fine and if you don't, it's fine too. I just thought it would be good for you to meet new people."

Wonder let out a breath. "I met a lot of people today. I'm a little tired of all the introductions." She smiled apologetically. "Don't get me wrong, it was fun. I love it. A whole community of immortals and everyone is so nice and welcoming. It was just a long day."

He had a good idea who were the friendly immortals who'd gone to the café today to introduce themselves.

An unattached immortal female was a big attraction, and they all had been trying to impress her.

"How did you like working with Carol?" Anandur chose the one safe topic that wouldn't enrage him.

"I like her a lot. She seems like an interesting person, but she's not really open. She hides behind a cheerful façade, but I have a feeling that she doesn't like to talk about herself."

Anandur chuckled. "Get her drunk, and you'll hear more than you've bargained for."

Wonder eyes widened. "Really? Like what?"

"You'll have to find out for yourself. Those are her stories to tell, not mine. Come on." He opened the door to the training room across from his. "Let me introduce you to Kri."

29

WONDER

"Kri," Anandur called out to get the Guardian's attention.

Wonder forced a smile, but as the instructor turned, her long blond braid whipping around to land with a thud on her back, the smile got broader and more natural.

Kri wasn't what Wonder had expected. So yeah, she was tall and muscular, her shoulders as broad as that of an athletic male, but her face was feminine, and her breasts were even larger than Wonder's.

Maybe they weren't so different after all.

"Wonder, I assume." She walked over and offered her hand.

"In the flesh. It's a pleasure to meet you, Kri. I heard a lot about you."

Kri narrowed her eyes. "What did the big oaf say about me?"

A big oaf? Wonder cast a quick glance at Anandur. He didn't seem offended at all.

"He thinks your intermediate class is a good fit for me."

A hand on her hip, Kri regarded Wonder with a critical eye. "From what I heard, my class might not be advanced enough for you. A beginner could not have taken down the undefeated duo."

"It was a fluke. I took them by surprise."

Kri snorted. "I bet." She gave Wonder another look over. "Well, if you want to join, you're welcome. But not in those clothes. Do you have a workout outfit?"

Wonder shook her head. "All I have are the things Amanda gave me. I guess I can use a pair of leggings and a T-shirt."

"You can borrow some of mine. I have a locker full of outfits, and you can grab whatever you want. Number one hundred and eight. It's unlocked."

"You mean now?"

"Yeah, why not? We are almost done, but I'll stay after class to assess your level."

"That's so nice of you. But I don't want to keep you here. Maybe I can come to your next class?"

Anandur tapped Wonder's shoulder. "I need to get back. I have another class after this one. If you stay with Kri, we can walk home together."

"Okay."

After an entire day of missing him, she wasn't going to give up a chance to spend time with Anandur, even if it was only the few minutes it took to walk back to her house.

Her house. It sounded so strange to say that.

"Do you know where the locker room is?" Anandur asked.

"Yeah, I do."

For a split moment, he looked disappointed, but then smiled and took her elbow. "I'll walk you there anyway. I don't want you to get lost."

"I'll see you in a few," Kri said and turned back to her students.

After making sure she could find her way back, Anandur dropped her off at the locker room and returned to his class.

Kri's locker was stuffed to bursting, and not only with

workout clothes. There were a couple of black T-shirts with cartoon characters printed on their front that didn't look like they were meant for exercise, a pair of black combat boots, and athletic shoes in a variety of colors. There was also a stack of fluffy pink towels on one of the top shelves. The one above it was home to a pink teddy bear with a big white heart on its tummy and the word 'love' stitched over it.

It seemed Kri had a softer side that she was hiding in her locker, or maybe not. Perhaps she didn't care if everyone knew that she liked fluffy pink things.

After changing into one of the Guardian's many outfits, Wonder found an empty locker, put her folded clothes inside, and headed back.

On the way, she passed several of Kri's students who were going in the direction she was coming from.

When she got to the classroom, the door was open, and the Guardian wasn't alone. There was a guy with her. The two were in a tight lip lock and had their hands on each other's butts.

Wonder started to back away, making as little noise as she could, but Kri heard her.

Releasing the guy, she turned around and smiled. "Wonder, come in and meet my boyfriend Michael."

"I can come later."

Kri waved a hand. "Don't be silly. We can continue smooching at home."

Michael glared at Kri. "I'm not your boyfriend. I'm your mate."

She patted his cheek. "I know, sweetie. But Wonder is new to our world. Mate might sound weird to her."

Kri was right. It did sound a bit strange but only because she hadn't heard people use it in reference to their partners.

The explanation seemed to mollify Michael, though. "I'll see you at home." He kissed Kri's cheek. "It was nice meeting you,

Wonder. I'll see you in the Guardian training program." He said it as if it was a foregone conclusion that she was going to join.

"I'm not sure about the program yet." She had no intention of joining but didn't want to get into the whole discussion with yet another person.

He shrugged. "I'll see you at the café then. I heard that you started working there today."

It seemed news traveled fast in small communities. "That's why I can't start the training."

"You can train with Kri in the evenings. She's an amazing fighter. It will take me years to get to her level." He looked at his mate lovingly.

It took a lot of confidence for a guy to admit that his girl was a better fighter than him. And he'd said it with so much pride.

"Let's start with what you know," Kri said as the door closed behind Michael.

"I don't know what I know. It just comes to me instinctively when I need to protect myself."

"In that case, let's get right to it. Stand in the middle of the mat, and I'll come at you. We'll see what you've got."

Wonder hesitated. "I'm very strong. I don't want to hurt you."

Kri lifted a brow. "I'm a Guardian with decades of training behind me, and I'm strong as well. If anyone is going to get hurt, it's you. Are you ready for that?"

Not really. But backing out was not an option.

"I guess I'm going to find out." Wonder walked to the center of the mat.

30

ANANDUR

"Good work, guys. I'll see you here same time tomorrow." Anandur pulled his shirt on, turned the lights off, and stepped out of the classroom.

Except for Kri's, the doors to all the other rooms were open, with sweaty people spilling out into the corridor and heading for the locker room.

That was why Anandur never used one.

What was the point? His house was a short walk away, and he could shower and change in his own bathroom, thank you very much.

He waited outside Brundar's classroom until everyone but his brother was gone. "Are you in a hurry to get home?"

"Always. Why?"

"Kri is training Wonder, I thought you would like to see her moves."

"Indeed." Brundar lifted his long, heavy gym bag off the floor and slung the strap over his shoulder. Unlike other people's bags, Brundar's didn't hold a change of clothes or shoes. By the rattling noise, he had more than one sword in there, and probably several knives.

Anandur glanced at the walls, looking for the evidence of Brundar's knife throwing. "Where are the holes?"

"I got a memo from Onegus demanding that I use targets for practice and stop damaging the walls."

A very reasonable explanation, except there were no targets in the room either. "Don't tell me you used your trainees for that."

One corner of his brother's lips lifted in a ghost of a smile. "The thought crossed my mind, but no." Brundar transferred the bag to his other shoulder and reached inside the exterior pocket to pull out his phone. "Interesting."

"What is?"

"Did you read the text from the chief?"

"Damn. I left my phone in the classroom. What is it about?"

"Go get your phone. We'll talk about it later."

"I'll meet you in Kri's classroom." Anandur turned around and jogged back.

Fortunately, his phone was still where he'd left it, and no one had taken it to the lost and found.

"Sweet," he murmured as he read the text from Onegus. Apparently, Magnus had been busy.

Tucking the phone into his pants pocket, Anandur jogged to Kri's.

Wonder turned to look at him as soon as he entered the classroom and smiled.

"Eyes on me, Wonder," Kri said. "Allowing yourself to get distracted in a fight is bad. No matter what goes on around you, you don't take your eyes off your opponent."

"Got it."

"Okay." Kri turned to Brundar and him. "Don't be quiet. I want to teach Wonder to ignore distractions."

"Yes, ma'am." Anandur gave her a two-finger salute.

"Let's try this move one more time." Kri assumed a fighting stance and Wonder mirrored it.

"So what do you think?" Anandur asked.

"There is nothing to think about. I want a piece of the action."

Did Brundar want to train Wonder?

Nah, he must've misunderstood. "Are we talking about Wonder's training?"

Brundar cast him a sidelong glance. "I meant the raid."

Now that made much more sense. "Onegus didn't say anything about a raid, but it's safe to assume there's going to be one."

Brundar's smile looked evil as he leaned against the wall and crossed his arms over his chest. "I'm looking forward to kicking some Doomer ass."

"Same here." Anandur leaned against the wall next to his brother. "The dog idea opens new possibilities. I'm not sure how we can utilize them, though. I'm pretty sure they can be trained to sniff out immortals. The problem is where to start. This time, Magnus had a lead, so he knew where to start looking."

"True. Maybe Turner can come up with something. If anyone can, it's him."

Anandur turned his attention back to Wonder. She was doing great, and it seemed that she'd learned how to tune out the background noise because she hadn't faltered again.

She was a natural, strong and fast, but her moves didn't seem to be the product of professional training. It was street fighting at best.

"Someone must've trained her," Brundar said.

"I'm not sure. She is powerful and quick and has good instincts, but other than a few basic moves I didn't see her performing any of the known sequences."

Brundar shrugged. "Nevertheless, she is not a complete novice. She has those basic moves down."

"Which proves once again that it's all in the attitude.

Wonder believed she could, so she did what needed to be done. No hesitation."

The primary tenet of combat training was to drill attack moves into fighters until they became automatic, second nature. When shit was going down, overthinking the next move was not an option. It took a lot of grueling training to achieve that level of mastery, but it seemed Wonder was one of the rare individuals who had it naturally. All she had to do was learn the moves, and they became part of her flight or fight instinctive arsenal.

Next to him, Brundar sighed wistfully. "I wish she would reconsider applying for the force. I've never had the pleasure of working with a natural. I could make her magnificent."

"She already is."

NICK

*N*ick glared at Eva. "Are you serious? You want me to go with Sharon on an assignment to Rio?"

Eva put her hand on her belly. "I can't go on assignments like this, and I need Sharon to take my place. She needs you to provide backup and handle the surveillance equipment."

The last thing Nick wanted was to go to Rio. Things were going great with Ruth. She was thriving because of the great sex they were having, and Nick had never felt as happy and as content as he did now.

Heck, he was planning to propose.

So yeah, he was young, but he was no fool. He and Ruth had a good thing going, and he didn't want to chance losing it. Not that marriage provided any guarantees, but it was a legal commitment that made it a little harder to walk away.

It was like a business contract. Any of the parties could break it at any time, but it provided a stronger pledge than a handshake, and there were consequences to violating the terms of the agreement. If he had his way, he would put a ring on Ruth's finger as soon as he could.

He had to wiggle out of this trip somehow. "Sharon is not ready, and I don't want to go."

Eva rolled her eyes. "When my biggest and best-paying client is asking me to do this for him, I'm not going to say no because my employee has a new girlfriend he doesn't want to leave behind."

"But you can still go. The pregnant belly is a better disguise than all the prosthetics you usually put on. Who is going to suspect a pregnant woman of spying on them?"

Eva waved a dismissive hand and wobbled over to the couch. Putting a hand behind her, she lowered herself slowly to the seat. "Look at me. I can barely move. And what if I go into early labor?"

He eyed her huge belly. She really looked like she was going to pop any day now. "Are you sure you don't have twins in there?"

She shook her head. "Although it feels like that. Just one very active boy who likes to kick and punch his mommy from the inside." She rubbed her belly lovingly.

"Come on, Nick, man up," Bhathian walked into the living room with two beers, and handed one to Nick.

"As if I have a choice." He took the beer and popped the cap.

"It's going to be fun." Sharon opened her mouth for the first time since Eva had dropped that bomb on them.

The thing was, she didn't sound sure at all. Eva had been training her for months to take her place, and Sharon had even gone on a few simple assignments already, but this was a big one, and if they screwed it up their agency would lose one of its best clients.

"Does Robert know?" Nick took a swig of his beer.

Sharon shook her head. "Eva told me about it right before she told you. I didn't have a chance to talk to him yet."

"He's not going to like it."

Sharon's boyfriend was the silent type, but he was very

protective of her. He was going to flip out. Not that Nick could blame him. If Ruth had told him she was going on a potentially dangerous mission, he would have flipped as well. In fact, he would have probably asked for a vacation and gone with her to make sure nothing happened to her.

"I bet Robert would want to come with you."

Sharon grimaced. "I'm sure he would, but I doubt he can get time off from work."

Bhathian sat next to Eva on the couch and wrapped his arm around her shoulders. "Since we became a couple, Eva has gone on missions many times. I won't lie to you and say that it was easy to let her go when I knew she would be facing danger. But that's her job, and I didn't want to make her life more difficult by giving her a hard time about it. I learned to live with it, and so will Robert and Ruth."

Sharon groaned. "I know Robert is going to be miserable without me. And I'm going to be miserable without him, but I'm really looking forward to the opportunity to prove that I can do it. My first big solo mission."

Resigned, Nick plopped down on the armchair and took a big gulp from his beer. "So, who are we going to be spying on?"

32

ANANDUR

"*D*id you have fun?" Anandur asked.

Wonder took her clothes out of the locker and tucked them under her arm. "I like Kri."

"I don't want to say it, but I told you so." He smirked.

"Ground floor," Wonder said as they entered the elevator.

Naturally, nothing happened.

"William needs to program the elevator to respond to your voice. Ground floor," he repeated. "Tomorrow I'll take you to him."

"Thanks. Can I use the buttons?"

"Until William debugs the voice recognition program to respond to the different accents, the buttons stay on."

"Why do you need it? Are there people in the village who are not allowed to use the elevators?"

"It's just another level of security."

They exited into the pavilion and then through the sliding glass doors into the cool evening air.

"I think Kri is cool, and she really is an amazing fighter," Wonder said. "She is also a very good teacher. But I don't think we have anything in common. Kri is a Guardian through and through. It's like this is who she is, not what she does."

Anandur arched a brow. "I'm the same way. Does it mean that we can't be friends?"

Wonder frowned. "You're more than that."

"I'm sure that Kri is too. You just need to get to know her better."

"I guess."

She sounded embarrassed and unsure, and he should've let it go. But he couldn't help himself. "So you think there is more to me than just being a Guardian, eh?"

Wonder nodded.

"Like what? I'm curious to hear all about my many good qualities."

Wonder cast him an amused glance. "The walk to my place is too short for that. I can't possibly list all of your attributes in ten minutes."

He took her elbow. "No problem. I'm all in for a long stroll."

"Sounds good to me. But can I drop off my clothes first?" She patted the bundle under her arm.

"Sure. Let me hold them for you."

"No, that's okay. I can carry them."

He pulled on the bundle. "Let me be a gentleman and do this little thing for you."

"Fine." She handed him the neatly folded and rolled clothes. "That's attribute number one, not in importance, it's just the first one that comes to my mind. You're a gentleman."

Anandur lifted his chin. "I've grown an inch. What's the next one?"

"You're polite, and you don't use crass language, at least not in front of me. I appreciate that too."

"Well, that's part of the first one. I watch my language in front of the ladies."

She cast him a sidelong glance from under her thick

eyelashes. "So you're different around other guys? Do you cuss a lot when hanging out with the other Guardians?"

"Not really. I can throw the f-bomb here and there or call someone a SOB, but not often. After working with Kian for so long cussing lost its appeal to me. We have very different temperaments. I'm a chill kind of guy while he is a stress ball waiting to explode. I suppose the frequent cussing is his way of releasing some of that pressure."

Wonder stopped. "Are you serious? Kian? He looks so regal and so refined. I would've never guessed it about him."

Regal and refined my ass.

Next thing she would start gushing about how handsome he was. No female was immune to Kian's godly good looks, and his crappy attitude probably made him even more desirable.

For reasons Anandur couldn't understand, women liked bad boys. Should he prod for more?

It was a masochistic move, but again Anandur couldn't help himself. "He is handsome, isn't he?"

"Gorgeous."

Figured that she would think that.

Wonder waved a hand. "He is almost too pretty, for a guy that is. I like more rugged types." She glanced at him and then blushed profusely.

"Do you think I'm rugged?"

She shrugged.

Sweet. "So I'm a gentleman who doesn't cuss and who is ruggedly handsome. What else?"

"You're funny."

"And? That's it?"

"What else is there?"

"Oh, there is much more."

As they reached Wonder's place, she took the bundle from him and put it on one of the steps. "No one is going to take it, right?"

"It's safe here."

"I know. It's a great feeling. I have not felt safe since I woke up from my coma."

At her admission, a wave of intense protectiveness swept through Anandur. Wrapping his arm around her shoulders, he brought her closer to him. "I promised to keep you safe, lass, and I always keep my promises."

"That's because you're a gentleman."

As Wonder sighed and leaned into him, resting her head on his bicep, he was ready to forget all about her being too young and kiss her senseless. It was the exact opposite of what her gesture of trust should've evoked.

He was a despicable old lecher.

"What's behind the fence?" she asked, saving them both at the last moment.

"The second phase. Originally, the village was supposed to house only the local clan, but then we got this big operation in motion, and many of the retired Guardians agreed to leave Scotland and come here to help us carry it out. We needed to supply housing for them. But it's much larger than that. Since we already have the crews here, Kian decided to provide for future expansion and enlarged the scope of work way beyond what was originally planned."

"Why? Does he expect more of the Scottish clan members to come live here?"

"It's not likely that many will. Maybe some. Sometimes he just gets carried away. Though this is a really bad time for it. The mission we've undertaken is leaching a lot of resources, and money is tight. This is not the right time for grandiose plans."

"Can you tell me about the mission, or is it a secret?"

It wasn't a secret, but it wasn't a pleasant topic for conversation either.

Except, strolling down the pathways with Wonder leaning

against him felt so good that Anandur didn't want it to end. Telling her about the mission would be the perfect excuse to keep on walking.

Hell, he could go on and on about the Chinese crews and their strange prejudices, then continue to tell her about all the special features that had been incorporated into the village, like the water filtration system and the trash incinerators. He had enough material to talk for hours.

"It all started with a luxury yacht and one rotten immortal who was making money on the side by luring young women and then selling them on the sex slave market…"

33

KIAN

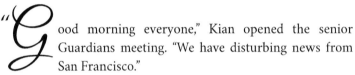"ood morning everyone," Kian opened the senior Guardians meeting. "We have disturbing news from San Francisco."

Anandur and Brundar, who'd also gotten the text from the chief, nodded. The other Guardians looked at him with worry on their faces. Turner, whom Kian had been inviting to all the senior Guardian meetings lately, showed no expression at all.

"No one of ours was taken," Kian qualified.

There was a collective sigh of relief.

"The news is about what the Doomers are up to. Apparently, they've ventured into drug dealing."

"They've always dealt in drugs," Yamanu said.

"True, but they used gangs for the distribution. It seems they decided to use warriors instead and took over the entire chain."

"More money for them," Arwel said.

"Right. In a way, it's a good sign."

Bhathian frowned. "How so?"

"It means that they are looking for ways to bring in more money, which in turn means that they are losing backers, or maybe just a single big one. If that is the case, lack of cash to run their organization is not their only problem. With no wars to instigate and fight, their army sits idle, and they have to find something for them to do."

"Like selling drugs," Bhathian said.

"Exactly. That in itself is worrisome, but what bothers me more is that they are using humans to manufacture and package the drugs. Onegus reports that they have a warehouse full of zombie-like humans who appear to have been thralled so many times that their brains are barely functional."

Anandur leaned back in his chair and grinned. "It was a good thing that Grud escaped. He led us right to their SF center of operation. I wonder how many more there are."

"It must be new," Arwel said. "The Doomers we interrogated didn't say anything about it."

Anandur waved a dismissive hand. "They might be under compulsion not to talk."

Kian didn't think so. "If they were under compulsion, they would not have talked at all. The other Doomers we've caught in the past couldn't tell us anything other than their names. It seems like they're loosening their security. Which makes sense. They can't have more than one immortal with the ability to affect other immortals' brains. They need to preserve his energy for when it counts."

In the past, very few Doomers had been sent on missions that put them at risk of capture by the clan. Compelling only a few individuals hadn't been a problem. But now that the Brotherhood was sending scores of warriors into clan areas, they had to be more discriminating about who to compel and to what extent.

The thing was that the majority of Doomers were so ignorant, even about the Brotherhood they were part of, that they had nothing of importance to tell.

"So what's the plan?" Brundar asked. "When are we raiding that warehouse?"

Kian smiled. "Patience, Brundar. This is just as much a hostage situation as the one at the monastery. To ensure minimum collateral damage, we need a good plan. Onegus is organizing the reconnaissance."

"Tell him to stay put," Turner said. "This is a job for humans. One sniff of an immortal male and you lose the element of surprise."

Fuck, he should've thought of that. Even after working with Turner for months, Kian's first instinct was to rely on his own people unless he was forced to outsource. He should start thinking of Turner's human subcontractors as part of his network and utilize them in cases where their humanity was advantageous.

"How soon can you have your people there?"

"Let me make a few phone calls. I can probably have a team meet up with Onegus later today."

"Do it."

"Budget?"

Kian waved a hand. "Whatever you think is reasonable for two or three days of reconnaissance. I want to know how many Doomers are working in that warehouse and how many humans they are holding there."

"Naturally. You also need to know where these Doomers are residing and who their commander is."

"The dogs were a brilliant idea," Anandur said. "Without them, Magnus could have never found Grud and followed his trail. We should consider getting us some."

Sounded good in theory, but it was a subject Kian knew nothing about. "It's not enough to get dogs. You need someone to train them."

Anandur leaned his elbows on the conference table. "I can

ask around. Maybe one of the old Guardians did that at some point."

Doubtful. Immortals didn't keep pets for the same reason they didn't have relationships with humans. Getting attached emotionally to those whose lifespan was a blink of an eye compared to theirs was a prescription for misery. The scientist who'd altered the gods' genes hadn't thought to do the same for pets.

Maybe there had been none where the gods had come from.

Bhathian shook his head. "I don't think we have anyone like that. But how hard could it be to learn to train the animals? We can have someone apprentice with a human expert."

"True. Do you have anyone in mind?"

For some reason, all eyes turned to Arwel.

The Guardian looked from one smirking face to the next. "Why is everyone looking at me? I'm not the dog whisperer."

"Do you like dogs?" Kian asked.

"Sure, but I don't want to run a kennel."

It was a pity. As an empath, Arwel could've done wonders with dogs. Except, having talent wasn't going to cut it if there was no desire.

Kian pointed at the Guardian. "I'm putting you in charge of finding someone who'd be interested in learning all about it and then implementing a program."

"I can do that. How large of a program are we talking about?"

"We will start small. Two or three dogs."

"Magnus is a good candidate," Anandur offered.

"Maybe, but I'm not sure I want to lose a Guardian for that. I prefer a civilian, just not someone who will run away at the first sign of danger. We need a person who can keep a cool head during confrontations."

Rapping his fingers on the conference table, Anandur looked at Kian. "I hope you're not thinking of letting the newbies raid the warehouse with only Onegus in charge. We all need to be there."

He'd never planned differently, but Anandur had earned himself some needling. "I think the decision should be left up to Onegus. He is the chief."

Anandur pulled out his phone. "I'm going to text Onegus. I want in, and I'm sure Brundar wants in too, right?" He glanced at his brother.

Brundar's smile was chilling. "Naturally."

Kian put a hand on Anandur's arm. "I was just messing with you. Of course all of you guys are going. I wouldn't dream of sending the newbies in by themselves."

34

SYSSI

"Do you have a moment?' Syssi poked her head into Bridget's office.

"For you, always. Come in."

"How are you holding up with Julian gone?"

Bridget sighed. "I wake up every morning and pray no one goes into transition, and that there will be no altercation with Doomers that I need to patch people up after. Heading the rescue project and working in the clinic is too much."

"When is he coming back?"

"Monday, thank the merciful Fates."

The week-long psychic convention Julian had gone to was a long shot, but it wasn't as if they had any better options for finding new ways to identify Dormants. Every avenue that might give them a clue was worth investigating.

"Did he find anything interesting?"

"I don't think so. He would've called me. But the convention isn't over yet. He might still stumble upon something."

"I'm crossing my fingers." Syssi lifted her hands, both with crossed fingers.

"Yeah, me too. So, what brings you here, Syssi?"

"You know how I've been obsessing about having a child lately, right?"

Bridget's gaze softened, and she reached for Syssi's hand. "Yes, and I still think you're being silly. You're so young. There is plenty of time for that."

Syssi sighed. That was what everyone was telling her, including her husband and her mother and her brother. Except, it did nothing to lessen the yearning.

"I know that it's irrational, but I can't do what all the other immortal females are doing and just wait for it to happen. It's not like I can expect it in a year or two. Centuries might pass, or even millennia. I'll go insane waiting."

Bridget leaned back. "What do you have in mind?"

"Fertility treatment. It helps human females conceive, so why not us? From what I understand, we are built basically the same way. The main differences are our fast regeneration ability and mind control. Although I still haven't mastered the second one. I guess you need to start as a child to get the hang of it."

"I'm not very good at it either, even though I started young." Bridget smirked. "Unlike us, the guys have a powerful motivation to learn how to do it. That might be what makes all the difference."

Syssi nodded. "Give a person a strong enough motivation and he or she can move mountains." She crossed her arms over her chest and narrowed her eyes at Bridget. "Just so you know, I'm extremely motivated to get pregnant. I'm willing to do whatever it takes."

The doctor sighed. "I understand. But the truth is that I've never researched immortal females' fertility. All I have is human data. A human female is born with all her eggs, between half a million and two million of them, but she starts losing them as soon as she is born and until she reaches puberty at a rate of about eleven thousand a month. Then the rate slows down to about a thousand a month."

"It sounds like such a waste."

Bridget shrugged. "It's the survival of the fittest—in this case of the healthiest eggs. Bottom line, from the onset of puberty and until menopause only three to five hundred eggs will reach maturity. Those are the only ones that can be fertilized, and it's not many."

Syssi rubbed her brows. "Then it must be different for immortal females. Otherwise, we would've run out of eggs at the same age human females do. I thought we remained fertile longer because we don't menstruate, but you say that eggs are lost regardless."

"In human females, yes. No one's researched it for immortals."

"Could you?"

"I can look into it. Are you willing to become my test subject?"

Syssi chuckled. "It seems to be my fate. I was Amanda's test bunny in the neuroscience lab, and now I'm going to be yours. But it's all good since it's for a good cause. Is it going to be invasive, though? I don't mind discomfort, I just don't want to risk damaging anything."

"I'll start with taking an ultrasound of your ovaries and some blood samples. Nothing too bad."

"Okay, when do we start?"

Bridget lifted a brow. "Do I look like someone that has time for research? Unless you want Julian to do it, it will have to wait until I have more time."

That sounded like never. But Julian was too young and inexperienced. If Syssi were to be a test bunny, it had to be with someone she felt comfortable with.

"After Julian comes back?" she asked hopefully.

"I wish, but no. This is not something I can do in my spare

time. What's the rush, though? A moment ago we were talking about a centuries-long wait. Now it's only a few months to a couple of years. I hope that in time I'll manage to streamline the operation enough so I can go back to research, at least part-time. I miss it."

"I still haven't adjusted to the immortal perception of time. I think in human terms."

Bridget chuckled. "I blame Phoenix. That baby has given you a taste of sweet and you can't wait to have some for yourself."

"True. She is so adorable. When I'm with her I'm smiling nonstop. She just makes me happy."

Bridget cocked a brow. "Also when she screams her head off? Or when she fills her diaper with toxic waste?"

"Even then. Besides, she never screams when she's with me because I spoil her rotten and give her whatever she wants. That's the beauty of being an aunt. Still, as much as I enjoy her, I want a child that will be Kian's and mine."

"Speaking of Kian, did you discuss it with him?"

"Not yet. I wanted to have your opinion first."

"Right now all I can tell you is that fertility treatments are not easy and they might not work on our bodies. And even if they do, you might be sacrificing your future ability to conceive by taking out your viable eggs ahead of time. And if the hormonal treatments don't do the trick and we need to do in vitro then there is the problem of too many fertilized eggs."

"I read that you can freeze embryos. That could be so cool. Whenever Kian and I want another child, we just unfreeze one. It sounds freaky, but think of the possibilities. If it works for me, it will work for the other females. We could have a village full of children. Wouldn't that be awesome?"

35

WONDER

"*H*i, girls." Holding a rectangular cardboard box, Amanda sauntered into the café. "I just came from the office building. There are packages waiting for you in the lobby." She looked expectantly at Wonder. "What did you get?"

"Shoes, and flip-flops, and a couple of bras."

Amanda lifted a brow. "I thought you didn't wear them."

"I don't. But Kri says I should wear a sports bra when training because my bouncy duo is distracting the guys in her class."

"I can imagine." Amanda chuckled. "You're the most sought after female in the village."

Wonder grimaced. "Yeah, just not by the one I want."

"Let's have a girl talk. Maybe I can help." Amanda wrapped an arm around her shoulders.

Waving her dishrag, Carol huffed. "Good luck with that. She dismisses everything I say, and we all know I'm an expert on the subject."

Just thinking about Carol's suggestions made Wonder blush. The woman used to be a pro who'd seen nothing wrong with exchanging her charms for material things from men.

When she'd told Wonder about her days as a courtesan, which she'd explained was a kind of paid mistress, Carol had sounded wistful, not remorseful.

Amanda waved a hand. "I can imagine what kind of advice you gave her. Wonder is still just a girl. She needs to learn how to be a woman first. Then, when she's confident in her femininity, she can use some of your tricks."

"I'm right here." Wonder pointed to herself. "You're talking about me as if I'm not."

"My bad." Amanda led her to a table. "Carol, can you get us all cappuccinos and put up the closed sign? We can't have guys intruding on our girl talk."

"I'm on it."

"So tell me, darling, who is that guy who's pretending not to be interested?"

"How do you know he is only pretending?"

"First of all because there isn't an unmatched male here who doesn't want you. But I assume we are talking about a certain tall and hunky redhead?"

Wonder nodded.

"What makes you think he is not interested? I hear that you guys are spending a lot of time together."

Where to start? And how was she going to explain Anandur's mixed signals when she didn't understand them herself?

"He says he's too old for me. But then he gets jealous when he sees young immortals talking to me. When he was my prisoner, he flirted with me all of the time, but that was only to make me cooperate with him. Now I don't know what he wants. He walks me home every evening, he comes to eat lunch here whenever he can, and we had dinner at his brother's house three times already." Wonder ran out of air.

"I see." Amanda regarded her while tapping a finger on her lips. "You need a makeover, darling."

"Amanda thinks everything can be solved with the right

clothes." Carol put down a cardboard carrier with three small paper cups inside it.

"Not just clothes, darling, it's the whole package. We need to make Wonder look like a woman, and even more importantly feel like one. Everything will be different when she is confident in her femininity." She flicked Wonder's braid aside. "Can you do me a favor and let your hair down?"

"Why?"

"I want to see it."

"Fine." She pulled down the rubber band holding the end and unraveled the strands.

"Ugh." Amanda looked at her hair with a grimace. "When was the last time you had a haircut?"

"I didn't. I just put it in a braid."

"Figures." Amanda finished her coffee in one gulp and pushed to her feet. "Get your packages from the office. I'll get my trusty shears and my makeup case and meet you at your place."

"And I'll bring my hair products and curling iron," Carol offered.

Oh, boy. The idea of a makeover was kind of exciting, but also a little scary. She didn't want to look too different.

On the other hand, she kind of understood what Amanda had meant. Dressing and acting the part would not only help Anandur see her as a grown woman, but also help her own her femininity.

"I appreciate the offer, but I'm not sure I want to change the way I look too drastically. What if Anandur doesn't like the new me?"

"Don't worry about it. I know what I'm doing. The change will be very subtle." She pointed at Wonder's chest. "Fifteen minutes. Your place."

"Oh, wait. What about training?" Wonder asked as she and Carol headed for the office building.

"Classes are canceled for today and tomorrow. Didn't you get the text?" Carol asked.

"No."

"That's probably because you're not on the list. I'll add you when I have the chance."

"Is it because of the raid?"

Carol nodded. "The Guardians are busy getting ready."

"Is Kri going?"

"If she is, it's not as part of the raiding party," Carol said. "Kian doesn't allow females anywhere near Doomers, not even Kri who can kick ass with the best of the guys. But she can do other stuff, like keep the humans calm and help evacuate them."

Wonder found her last package, tucked it under her arm, and waited for Carol to find all of hers.

"Why is that? What's the difference? If she can fight as well as a guy, then why not?"

Carol's pretty face contorted into a snarl. "Trust me. There is a good reason for it. I agree with Kian on that."

36

ANANDUR

*B*y the end of the pre-mission orientation with Kian, Anandur was all hyped for the upcoming action but bummed about missing his daily walk with Wonder.

As he passed Kri's empty classroom, he glanced inside hoping to see Wonder training by herself, or maybe with Carol, but the place was vacant, as were all the other classrooms. Apparently, no one was overly upset about the self-defense classes getting canceled or eager to continue training on his or her own.

Talk about disappointment.

With Kian spending half a day at Turner's office in town, and then the video conference with Onegus and Magnus in the afternoon, Anandur hadn't seen Wonder all day.

He missed her.

She was so much fun to talk to, finding everything he told her fascinating. After nearly a millennia of eventful life, Anandur had an almost endless supply of stories to share. The problem was that most of his Guardian buddies had either taken part in the action or had already heard all about it. But Wonder hadn't, and he loved the way she listened intently, with her eyes peeled wide and the occasional uhh and ahh.

The other benefit of the storytelling was to help focus his attention on something other than his desperate need for her.

While his head was in the past, reconstructing this or that event, he wasn't thinking about how beautiful she was, or how soft her feminine curves were, and how it would feel to touch her all over.

Without making a conscious decision about it, Anandur was living like a monk.

Since the day Wonder had caught him with his pants down in the back alley of her club, Anandur hadn't gone hunting for sex even once.

He'd lost his appetite for all others, but he couldn't have the one he craved.

Wanting Wonder and keeping his hands off her was torture.

And the worst part was that he knew she wouldn't object if he crushed her against him and kissed the living daylights out of her.

Wonder wanted him too.

Except, as the responsible adult in their relationship, it was his moral obligation to make sure that she made the right decisions for the right reasons. He'd promised to protect her, and that included from himself. But he'd also promised to take care of her, and that meant being her friend and spending time with her.

Or at least that was what he told himself every time he came to the café to have lunch with her, or took Wonder to dinner at Callie and Brundar's, or waited for her outside Kri's classroom.

And in that spirit, he pulled out his phone and texted her. *Are you up for our nightly walk?*

Her answer came mere seconds later. *Yes.*

Anandur smiled. His Wonder wasn't much of a talker. She

used her words frugally. But that was good because he could talk enough for the two of them.

I'm heading in your direction. Can you be ready in ten minutes?

Yes.

When he got to her house, he was half expecting Wonder to wait for him on the porch, but she didn't, and he had to knock on the door which made him feel awkward. Gertrude and Hildegard could get the wrong idea and then spread the rumor around the entire village.

Anandur had been the source of enough rumors to know how it worked.

Instead of one of the nurses, though, Carol opened the door with a big smirk on her lovely face. "Wonder will be out in a minute. Take a seat." She pointed to the wooden swing on the porch.

He quirked a brow. "Aren't you going to invite me in?"

"No." She grinned and closed the door in his face.

Anandur shook his head. What was this? Elementary school? But he did as Carol had instructed. Sitting on the swing, he pushed with his legs to start the swaying motion and closed his eyes.

The creaking of the door opening got him to turn his head, and then immediately jump up to his feet.

Wonder had gone through one hell of a transformation.

Instead of looking like a high-school girl, she looked like a freaking supermodel. And not just any supermodel, a Victoria's Secret supermodel.

For the first time since he'd met her, her long, nearly black hair hung loosely around her shoulders and down her back, the moonlight reflected from the thick and glossy waves framing Wonder's beautiful face in a halo.

"Wow," he said, suddenly lost for words.

Smoothing her hand over one long strand, Wonder smiled. "Do you like my new hairstyle?"

"I love it. You always wore it in a braid before."

"What about these?" She lifted her sandaled foot.

"Are you asking about the sandals or the red nail polish on your toenails?" She had the most beautiful feet, with pretty slim toes and perfectly shaped toenails that the red nail polish accentuated.

In short, everything about the girl was perfect.

"Both."

"I like both. What's the occasion?" He put his hand on the small of her back and led her down the steps.

She shrugged. "Amanda and Carol gave me a makeover. Amanda trimmed my hair, and Carol styled it. Amanda also did my makeup and dressed me up, and Carol gave me a manicure and a pedicure." She chuckled. "I feel so pampered."

"You look beautiful. Not that you weren't beautiful before," he added quickly.

Giving women compliments was tricky, and there were many pitfalls, which Anandur was usually smart enough to steer clear of. But it was hard to think and come up with the right things to say when all he could think was beautiful, gorgeous, alluring, tempting...

It had been much easier to fight temptation when Wonder looked like a schoolgirl. Looking like she did now, elegant and sophisticated, Anandur felt like he was fighting a losing battle.

Tonight, he wasn't going to even wrap his arm around her shoulders, or encourage closeness of any kind. It was too dangerous.

After several minutes of strained silence, Wonder asked, "How was your day?"

"The usual. Brundar and I followed Kian around to his meetings in the city, and when we returned, we had the video chat with our guys in San Francisco."

He'd already told her about Grud leading Magnus to the warehouse and what was in it, and he doubted she would be interested in hearing about the mission details. Wonder had made it clear that warfare and combat were not subjects she wanted to learn or talk about. Which was a shame because some of his better stories were from the battles he'd fought.

"What they did to those poor humans is horrible. In my opinion, it's just as bad as murder because with the damage to their brains these people are no longer who they used to be. It's like they are dead." Wonder shivered and wrapped her arms around herself.

Without thinking, Anandur wrapped his arm around her shoulders and brought her closer to him. He intended to provide comfort, but the jolt delivered by the feel of her against his body reminded him why touching her was a bad idea.

Except, he couldn't undo what he'd done. Wonder sighed, her entire body sinking into him, and put her head on his bicep. "Thank you. I needed that," she murmured.

Fates. What the hell was he doing?

By denying what was obviously between them, he was torturing not only himself but Wonder too.

The poor girl had thanked him for putting his arm around her.

"Don't thank me, lass. I don't deserve it."

37

WONDER

*W*hat an embarrassing slip of the tongue.

All throughout their walk, Wonder had waited for Anandur to wrap his arm around her, so she could lean against his strong body. This was the only intimacy he allowed, and she'd been looking forward to it, yearning for it.

It had been such a relief when her wish had finally been granted that the words of gratitude just slipped out.

Talk about pathetic.

She needed to salvage what remained of her self-respect. "Why would you say you don't deserve my thanks? You gave me this." She waved her hand in a circle. "I have new friends, Gertrude and Hildegard treat me as if I were their beloved niece, and I even got a makeover from a goddess's daughter. I still can't believe Amanda did this for me."

Anandur chuckled. "She lives for stuff like that. But yeah, Amanda is cool. I like her a lot."

"I'm still a little intimidated by her. She is so beautiful and confident and a professor on top of that. And she has great taste in clothes."

"With how much money she spends on them it's not diffi-

cult. The trick is to look amazing on a budget. Like me."
Anandur waved a hand over his plain T-shirt and Levi jeans.

He'd meant it as a joke, but the truth was that Wonder
couldn't imagine him in anything else. The simple style he'd
adopted fit his rugged good looks perfectly. He was too tall
and too broad and too redheaded for fancy stuff. A man like
him would've looked ridiculous in designer jeans or a suit
and tie.

Gods, he was everything Wonder could've ever wanted in a
man, except for his attitude toward her.

She wasn't his little sister.

The thoughts he evoked in her were as far from sisterly as
it got.

For several moments, they walked in silence with Anandur
looking ahead into the night and Wonder trying to keep her
heart from racing. It was hard to hide things from an immortal
guy who could hear her heartbeat and smell her emotions.

Her desire for him.

But then she was an immortal too. Why couldn't she figure
out what Anandur was feeling for her? His real feelings, not the
ones he was portraying.

Was he better than her at masking his emotions?

Or maybe her senses were not as sharp as his?

Or maybe she'd been so busy focusing on her own feelings
that she'd missed on clues another immortal female could've
picked up.

"Did you ask Amanda to style your hair?" Anandur asked.

"No, she volunteered, and then Carol joined in on the
effort."

"I'm curious about what prompted it. Did any of the guys
invite you on a date?"

She didn't need immortal super senses to detect the note of
jealousy in Anandur's voice.

The nerve of the guy.

If he wasn't interested in her romantically, he had no right to envy others that were.

"And what if they did? It's not like I have something going on with anyone else."

Shit on a stick, she shouldn't have said that. It was as if she was accusing him.

Well, she was. The big oaf was acting dumb.

Anandur sighed. "You're right. I'm sorry."

Gods, what a clueless male. Wonder felt like taking off one of her sandals and beating him over the head with it. Maybe it would clear the tangled mess he had up there, and she wasn't referring to his hair, although that needed a trim as well. Birds could build a nest in there.

The guy needed a woman in his life. He needed Wonder. Except, he was too stubborn and opinionated to realize a good thing when he saw it.

She might be inexperienced, but that didn't mean she couldn't learn. Besides, relationships were about more than just sex. The two of them enjoyed each other's company, and they had plenty of things to talk about.

Even a young woman like her knew that it was a good foundation.

If only Anandur would open his eyes and see her for who she really was. Not a child, and not a teenager, but a grown woman who knew how to take care not only of herself but also of others.

If she didn't do something about it, though, Anandur would keep playing his dumb game for gods knew how long.

Ugh.

Her anger rising with each passing moment, Wonder was ready to tell Anandur precisely what she thought about his supposedly noble restraint.

"I like it when you get jealous over me. That's how I know you want me even though you like to pretend that you don't."

She stopped and turned to face him. "You're not fooling me, Anandur."

His face looking pained as if someone had punched him in the gut, Anandur let his arm drop by his side. "Fates, Wonder, I'm not a saint. I can't help being attracted to you. But for both our sakes, I'm doing the best I can to keep my hormones from taking control of my brain."

Ooh, he was really making her mad.

Wonder put her hand on her hip and glared at the stupid male. "You're doing it for the sake of some dumb notion you've gotten into your head that I'm too young for you. You're not doing it for my sake, that's for sure."

She waved a hand over herself. "I did all of this for you, so maybe you'd finally see me as a woman."

Indecision danced over Anandur's handsome face. "What do you want from me, Wonder?"

"I want you to take me into your arms and kiss me. But if you're not up to it, there are plenty of perfectly fine immortal males who would be thrilled to give me my first kiss."

Wonder turned on her heel and started walking away. "Or the first that I'm going to remember," she mumbled under her breath.

The whoosh of air coming from behind her was the only warning Wonder had before Anandur caught her elbow and flung her around. Caging her in his arms, he dipped his head but stopped an inch away from her lips.

Her heart beating a drumroll against her ribcage, Wonder could barely breathe. "Kiss me already. Don't make me wait a moment longer."

38

ANANDUR

a man could resist only for so long.

Holding Wonder in his arms and looking into her mesmerizing jade-colored eyes, Anandur no longer cared about all the reasons why he'd thought this was a bad idea.

Denying her was worse.

For an inexperienced girl who wasn't naturally forward to proposition him so blatantly required guts. If he kept saying no, he would hurt her feelings, and her self-confidence might take a nosedive.

He couldn't do that to her.

Yes, that was it, the justification he needed for taking what Wonder was so eagerly offering.

Gathering her to him with an arm around her middle, he smashed her body against his and cradled the back of her head with his palm,

Her heart hammering in her chest, she breathed, "Kiss me already. Don't make me wait a moment longer."

Never before had a kiss been so important. A very long time ago, when Anandur was a young lad, he had given girls a few first kisses, but that was then, and this was now, and there was no comparison.

Wonder meant something to him, and he was going to make sure that her first kiss was the best he'd ever given.

Ever so gently, he grazed his lips against hers, the contact sending shockwaves throughout his body.

Electrifying him.

And just like that his primal instincts roared to life, spurring him to smash her mouth and possess it with his tongue.

It took all he had not to succumb and take her the way his body was demanding he did.

But this wasn't about him and what he needed. This was about Wonder.

Her first kiss was going to be magical no matter what it cost him.

Instead of launching an attack, he flicked just the tip of his tongue over her full lips, seeking permission for entry.

Wonder moaned, parting her lips immediately.

And yet he didn't plunge right away, teasing her with soft flicks and tiny nips.

She let him play for a few seconds, and then threw her arms around his neck and tried to take over, her own tongue darting out to meet his in welcome.

Impatient girl.

Passionate girl.

The time for teasing was over. If he kept it up, Wonder was bound to explode. Worse, she was going to be disappointed.

The only reason she was trying to take the lead was that he wasn't moving fast enough for her. The girl was assertive, but he had no doubt that she would've preferred for him to take charge.

It was a rare female who wanted to dominate her male, and he'd encountered only a handful throughout his long life.

Despite her incredible physical strength, Wonder didn't belong in that group. Anandur was willing to bet his life on it.

Tightening his grip on her nape, he kissed her harder, plundering her welcoming mouth until her knees gave up, her body going lax against his.

If he hadn't been holding her up with an arm around her middle, she would have collapsed.

He must've been doing something right to get such a reaction. Either that or she'd been absolutely starved for it.

As guilt washed over him, Anandur felt like banging his head against a wall. He'd been so obtuse. If he'd paid closer attention, he would've realized that Wonder had been suffering as much as he had.

Idiot.

Focusing inwardly, he'd ignored what was right in front of his eyes.

As Wonder regained her senses and started kissing him back, her sweet tongue darting into his mouth for a taste, it was Anandur's turn to go weak at the knees. Except, he couldn't let himself go.

He would've loved nothing better than to let her explore, but his fangs were fully elongated, and he was afraid to hurt her.

Crap, once again he was acting dumb.

He wasn't dealing with a fragile human. Wonder was an immortal too, and if he nicked her, she would heal in no time.

The implications sent a jolt of desire down to his straining shaft.

This was going to be a first for him too. Never before had he allowed a female entry into his mouth.

Relaxing into the kiss, Anandur let go of her nape and lowered both hands to grip at her gorgeous butt.

As he ground his aching shaft against her soft lower belly, she swept her tongue against his. He groaned in pleasure, and as she licked at one of his fangs, he nearly orgasmed right then and there.

Looking dazed, her eyes still closed, she drew back and touched a finger to her swollen lips.

So beautiful.

He kissed her eyelids, and then took her mouth again.

Threading her fingers into his curls, Wonder held him to her as if she was never going to let go.

"Oh, Esag," she mumbled into his mouth.

Had he heard her correctly?

Had she just moaned another male's name while kissing him?

Leaving her mouth, Anandur leaned away. "Who's Esag?"

Still dazed, Wonder opened her eyes just a crack. "What?"

"Not what, who. You said Esag while kissing me."

Wonder's eyes rolled back, and her knees buckled. She would've slumped to the ground if he hadn't caught her.

Lifting her into his arms, Anandur carried her to the nearest bench and put her down, then knelt in front of her.

During all the time he'd known her, he'd never seen her in such a state. His initial anger gave way to worry.

"What's going on, Wonder? What's happening?"

"There was someone." Wonder touched her lips with trembling fingers. "He kissed me." The trembling intensified. "He was tall, not tall like you, but tall. Taller than me."

Anandur felt like the ground was slipping from under his feet. Wonder's first memory had just resurfaced, and it was of another man kissing her.

"Could he have been the one who hurt you? The one who put you in a coma?"

Wonder shook her head. "I don't remember his face, only his smile." She touched a hand to her belly. "All I have are shadows of impressions. Esag smiled a lot, like you." She lifted a pair of teary eyes to him. "I think I loved him, but I can't remember anything more."

Fuck, fuck, and fuckety fuck.

What if Wonder had someone back in Egypt?

What if she was already mated?

No, that didn't make sense. If she were, she would've been repulsed by Anandur, not attracted to him. On the other hand, nine months was probably long enough to get over the addiction.

He should ask Bridget. Maybe she knew how long it took for the venom addiction to wane.

Suddenly, Wonder's maidenly delicate scent of arousal made sense. It wasn't because she was too young, it was because she was at the tail end of getting over her addiction.

"Do you think he was your mate?"

"You mean like a husband?"

"Yes."

Wonder shook her head. "I'm sure I've never been married."

"How can you be sure of that? You said that you remembered loving him."

"I might have been in love, but I've never been with anyone."

Anandur scratched his head. "You could've forgotten."

Wonder smiled sadly. "It's not a question of remembering or not."

Finally, her meaning got through his thick head. "You're a virgin."

She nodded. "I asked Bridget to check."

39

WONDER

*O*onder managed to keep the tears at bay until Anandur dropped her back at home. But the floodgates broke free as soon as she closed the door behind her.

"What happened?" Gertrude asked.

Shit on a stick. She hadn't noticed the nurse sitting on the couch. If she had, Wonder would've held off the crying fit until she reached her bedroom. Now she was stuck having to explain something she didn't understand herself.

"It's complicated." She wiped her face with the sleeve of her blouse.

Gertrude frowned. "Did Anandur say something to offend you? Because if he did, he probably didn't mean it. He just likes to joke around and sometimes it comes out the wrong way."

Wonder shook her head. "Can we talk about it tomorrow morning? I just want to take a shower and get in bed."

"As you wish. But I think that getting whatever troubles you off your chest will help you sleep better."

There was truth in that.

Wonder was so used to being alone that the idea of sharing

her troubles with anyone was foreign to her. But Trudy and Hilde had made her feel so at home with them, that she was starting to think of the nurses as her family. Especially since she didn't have a real one of her own.

"Okay." Wonder sat on the couch and kicked off her sandals. The straps were pretty, but they were starting to pinch.

Trudy rose to her feet. "Let me make you some calming tea first."

"Thank you."

A few minutes later the nurse returned with two cups of steaming, weird-smelling tea.

Wonder lifted the mug and scrunched her nose. "What's in it?"

"It's a secret recipe. If you want to know, you'll have to become my apprentice, and I'll have to swear you to secrecy." She winked. "Let it cool a bit and then drink up."

"Okay." Wonder put the mug down on the coffee table.

"Let's hear it. What did the big oaf do to upset you so much? Is he still playing hard to get?"

Wonder wasn't too happy about letting her roommates in on her secret infatuation with Anandur. As far as they were concerned, he'd been supposed to be a friend or a big-brother style mentor.

Except, whether they'd believed her or not had become irrelevant after the makeover. Naturally, it had been impossible for Amanda to keep her mouth shut about what had prompted the beautifying session, and both Gertrude and Hildegard had voiced their opinions on the subject of Anandur's reluctant attitude.

Or stinky attitude, as Hilde had called it.

Trudy had called him a condescending prick and had suggested Wonder hit him over the head with her sandal.

"I confronted him and told him to kiss me."

"High five." Trudy lifted her hand. "Good for you, girl." She smiled and leaned forward. "How was it?"

"Amazing." Wonder sniffled.

"What's going on?" The blurry-eyed Hildegard walked into the living room in her Hello Kitty sleep shirt. "Why are you crying?"

Trudy wrapped her arm around Wonder's shoulders. "Anandur kissed her."

"Wasn't that what you wanted?" Hilde plopped into an armchair.

"Yes, and it was a great kiss."

"But?" Hilde made a circular motion with her hand.

"It brought back a memory of another kiss."

As Wonder wiped her tears away with her sleeve and picked up the mug, her roommates gaped at her with their eyes peeled wide.

"That's excellent news." Trudy clasped Wonder's hand. "If one memory resurfaced, then there is a good chance others will too. It means your memories are not lost forever."

"I think that calls for a celebration." Hilde rose to her feet. "Wine, anyone?"

Wonder shook her head. "No, thank you. I don't drink alcohol."

"Right. What about you, Trudy?"

"I'm always game for wine." She turned to Wonder. "I understand that having a memory come back can be emotionally laden, but I have a feeling these tears are the sad kind, not the relieved or grateful kind."

Wonder closed her eyes and groaned. "I finally got Anandur to kiss me, and then I moan another guy's name into his mouth. You should have seen his face. He looked as if I punched him in the stomach."

"Ouch." Gertrude grimaced. "That's bad. You'll have to reassure Anandur that the other guy is just a memory. Tell him that his kiss was so electrifying that it helped reboot your brain. That should mollify him."

Another tear escaped the corner of Wonder's eye and made its way down until it detached from her chin and landed inside the tea.

Great, now the tea was going to be salty.

"What? You don't like my idea? Guys have fragile egos. It always helps telling them how great they are, especially as lovers." Trudy winked.

"I'll drink to that." Hilde handed the other nurse a wineglass. "There is nothing wrong with a little white lie if it makes someone happy, right?"

"It's not that," Wonder said. "I think I was in love with the other guy, Esag."

Hilde frowned. "Esag, that's a name I've never heard before. Are you sure you remember it right? Maybe it was Esau? Not that Esau is popular nowadays, or ever. He wasn't exactly a hero to name your little boy after."

"On the other hand, Wonder can use Esau as a good excuse. Wasn't he a big redhead too?" Trudy asked. "You can say that Anandur reminded you of the biblical Esau."

"That's not a little white lie, Trudy," Hilde said in a stern voice. "That's a big fat one."

Gertrude shrugged. "All is fair in love and war."

"You're missing the point," Wonder said quietly. "Before my coma, I was in love with another guy. Maybe I'm still in love with him but can't remember it. What if more memories of him resurface?"

Hilde lifted her wineglass. "That's a good problem to have."

"I'm not sure about it. I have feelings for Anandur. I want to see where it could go, but not if I have a boyfriend somewhere who's waiting for me, and worries about me, a boyfriend I still love."

"Or a husband," Trudy said.

Wonder shook her head. "No, not a husband. Bridget says I'm still a virgin. But it doesn't make a difference. Shouldn't people be loyal to the ones they love? Shouldn't my heart stay true to Esag?"

Hilde finished her wine and put the glass on the coffee table. "Not if he's dead. Maybe whoever or whatever put you in a coma has killed Esag. Otherwise, he would have been searching for you. How long did you stay in Alexandria after waking up?"

A feeling of dread gripping her insides, Wonder put a hand over her heart. "For about six weeks."

"If he were alive and in love with you, don't you think he would've found you by then?"

"It's a big city."

Still, she'd spent many hours of every day at Alexandria's central market. Anyone looking for a lost person would've started there. It was the city's hub.

40

SYSSI

*K*ian wasn't going to like her idea, Syssi knew it, but at some point, she would have no choice but to tell him.

This wasn't a trivial thing she could get away with hiding. Taking fertility drugs wasn't like deciding to add highlights to her hair and then asking him if he liked it after it was done.

She loved him to pieces, but sometimes he could be so overbearing. She hated to see him frown at her.

Stop being a mouse.

It would be a long time before Bridget got back to her, but it didn't feel right to keep Kian out of the loop. He needed to know what she was planning even if it was months away from happening. If the roles were reversed, Syssi would've wanted to know right away.

Kian might huff and puff, but it was all bluster. In the end, Syssi always got what she wanted. In fact, she needed to be careful with what she told him because he often interpreted her musings as requests and had them immediately fulfilled.

With that in mind, she strode into his home office and took a seat. "I need to talk to you."

He lifted his head from the report he'd been reading and smiled. "That sounds ominous. What did I do this time?"

Right, as if she was so scary. Syssi rolled her eyes. "It's not about what you did. It's about what I want to do."

He sighed. "I know I promised you another vacation in Hawaii. But with the way things are going, it will have to wait."

"It's not about a vacation." She took a deep breath and plunged right ahead. "I talked with Bridget about our fertility issues and suggested attempting some of the treatments that work for humans."

He lifted a brow. "Our fertility, as in yours and mine, or the clan's in general?"

"Both. You know how much I want a child, but this is bigger than just me and my longings. This village is perfect for raising children, but one baby and one more on the way are not enough. Every time I walk by the deserted playground my heart squeezes a little." She put a hand on her chest.

"Oh, my sweet girl." He pushed to his feet and walked over to the other side of his desk. "What do those fertility treatments entail?" He sat in the chair next to her and took her hand.

"Bridget is still checking up on that, but from what I read it seems that drugs that increase ovulation are the first step."

Kian shook his head. "The problem is not limited to immortal females. Immortal males are not all that fertile either. Are there any drugs for that?"

"There are for humans. I didn't discuss it with Bridget yet, but there might be many reasons for the infertility, and we can't treat something until we know what that something is. The low fertility of immortal males can be caused by a low sperm count, or by weak compatibility with human females, or by other factors we are not aware of."

"The same is probably true for immortal females as well."

"Yeah, but the explanation seems simpler. We don't ovulate

as frequently as human females. But males produce sperm all of the time, so the limiting factor must be something else."

"We need more research to be done on the subject."

"Exactly, but there are several problems with that. Bridget doesn't have time to conduct in-depth research, and we need volunteers who are willing to get tested."

"What about Julian?"

Syssi shook her head. "He's too young and inexperienced. I don't know about you, but as much as I like the guy, I wouldn't entrust something like this to the hands of a doctor who didn't even finish his internship." Not to mention that she would feel very awkward with the handsome young doctor who looked a lot like her husband.

Kian raked his fingers through his hair. "So what are you suggesting? I assume that you have a plan."

"Not really. I'm willing to be the first test subject and start taking fertility drugs. Maybe that would be enough, and no further research would be needed. If that doesn't work, we can try in vitro fertilization. That should work for sure."

As she'd expected, Kian didn't like her idea at all. "No way. You're not subjecting yourself to anything before it's thoroughly researched. Are you out of your mind? What if the drugs cause irreversible damage and you wouldn't be able to conceive at all?"

A shiver ran down Syssi's spine. Was that even possible? The truth was that she didn't know enough. No one did. Immortal bodies functioned differently, and until research was done on them, it wouldn't be prudent to take risks. It was like taking shots in the dark and hoping no one would get hurt.

"Then what do we do? Just wait?"

"Why not? Let nature do her thing."

Syssi pulled her hand out of Kian's and crossed her arms over her chest. "I don't want to wait. And it's not only because

I'm impatient for a child. If the clan is to survive, it needs to grow at a faster pace."

That was the backup argument she'd prepared in case Kian wasn't willing to risk her health. As a leader, this was a consideration he couldn't dismiss out of hand.

But her husband wasn't a fool. Wagging a finger at her, he smirked. "Good one, Syssi. How long did it take you to come up with this argument?"

She lifted her chin. "Not long. It crosses my mind every time I walk by that empty playground."

That had gotten rid of the smirk pretty quickly. "As I see it, we have two options. One is do nothing and let nature take her course like we've always done. The second one is to start serious research. But since Bridget is busy with running our humanitarian undertaking and Julian is not experienced enough, we need someone else to do it."

"Like who?"

"We have two more medical doctors in the other clan locations. Merlin in Scotland and Rebecca in Alaska."

"Merlin? Like in Arthurian Merlin?"

Kian chuckled. "No, he is not the legendary one. His mom liked the name."

"I can just imagine how much he got teased about it."

"He did. But instead of getting annoyed, he grew a long beard."

"That's funny. Is he any good?"

Kian shrugged. "He is older than Bridget, but just like her he stays on top of the most recent developments in the medical field."

"What about Rebecca?"

"Rebecca was a nurse for a long time before becoming a doctor. She has a lot of experience both with humans and immortals. Either one of them is capable of doing the research.

The question is which one would agree to actually do it. That's a major undertaking. I'll make the calls tomorrow."

Was he the best or what? As always, all she had to do was ask, and Kian would jump through hoops to fulfill her every wish.

Syssi got up, sat in Kian's lap, and wrapped her arms around his neck. "I love you to pieces. Thank you for being you."

He arched a brow. "Meaning?"

"Meaning that I can always count on you to do your best to get me what I want. Even when you're not too enthusiastic about it."

"You don't ask for much. So when you do, I'm glad for the opportunity to finally give you something."

Syssi chuckled. "Poor baby. I know I'm a problematic wife. I don't like expensive gifts or fancy clothes. But I think this research is going to compensate for all of that. It's going to be costly. I would assume that a lot of expensive equipment is needed. Can we even afford it? I know that money is tight."

"Don't worry about it. We'll find the funds for that."

Syssi lowered her eyes. "We can sell the jewelry you bought for me. I think that alone could fund the research."

"Not going to happen."

"Why? You said it was an investment, and that we could sell it if we needed the money."

"I meant in case of an emergency, and funding research doesn't qualify as such."

"But…"

Kian put a finger on her lips to shush her. "This is not up for discussion."

Syssi swallowed the rest of her argument. As it was, she'd already achieved more than she'd expected. A smart woman knew when to quit.

"Okay."

KIAN

"*T*hat's it?" Kian frowned. "No more arguments? That was way too easy."

Syssi leaned up and kissed him lightly on the lips. "You married a very sensible woman. I'm always willing to compromise. Besides, you're right. The jewels should be saved for a real emergency. A last resort kind of thing."

"I'm indeed a lucky man." He pushed up to his feet with his treasure in his arms. "How about we give making a baby the natural way another try?"

Syssi chuckled. "We've been giving it a twice and thrice and sometimes more tries a day for a long time."

He kissed her nose and kept walking. "True, but you see, it's not entirely up to us. The Fates decide the right time for adding that special life-giving spark, and we can never know when that is."

"You and your Fates. They are just a trio of capricious ladies."

Kian sat on the bed and hugged Syssi closer to him. "Whenever I mention the Fates, I have the same image pop into my head."

"What is it?"

"Do you remember when you took me to the retirement home? You were supposed to read to your nana's friends."

"How can I forget. The nasty old crones had me read a racy romance novel in front of you and Brundar. I almost died from embarrassment even though you saved me and did the reading for me. Just listening to you read it was mortifying."

"Yeah. I remember you turning redder than a beet. But I also remember falling a little more for you in that room."

"Why?" She narrowed her eyes at him. "Do you like seeing me squirm?"

"That too." He kissed her forehead. "You look adorable when you blush. But I also liked that you kept on listening despite how uncomfortable it made you, and that you didn't try to stop me. You're not a quitter. That is one of the many things that I love about you."

His compliments seemed to mollify Syssi. "And I love that you notice every little thing about me and find a reason to love it." She put her head on his chest.

He breathed easier when she did that. The closeness, the trust, it was like a soothing balm on his frayed nerves. "Anyway, in my mind, these three old ladies helped us get closer, and when I think of the Fates, their smug wrinkled faces pop into my head. I remember thinking that they looked as if they'd won a bet or something."

"Yeah, me too. But I thought they were so smug because they got you to read aloud that incredibly embarrassing book."

Kian waggled his brows. "A very arousing story about vampires if I remember correctly. It got you all hot and bothered."

"Oh, shit." Syssi slapped her forehead. "You smelled my arousal, didn't you?"

"Yep."

"No wonder you looked just as smug as them."

"I was in no better state. They got us both exactly where they wanted us."

Syssi's brows dipped in a frown. "Hmm, maybe you're on to something. Not long after that most memorable visit, the three of them moved to Florida. The pretext was finding a retirement home closer to Leonora's granddaughter. But when I tried to contact them at the place they'd mentioned, no one had heard of them. I thought that maybe I didn't remember the name right, and I called a bunch of others with similar names, but they weren't there either."

"There you go." He waved a hand. "A mystery."

Syssi smirked. "If they are indeed the three fabled Fates in disguise, maybe I should resume the search, find them, and ask them to give us a baby."

"Or we can give the natural way another try."

"We can do both."

"Always the voice of reason. Tomorrow, I'll contact Turner and ask him to look for your missing ladies. But right now, I want to make love to my wife."

She scrunched her nose. "Maybe you shouldn't."

"Make love to my wife?"

"No, have Turner look for them. What if one of them died? They were so old. So it's not a remote possibility. I'd rather not know."

"As you wish. When you decide you want to find them, tell me, and I'll ask Turner to do his thing."

"Okay."

He loved that word coming out of her luscious lips. Usually, it meant that fun times in bed were about to start.

"How about you get naked and put on that jewelry we were talking about?"

She narrowed her eyes at him. "I would rather you undress me first and then put those jewels on me yourself."

That was even better. "I like the way you think."

RUTH

*P*hone clutched in her hand, Ruth sat on the couch and waited for Nick's call. It had been three days since he'd left for Rio, and she was missing him something fierce.

He called her twice a day every day, once in the morning before leaving his hotel room, and once at night when he returned. The problem was that unless he stayed up late to call her, they couldn't talk long because of the four-hour difference between Rio and Los Angeles. Ruth's workday ended at seven in the evening, and she usually got home half an hour later, which meant that Nick had to wait until twelve-thirty at night Rio time to call her at home.

It was seven forty-two.

Did something happen to make him late? Or had he simply fallen asleep?

Should she call him instead of waiting for his call?

Before leaving, Nick had told her that while working he left his personal phone at the hotel. In case Ruth needed to get in touch with him urgently, she was to call Eva. He wasn't allowed to give out his work number to anyone other than his team members, but his boss could reach him in case of an emergency.

Ruth glanced at the phone for the hundredth time, then shook her head and put it down on the coffee table. She was being silly, getting all worked up over a twelve-minute delay.

Instead of acting like the mature partner in their relationship, she was turning into a lovesick teenager who couldn't live without her boyfriend for more than a day.

Was it Nick's influence? Was his youth rubbing off on her?

Ruth smiled.

In some ways, Nick acted even younger than his twenty-two years, and in some ways, he acted way older.

She loved the polarity.

His youthful exuberance was contagious. Ruth couldn't remember ever being as happy as she was with Nick. Not only was he sharing with her his innocence and the discovery of all the wonders of intimacy, but he was also giving her a second chance at a complete do-over of her own messed-up youth.

Despite Nick being just as socially inept as her, he didn't feel awkward around people or shy away from them. His attitude was basically; so what?

And how liberating was that?

He'd shown her that it was possible to have a full life, despite what she considered a disability.

Ruth wasn't there yet, but she was working on adopting Nick's attitude. She was finding out that it was okay to be around people and not say much, or anything at all. Most people were forgiving and accepting of her and her limitations.

And those who weren't?

Screw them, as Nick loved to say. Judgmental assholes weren't worth an iota of her mental energy.

In Ruth's opinion, that attitude of 'so what' was very grown up. In fact, most humans didn't achieve that wisdom until old age. On top of that, Nick's maturity was evident in how hard-working and responsible he was.

He was also highly intelligent.

Unlike many others of his generation, Nick wasn't a follower. He formed his opinions after researching the facts instead of parroting meaningless slogans. Just because everyone else around him accepted something one idiot or another had spewed as immutable truths, didn't mean that they were.

Maybe it was the flip side of social ineptitude. Followers weren't contrary, they didn't voice opposing views, they said amen, and by doing so became part of the herd instead of looking on from the sidelines.

If this was indeed so, Ruth was grateful for her nonconformity. She'd rather be true to herself and retain her independent thinking than sacrifice it in order to belong. Not that this was the only way one could do that. She knew enough people who could combine independent thinking with easy socializing, but that required skills neither she nor Nick had.

When her phone finally rang, it was seven fifty-five.

"Hi, Nick. Did you fall asleep?"

"No, I was reading on the crapper and lost track of time."

Ruth laughed. "T.M.I., I could've done without that mental image. What were you reading?"

"A book about the plasticity of the mind. Did you know that the number of connections in our brains can double in just one hour of repeated stimulation?"

"No, I didn't. What does it mean?"

"It means that the brain rewires itself according to its activity in real time. What you think about the most is what it creates more neural pathways for, and therefore what it becomes better at. So if you spend your entire day solving math problems, your brain becomes more adept at math, and if you spend the entire day thinking about me, you become horny."

That was Nick to a tee. Perhaps other women would have found his comment crass, or immature, but Ruth found it not only funny but also true.

"I was thinking about you the entire day, and I have to admit that I was somewhat perturbed."

"Perturbed? That doesn't sound sexy."

Smirking, Ruth switched the phone to her other ear. "How about hot and bothered?"

"That's better. Where are you now?"

"On the couch in the living room."

"Are you comfortable getting naked there?"

"I've done it before."

"True, but that was while Mr. Big Schlong and I were distracting you.

Ruth laughed. "Would you stop calling him that?"

"What do you want me to call him?"

"The Professor."

"Fine. But I don't want to talk about him. I want to talk about you in the nude."

"Oh, yeah? And what exactly should I be doing in the nude?"

"Get naked, and I'll tell you."

This should be interesting. But he was right about her not being comfortable doing so in the middle of her living room. It wouldn't feel private even if she closed all the drapes and locked the door.

"Give me a moment, I'm going to my bedroom."

Ruth regretted the choice of words as soon as she'd said them. It should have been their bedroom, not hers. But there was one huge obstacle to her asking Nick to move in with her.

He was a human, and she was an immortal.

Ever since she started working at the café, Ruth had become quite adept at hiding her immortal tells, and she was confident in her ability to hide them from Nick. But what happened if he wasn't a Dormant? How the hell was she going to erase herself from his memories?

What if he were an immune?

She would have to disappear, which meant giving up her house, moving into the village, and managing the café over there.

But none of that would be as difficult as trying to forget Nick. How would she go on without him?

Oh, dear merciful Fates!

This was it. This was the certainty she'd been looking for.

Nick was her one.

If she had doubts before they were all gone now.

"Ruthie? Are you there?"

"Yeah, I'm here. I zoned out for a moment. Give me another minute."

"No problem. Just so you know, I'm naked in bed, and my schlong is pointing at the ceiling just from imagining you getting undressed. Can you narrate while you do it?"

It might be a bit embarrassing, but describing her striptease might divert her thoughts from her newfound revelations and put her in the right mood for their nightly naughty phone time.

"I'm putting you on speaker."

"Are you sure about that? What if anyone overhears us?"

Ruth smiled. "So what?"

"That's my girl."

43

ANANDUR

$\mathcal{A}$s Anandur took his seat in the war room, also known as Kian's office in the underground, he was all hyped up about the opportunity to kick some Doomers' asses. Tonight's mission was exactly the type of distraction he needed.

Hopefully, the lack of sleep wasn't going to affect his alertness.

After the double explosions Wonder had detonated under his feet last night, he'd spent the rest of it seething with anger and punching his pillow into submission.

The thing hadn't survived, and the first thing he had done this morning was to order a new one. Tiny feathers were still floating all around his bedroom because he hadn't had time to vacuum the suckers.

"What's with you?" Brundar asked as he sat next to him. "Your frown could give Bhathian's a run for its money."

"I had a fight with my pillow last night."

Brundar lifted a brow. "Who won?"

"The pillow lost. Services are being held tomorrow after we come back from the mission."

"My condolences." Brundar dipped his head.

Since Callie, Brundar was developing a sense of humor, which was absolutely awesome. Finally, after centuries of trying to get a rise out of his brother, Brundar was picking up the banter Anandur was throwing his way.

And since he was doing it in his toneless, expressionless, robot-like manner, he was cracking people up without even trying.

Good times.

But as it was often the case, life or the damn Fates couldn't let a guy enjoy a peaceful, content moment for too long. Something always had to go wrong.

Like a woman-child who was too tempting to say no to, and when he finally succumbed, giving her a kiss to trump all kisses, she'd moaned another man's name in his mouth.

If Anandur could find that Esag dude, he could challenge him to a fight over Wonder. When Anandur turned on the charm, no other dude stood a chance. Unless said dude was missing in action, and the only place he could be found was in Wonder's head.

Fighting phantoms was a losing proposition because they were as perfect as their host wanted them to be. They never screwed up to prove themselves unworthy.

"Dalhu, what're you doing here?" Brundar asked.

"I'm going with you on the mission." Dalhu sat on Anandur's other side. "I haven't seen any action since the monastery, and I'm getting twitchy."

Anandur quirked a brow. "You haven't trained for months. What makes you think you're ready for action?"

Dalhu pushed back up to his feet and stretched his body to its full height. The guy was huge even compared to Anandur. A smirk lifting one corner of his lips, he crooked a finger at Anandur. "Let's get on the mat, and I'll show you exactly how ready I am."

With a big grin stretching his face, Anandur stood up. "You're on." The ex-Doomer was a formidable foe, but Anandur was the undefeated wrestling champion. This was exactly the kind of challenge he needed to release the frustrated energy swirling around his gut and slowly poisoning him from the inside.

Regrettably, Kian had chosen that moment to arrive. "Sit down, gentlemen."

Anandur pointed a finger at Dalhu. "After we come back from the mission."

"You're on."

Kian waited until all eyes were on him. "I just got off the phone with Onegus. Turner's guys completed their reconnaissance, and we have the final numbers."

He clicked the monitor on. "This is the apartment building the Doomers are using as their quarters. There are a total of twenty-two of them. Six operate the warehouse and are in charge of the thirty-one humans they have doing slave work for them. Fifteen are in the field, selling the drugs mainly in clubs. They take turns working in the warehouse. The last one is their commanding officer, a guy named Gommed. Ring a bell, Dalhu?"

The ex-Doomer shook his head. "Nope."

"Makes sense," Bhathian said. "They are never going to get caught because they can thrall their customers and the security people in the clubs to forget them."

"Nah," Arwel said. "A good dealer forms relationships with his clients. They need the humans to remember them. Otherwise, they will go and buy from someone else. The Doomers are not the only game in town."

"Then they thrall the security and the police," Bhathian acquiesced. "That's enough to keep them doing business with impunity."

"Right." Kian frowned. "What I would like to know is

whether this is a pilot program and more are coming in the future, or do they already have warehouses like that spread out all over. The Brotherhood works on a large scale; if there is one location, there are others, or there are going to be."

"Depends on who runs it," Dalhu said. "And I don't mean the commanding officer in the field. If he is the only one in charge, then there are more distribution centers like this one. But if one of the head honchos is in charge, then this is a test run."

"That's what I thought," Kian said. "Turner's team didn't report anyone other than that Gommed guy, so we have to assume there are more. We will have to question the Doomers we catch."

"Won't work," Dalhu said. "The only one who might know about other centers is their commanding officer, though he probably doesn't. And if he does, you should assume that he is under compulsion not to reveal anything of importance."

"Don't you know it for sure?" Anandur asked. "Didn't they do it to you?"

"I suspect that they did, but I have no recollection of it. What I remember, however, is that my thought process became clearer the longer my mission was. Which made me think that I had been put under compulsion, but that it had weakened over time."

Anandur thought back to his time in the facility. "The Doomers I was locked up with talked quite freely, but then they thought I was one of them."

Dalhu shook his head. "The simple soldiers know so little that no one bothers with them."

That had been Anandur's impression too. "What about my buddy Grud? Did Turner's guys mention him?"

"No, and it's not important," Kian said. "The other two Doomers that Wonder caught gave us the names of their comrades. But having the names gives us no advantage."

Arwel lifted his finger. "What are we going to do with the humans?"

"That's a good question. I'm still trying to come up with the answer. As far as we can ascertain, those working in packaging are illegal immigrants. We can try to send them back to their families with some money to tide them over. Even if they remember anything, the most they can suspect is being drugged or hypnotized. But if the damage to their brains is so severe that they don't remember where they are from, then we have a problem."

"What about the others? I assume they have chemists manufacturing the drugs?" Yamanu asked.

"The chemists are a different story. I don't believe they were thralled like the others because that would've been counterproductive. They needed their brains functioning well. We need to find out if they were bribed or coerced by threatening their families."

Bhathian leaned back in his chair and crossed his arms over his chest. "So we round them up and ship them to the airstrip?"

"No. The San Francisco airport is small and private, but it's not exclusively ours. Someone might wonder why a bunch of zombie-looking humans is being herded through it. We are going to transport them via bus. Shai is working on renting a place near the sanctuary so Vanessa can hop between the two."

"And the chemists?" Yamanu asked.

"We'll run them through our probes, meaning Edna and Andrew."

44

WONDER

"One roast beef sandwich and one tuna melt," Carol repeated the order for Wonder's sake. "Did you get it?"

"I did. Coming right up."

She'd been scatterbrained all day, forgetting the orders as soon as she'd heard them. Most of the time she caught herself staring into the distance as if the answers to her problems could be found in the treetops.

It bothered her tremendously that she hadn't had the chance to wish Anandur good luck on his mission or to talk to him about what had happened last night.

After the restless night she'd had, she overslept, waking up after he and the other senior Guardians had left for San Francisco.

Not that there was anything she could say to make things right between them. Not unless she wanted to use Gertrude's suggestion and make up a lie.

Then there was the worry. He hadn't shared any details about the raid with her, so she didn't know whether he was going to be in any real danger.

"Do you think I should call him?"

"I assume that by him, you mean Anandur."

"Who else?" It's not like she could call Esag. All she had was a name and a vague image of a tall, smiling guy, that and the tight feeling in her chest whenever she said his name in her head.

"Calling or texting the Guardians during a mission is prohibited. Besides, their numbers are temporarily blocked, and they can't receive or even see calls from civilians. Only Kian and Onegus can call them."

"But they can call out, right?" Wonder stuffed the tuna sandwich inside the panini maker.

"It's likely. The raid won't happen until late at night. They might be allowed to make calls before that."

Wonder used tongs to take out the tuna melt, placed it on a plate, added a scoop of potato salad and a pickle, then handed it to Carol who took the order to the table.

"Start making two cappuccinos," she told Wonder as she came back. "I saw Amanda and Syssi heading here."

On their way back home, the two stopped by the café almost every day. It was so cool how well the sisters-in-law got along, carpooling to and from the university where they worked together. It seemed like the two were spending more time with each other than with their respective mates.

Wonder couldn't help but feel a little envious. She would've loved having a best friend who never tired of her company and vice versa.

"Wonder, darling." Amanda sauntered behind the counter as if she owned the café and pulled her into her arms. "How did it go last night?" She leaned to whisper in her ear. "Did you get what you wanted?"

Wonder sighed. "Let's just say that I've gotten more than I bargained for."

Amanda frowned. "Really? What happened? Anandur is a

sweetheart. There is no way he did something he wasn't supposed to."

Why did everyone automatically assume it was the guy's fault? Wonder had seen enough bitchy and underhanded moves in the club to realize that often it was the girl's fault and not the guy's.

"I need to finish making your cappuccino. Anything you'd like to eat?"

Amanda smacked her lips. "Goat cheese and roasted red peppers melt. Usually, I wait to eat with Dalhu, but he went with the Guardians to San Francisco and won't be back until tomorrow." She turned around to her sister-in-law. "Syssi, do you want a sandwich?"

"I'll have the same one you're having."

Wonder pulled out two more slices of bread. "Is Kian gone too?"

"No, he's here. But he is going to spend most of his time in the war room until the mission is over. Our butler is going to bring him his meals there."

As Wonder made the sandwiches, she remembered Anandur mentioning that Dalhu was an ex-Doomer. She hadn't met the guy yet, but Anandur seemed to like him.

"Is Dalhu going on the mission as a consultant?" Wonder handed Amanda the two cappuccinos.

"No, my Dalhu needs to flex his muscles a bit. He's been holding a paintbrush for far too long. He's going to fight with the guys." She took the cups and sauntered away to where Syssi was sitting at a table. "Why don't you join us, girls? We can have a fab gossip session."

Amanda didn't sound worried at all. Was it because she knew Dalhu was a formidable warrior, or was it because the mission was not dangerous?

Carol glanced around the café and then lifted her wrist to look at her watch. "It's ten minutes to six. We can get away with closing a little early. Whoever comes now can use the vending machines." She flipped the sign to 'closed' and grabbed a can of cola from the fridge. "Can I get you something?"

"I'll take one of these too." Wonder took the two sandwiches out of the griddle, put them on plates and brought them to the table.

Amanda lifted her sandwich. "I'm waiting to hear the story, entertain me while I'm eating."

Wonder cast a sidelong glance at Syssi. Did she know about her and Anandur too? Probably. At this rate pretty soon every immortal in the village would know.

"Can this stay between us, please? It's bad enough that Trudy and Hilde know. Don't tell anyone else, will you?"

Amanda made the zipping motion over her lips.

"I promise," Syssi said.

Carol shrugged. "I didn't tell anyone."

"Talk, girl. I don't have all night." Amanda winked. "Well, actually I do. It's not like I have any plans for later. But I have no patience."

Wonder took a deep breath. "The long and the short of it is that Anandur kissed me and I said another guy's name. Apparently, I've been in love with someone named Esag." She grimaced. "What a bad timing for a memory to resurface. I was enjoying the best kiss imaginable, and then poof; all the effort of dressing up and looking nice so Anandur would notice that I'm all grown up was gone up in smoke. I ruined it for us before it ever began."

"Was Anandur mad?" Syssi asked.

Amanda rolled her eyes. "No, he was so happy he went dancing naked in the woods. What kind of question is that? Of course, he got mad. Who wouldn't?"

Syssi waved a hand. "You're obsessed with that dancing naked in the woods idea. Just do it already and stop talking about it."

Baffled, Wonder looked from one woman to the other. What were they talking about?

Carol leaned over to whisper in her ear. "Ignore them. They're being silly."

Oh. So it was some kind of a private joke.

Amanda smirked. "Only if you join me, darling. We need seven beautiful women to perform the ritual. Are you game, Wonder?"

"Keep ignoring them," Carol said.

"Maybe some other time. I'm too anxious to go dancing, in the nude or otherwise."

"Right." Amanda put her half-eaten sandwich down and wrapped it in a napkin. "I say forget about that Esag guy whoever he is and concentrate on Anandur. You are obviously into him, and he is into you. What was in the past, should stay in the past."

That was actually not bad advice, even if it was somewhat simplistic. Sometimes it was better not to overthink things and just go with one's gut.

"You should talk to Vanessa," Syssi offered. "Now that you've gotten one memory back, she might help you retrieve the others."

"I don't have her number."

Syssi pulled out her phone and found the contact. "What's your number? I can text you the contact information."

As Wonder dictated the numbers and Syssi sent the contact over, Amanda tapped her long-nailed fingers on the table impatiently.

"Vanessa is too busy now to schlep over here. Kri is going to the monastery tomorrow for the bi-weekly self-defense classes she's giving the girls. She can take you with her."

"Didn't she go with the guys on the mission?" Wonder asked.

Carol shook her head. "I told you that Kian doesn't allow it."

"You did. But you also said that she could do other things, like calming down the humans."

"True, but I think what she does with the girls is more important. She is helping them gain confidence. After what they've been through, that's crucial."

Wonder couldn't argue with that. Carol's comment reminded her of her old roommates' haunted eyes. Gods only knew what those two girls had been through. Maybe the shelter should offer self-defense classes as well.

If she ever went back there, Wonder might volunteer to do that. She wasn't anywhere near Kri's skill level, but somehow she knew how to street fight, which should be enough.

45

RUTH

"*J*ackson, can I have a word with you in the kitchen?" Ruth asked as soon as he entered the café. He'd been supposed to be there hours ago.

"I'm sorry about coming in late. Carol and I were brainstorming ideas and time flew by."

"That's okay. I just wanted to ask if you can cover for me for the rest of the day? I need to leave early."

"Sure, no problem." He frowned. "What's up? Everything okay?"

"I'm going to the village." She motioned for him to follow her outside the back door and closed it behind them. "One of the Guardians is giving me a lift."

Jackson glanced left and then right, making sure that the alley behind the café was free of eavesdroppers. "You should get your own modified car. It doesn't matter that you don't live there yet. Kian will gladly hook you up with one."

"I know. But the idea of a self-driving car scares me."

"They are perfectly safe."

"Yeah, until they aren't. Computers malfunction, Jackson. It might not happen often, but it's not such a remote possibility."

"There are plenty of safety features incorporated into our cars. You have nothing to worry about. If you want, you can stop by William's, and he will explain everything. Trust me, after you hear him out, you will request a modified car right away."

She waved a hand. "If I have time after my meeting with Bridget I will."

"What are you seeing Bridget about?"

This time Ruth glanced both ways to make sure they were alone, then stepped closer to Jackson and whispered, "It's about Nick. I want to ask her things about the transition process for guys. I don't know much about it."

Jackson grinned. "Congratulations." He clapped her on the back. "So you're finally ready for the next step?"

Ruth felt her cheeks getting hot. The next step Jackson was talking about had already been taken, but she wasn't about to share that information with him. Her relatives were way too nosy for her liking.

"If by the next step you mean that I'm finally sure Nick is the one for me, then yes, I'm ready for the next step."

An even wider grin split Jackson's face. "I'm glad. When are you going to break the news to him?"

"That's what I need to talk to Bridget about. I need her advice on how and when to do it. Especially since we suspect that he might be difficult to thrall. What if he's an immune, and then we find out that he is not a Dormant? How are we going to erase the memory of the experiment from his mind if we can't access it?"

The smile evaporated from Jackson's face. "You're right." He pushed his bangs back. "I suspected he would be hard to thrall when I brought him to the wedding. I didn't even try to do it, getting him drunk instead. Now I regret not testing him to see if it was even possible."

"You can still do it." Ruth perked up as an idea started

forming in her head. "We can test him. I'm not good enough to thrall someone who is naturally resistant. But maybe you are? How is your thralling, is it strong?"

"I'm okay, but some of the guys are much better than me. Yamanu and Arwel are excellent, and Kian is probably the best at it. You know how it works. The less diluted your blood is, the stronger the abilities."

It was a misconception, but before Ruth could answer Jackson, Lori opened the back door and poked her head outside.

"Guys? Are you coming in? There is no one manning the register."

Jackson lifted two fingers. "We'll be back in two minutes."

"What do I do with the customers until then?"

"Write down the orders, and they will pay for them when they leave."

"Oh, why didn't I think of that?" The girl waved a hand. "Take your time."

Given the smirk on Lori's face, she probably thought that there was something going on between Jackson and Ruth, even though it was a ridiculous notion given that both of their partners visited the café often.

The girl had to be clueless not to realize that the two of them were in committed relationships with other people. Even a blind person could see that Jackson was totally in love with Tessa. Ruth wasn't as extroverted with her feelings toward Nick, but still, they should've been obvious as well.

"It's not true what you said about the abilities being stronger the closer an immortal is to the godly source. As far as I know, Sari has no special abilities aside from being a great businesswoman. And Alena is wonderfully fruitful for an immortal female, but she has no other special talents. I'm not aware of Amanda having any either, does she?"

"Aside from being a freaking neuroscience professor? I don't think so."

"You see?" Ruth waved a hand. "That proves it. Annani's daughters have the least diluted genes of all of us, and they are not more powerful."

Jackson frowned. "Yeah, I guess you're right as far as special talents go. Thralling is something every immortal can do to some extent. But males are much better at it than females because we get more practice. Everyone knows Kian is the best at it."

"True. So what are you trying to say, that I should ask Kian if he is willing to thrall Nick?"

"What I'm saying is that if nothing else works, you can ask Kian as a last resort."

Ruth sighed. "I'll keep it in mind. First, I want to see what Bridget has to say. She has a lot of experience with transitioning Dormants."

"We should get back inside."

"Yeah." Ruth glanced at her watch. "Rick is picking me up in ten minutes."

46

KIAN

*K*ian picked up his phone. "What can I do for you, Bridget?"

"Do you have a few moments to discuss Nick's transition? I hate to bother you with that, but Ruth has some concerns."

"Of course." He got up and opened the door. Conveniently, Bridget's office was down the hall from his. That was when she could get away from the clinic and actually do the job she'd volunteered for instead of filling in for Julian. "Come right in. The door is open."

It was about time Ruth and Nick made up their minds whether they were meant for each other or not. Eva could go into labor any day now, and she was still refusing to move into the village until Nick transitioned.

In her mind, there was no doubt that he would. And since she'd been right about Tessa and Sharon, whose talents were much less apparent than Nick's, Kian had little reason to doubt that either.

What irked him, though, was the doctor's apologetic tone. She'd made it sound as if the guy was of no importance, and as if dealing with whatever troubled Ruth about his transition was a nuisance Bridget was loath to bother Kian with.

It couldn't have been further from the truth.

Maybe he needed to remind her that potential Dormants were of utmost importance to the clan. All other considerations, economic and humanitarian, took a backseat to this. The future of the clan depended on finding Dormants and their successful transition to immortality.

Apart from the obvious problem of extinction, the effect of solitary life was corrosive to the mental health of his clansmen and women. Finding Syssi had changed Kian's life so profoundly, giving it a meaning and a future he hadn't dreamt of, that he often felt guilty about having been granted such an incredible boon while others remained lonely.

That was why he'd approved Julian's week-long absence to attend a psychic convention even though it put additional strain on Bridget's time. Every possible avenue, no matter how improbable, was worth investigating.

"Come in." He waved Ruth and the doctor in.

"Thank you for agreeing to see us," Bridget said.

"Yes, thank you," Ruth mumbled under her breath.

"Never hesitate to come to me with anything that has to do with Dormants. I will always make time for that." He motioned to the two chairs facing his desk. "Please take a seat."

When they did, he walked over to the bar and opened the fridge. "Can I offer you anything to drink? Water? Soda? Something stronger?" As was his habit, he managed to get himself all riled up and needed something to calm him down.

"No, thank you," Ruth said.

Bridget put her tablet down. "I'll have whatever you're having."

It was late afternoon, a perfect time for a drink, but maybe he should wait for his meeting with Onegus. The ladies might frown on him grabbing a beer in the middle of his workday.

With Syssi's encouragement, he was putting some effort into improving his public image. The squeeze balls she'd gotten him for stress relief would do for now.

He pulled out three small bottles of carbonated water and put two in front of his guests, even though Ruth had declined his offer. The way her eyes were darting around, she was nervous as hell, which usually resulted in a dry mouth.

And people thought he had no empathy.

"What can I help you with?" he asked.

"Ruth, could you tell Kian what you've told me?"

Clutching the plastic bottle, Ruth nodded, took in a breath, and then finally looked him in the eyes.

Good for her. It was about time the woman developed some backbone.

"I'm ready to tell Nick about the possibility of him being a Dormant."

Kian smiled in what he thought was an encouraging way. "Congratulations." Dialing down his intensity was one more thing Syssi had told him he needed to work on. According to his wife, it came through as aggression and intimidated people, which was probably doubly true for someone as timid as Ruth.

She shook her head. "But there is a problem. He might be an immune. The one time I tried to peek into his mind, I couldn't. I know I'm not very good at it, but I had no problem with other humans." Suddenly aware of the incriminating implications of her admission, Ruth looked up at him with worried eyes. "I didn't thrall anyone. I just took a quick peek once in a long while. I hope that's okay. I'm not a lawbreaker."

He lifted his hand. "That's okay, Ruth. No need to apologize. Did anyone else try to thrall Nick? Wasn't Jackson supposed to do it for Eva's wedding?"

"Yes, but he didn't. Instead, he got Nick drunk."

"Because he couldn't?"

"Jackson didn't try. He said he had a feeling that Nick might be a hard nut to crack."

Kian leaned back in his chair. "Well, it seems like no one really tried to thrall the kid except for you, and you admit to being not so good at it. The first course of action should be an actual test. I'll ask Bhathian to attempt thralling Nick. It's convenient since they live in the same house."

"If you don't mind, I'd rather have Jackson try first," Ruth said in a small voice.

"Be my guest. I don't know how good Jackson is, but I know Bhathian is decent. If both of them fail, we will have to test him with someone better. Yamanu and Arwel are both very strong. Yamanu more than Arwel, but his appearance might raise Nick's suspicions. Is he a suspicious guy by nature?"

Ruth shook her head. "Not at all. He's open and talkative and has no filter, but he is also very smart." She sighed. "What are we going to do if he can't be thralled? Could we even offer him a chance at transition? Because if we do and he turns out not to be a Dormant, and we can't erase the experience from his memory, we will have to imprison him, right?"

"Right. But let's not panic just yet. If everyone else fails, I'm willing to test him myself. If I can't thrall him either, we will figure something out."

Bridget arched a brow. "Like what?"

"I don't know yet. I need to do some thinking."

She eyed him suspiciously and for a good reason. The way he'd first healed and then turned her mate was still a mystery Bridget was thankfully unable to solve.

Keeping his expression schooled under her scrutiny, Kian thanked the Fates that neither Bridget nor Turner, both extremely smart people, had managed to figure out what he'd done.

After a few seconds of a stare down, Bridget gave up and

pushed to her feet, with Ruth quickly following suit. "Thank you for seeing us."

"Anytime." He stood up and escorted them to the door. "You know what to do, Ruth, right?"

"Yes, start with Jackson, and if that doesn't work, try with someone stronger."

He put a reassuring hand on her shoulder. "Exactly. And if all else fails, don't hesitate to call on me."

"Thank you. I appreciate it."

As Kian closed the door behind them, he let the smile slide off his face.

Nick presented a similar problem to Turner, but with the added complication of having no knowledge of immortals.

The guy must have been pretty oblivious if he hadn't noticed anything peculiar about the people surrounding him. Either that or his roommates and Ruth were doing a fantastic job of hiding their otherness.

But that was neither here nor there. If Nick proved to be an immune, they couldn't tell him anything. Turner had been the only exception to the rule of keeping their existence secret from humans, and there had been plenty of good reasons for that.

That reasoning was absent with Nick.

He was a young guy who according to Ruth had no filter. Turner was an operative whose entire life revolved around keeping secrets.

Bottom line, Nick would have to be induced without his knowledge, which was morally wrong but the lesser evil. If he were told the truth and then didn't transition, his life would be ruined. They would have no choice but to keep him locked up, either in the keep or the village.

The question was how to do it.

Kian could drug Nick the same way he'd drugged Turner,

but this time he wouldn't have the benefit of the goddess's miracle-producing blood.

Without it, the only way to induce Nick was by a venom bite, and there was no way Kian could summon enough aggression out of thin air to bite an unconscious man, not even if he listened to vile lyrics of slam poetry. That trick had worked once. It wasn't going to work again.

He couldn't do it, but Brundar might.

The Guardian prided himself on the ability to produce venom and elongate his fangs on demand.

With Turner, the goddess's blood had been necessary because of the cancer, and since no one was supposed to know about her blood's miracle-producing properties, Kian had no choice but to do everything himself.

Nick, on the other hand, was a healthy kid who any immortal male could induce, provided said immortal could do it to an unconscious Dormant.

MAGNUS

*A*s Magnus glanced at Anandur, he thought his partner didn't seem battle ready at all. Instead of being all pumped up with pre-mission adrenaline, the guy sat slumped in the passenger seat with his eyelids drooping like he was about to fall asleep. "You look tired."

"It's after three in the morning, and I didn't sleep much the night before."

Magnus shook his head. "I'm not going to ask what has kept you awake."

"Much appreciated." Anandur crossed his arms over his chest and closed his eyes.

"You need to wake up, buddy. We are on at exactly four a.m."

"That means that I have half an hour of shuteye. Bug off."

If it were up to him, Magnus would have preferred the Doomers to know that he was coming, not only because taking them by surprise in their beds wasn't the Guardian way, but because he would've loved a decent fight.

But that's how Kian and Onegus wanted it to play out.

Assigning one Guardian per Doomer was overkill too, but

the idea was to take them out simultaneously so no one could sound the alarm and bring reinforcements. In fact, the plan was to make it look as if the Doomers defected. Meaning that any signs of struggle had to be cleared up before the mission was considered completed.

According to the ex-Doomer, Dalhu, that would put the top man of the entire drug-dealing operation in a very bad light. Maybe even cost him his head.

But that wasn't the main reason for it. The overriding consideration was to keep the raid quiet and not alert the humans living in the nearby apartment buildings that something was going on. It was also important not to leave a trail to follow for the human authorities, as well as the higher-ups in the Doomer organization.

Except, with Yamanu—the ultimate thrall master—shrouding the area, no human would have heard or seen anything anyway. Luckily, the apartment building the Doomers used for their quarters was so close to the warehouse that Yamanu could cover both, which allowed for a simultaneous attack.

Arwel, who was with the team going for the warehouse, could've done a decent shroud too, but he didn't come close to Yamanu's powers.

At a quarter to four, Magnus nudged Anandur's shoulder. "It's time. We need to get into position."

"I'm up." Anandur stretched his arms as much as the rental vehicle allowed. "Do you still have any coffee left in that thermos?"

"Plenty, here you go."

"Much obliged."

Anandur gulped the thing as if it were water, then handed the empty container back. "I'm afraid there is not much left. I'll buy you coffee after we're done."

"You got it."

Taking out the Sig Sauer from its holster, Magnus checked the safety. Next, he screwed the silencer on and put it back.

Lastly, he tapped his earpiece. "Testing."

A moment later Onegus's voice came in. "Test complete. Carry on, Magnus."

Next to him, Anandur went through the same sequence.

Magnus reached behind to the back seat and grabbed his Kevlar vest and the jacket to go over it.

"We're going to be cooked with all of that on."

Securing his vest, Anandur reached for his jacket. "I wish William would invent a cooling jacket."

Shaking his head, Magnus opened the door and closed it as quietly as he could. "When did we become so spoiled?" he whispered as Anandur did the same.

"Yeah, this is nothing compared to the full body one. That thing is awesome, but it's cumbersome and hot as hell."

They didn't bother locking the car. Even though they were parked two blocks away from the apartment building, sound carried in the quiet of the night. A small thing like a car door closing or the beep of the lock engaging could alert the Doomers.

The good thing was that the Doomers' commander hadn't thought to post guards in their living quarters. The warehouse, on the other hand, was guarded at all times.

The Doomers had no reason to expect a clan attack, but they had plenty of reasons to expect one from the gangs they'd disenfranchised, or other thugs who were after the drugs and the money.

Anandur covered his nose. "I didn't expect it to stink that bad."

"The stinkier, the better. Turner is a genius."

Magnus had to hand it to the operative. Turner's idea to have a pretend crew work on the sewer near the apartment building and leave it open overnight was brilliant. The stench was going to mask the Guardians' immortal scent, so the Doomers wouldn't smell them coming.

The warehouse, even though it was nearby, was too far for the stench to reach, but then the night watchmen guarding the drugs wouldn't be sleeping like the Doomers in the apartment building. Those two would have to be overtaken by force.

Magnus sighed. The guys assigned to the warehouse unit were going to have fun. He wished he were one of them. But unfortunately, he hadn't been that lucky, or maybe the chief didn't think he was ready for action, which was ridiculous. He was ready and then some. Besides, he knew how to unlock a safe, which he was certain the Doomers had to have in there.

"Do you think they keep the money in the warehouse?" he asked.

Anandur shrugged. "I don't know. Onegus didn't say anything about it. He only said to destroy the drugs."

"If there is any money, it should go toward taking care of the humans the Doomers turned into zombies, but some of it needs to go to the old couple whose bank account Grud cleaned out."

Anandur's face twisted in a grimace. "If I were lucky, I would've been assigned to the apartment the piece of shit sleeps in. He would not have gotten away with stasis. I would've finished him off."

"That's not allowed, mate."

"I can miscalculate, right? Putting an immortal into stasis requires precision, and I'm known for being deficient in that respect."

That was true. Where Brundar was like a sharp blade, Anandur was like a battering ram. But it was beside the point. Turner's team had supplied the numbers, not who slept in which room.

They'd taken photos with a long-range camera, so the Guardians could recognize the faces, but they hadn't collected names. The only room they had differentiated from the others was the one belonging to the commander and his second. That was the one he and Anandur had been assigned to.

For all Magnus knew, Grud could be in the warehouse. The last update Turner's team had provided was yesterday morning. Later in the day, they had been dismissed to make room for the Guardians. What was about to go down was not for human consumption.

Naturally, Turner's people hadn't known that they had been keeping tabs on immortals, and even if one of them had noticed something strange, they weren't the kind of humans who talked. Ex-commandos knew to keep their mouths shut.

Just before the raid, their own Guardian team was going to do the last check. Using electromagnetic radar equipment, they were going to count bodies and make sure that all the Doomers were accounted for.

A block away from the apartment building, Magnus and Anandur stopped where several Guardians were already waiting.

No one talked.

A few minutes later, when everyone was in place, the chief's voice came through Magnus's earpiece as well as everyone else's. "One last test before we go in. Tap your earpiece if you can hear me."

48

ANANDUR

"Okay, I have everyone tuned in," the chief said through Anandur's earpiece. "Our team has verified that all twenty Doomers and thirty-one humans are in the building. The Doomers are on the bottom floor, and the humans are on the second. You're clear to go."

There were a total of ten two-bedroom apartments in the crappy old building, five downstairs and five upstairs. The twenty-two Doomers shared the bottom five, and the thirty-one humans shared the top ones.

The beauty of this arrangement was that the five ground level entry doors faced the street, with the Doomers' cars parked in front of them, so there was no hallway with a creaking floor to traverse. It was concrete all the way.

This part of the raid was going to be so easy that it almost disappointing. The Guardians assigned to the warehouse were going to have so much more fun.

It wasn't fair, but that was the life of a Guardian. If Anandur wanted to call the shots, he should've vied for the chief's position. But since he wasn't interested, he had to abide by Onegus's decisions of who went where.

Besides, the chief wasn't taking part in the fun either. Onegus was sitting in the control van together with William and monitoring everything via cameras that Turner's people had attached to the utility poles outside the building. Once the mission started, William was also going to launch his drones.

At the rate technology was advancing, Anandur was sure that pretty soon warriors would become obsolete. Battles would be fought from afar by pimpled teenagers with joysticks because this would happen way before they found a cure for acne.

As the five teams of Guardians took position in front of the five doors, the one holding the bump key in each team did the honors of opening the way.

Anandur and Magnus had gotten the commander's apartment, which housed only him and his second.

Crouching by the door, Magnus used his bump key for breaking and entering, doing it almost soundlessly, which was quite impressive.

As soon as they had the door open, they rushed inside. In the couple of seconds it took Anandur to reach the bedroom, his Doomer had woken up and bolted out of bed, making Anandur so happy he was ready to kiss the dude before biting him.

The guy didn't wait for Anandur to launch his attack, leaping three feet in the air and using his momentum to topple Anandur down.

Anandur didn't fight it, letting himself fall back with the Doomer on top of him. But the Doomer's victory didn't last long. A millisecond before hitting the floor, Anandur flipped them both around and landed on top of the Doomer, immobilizing him immediately.

"It was a good fight, buddy." Anandur smiled down at the Doomer's shocked expression. "But you're out."

The guy struggled, trying to get free of Anandur's grip, but it was no use. Once down, it was game over. No opponent had ever succeeded in dislodging Anandur's grip, not Bhathian with all his muscles, and not Dalhu with his formidable size and strength.

Well, there was that one time when he'd been distracted by Wonder during training, but that had been a fluke and was never going to happen again.

As the Doomer realized it was over, he closed his eyes in resignation.

For some reason, Anandur felt magnanimous. "Don't worry, buddy. You're just going to sleep for a very long time."

The Doomer's eyes popped open. "You're not going to kill me?"

"You're going into stasis."

The lack of comprehension in the Doomer's eyes was pathetic. Those suckers were told nothing.

"As I said. Long sleep." He hissed before sinking his fangs in the guy's neck.

Contrary to what he'd told Magnus, Anandur was very careful. He listened to the Doomer's heartbeat slowing, and retracted his fangs before it stopped.

One day this Doomer would get to live again. Lifting the guy over his shoulder, Anandur checked the other bedroom, but Magnus and his Doomer were already gone. He hadn't heard any sounds of struggle coming out of there, which meant that Magnus got the guy while he was sleeping.

As Anandur emerged from the building with a Doomer draped over his shoulder, Magnus tapped his earpiece. "That's the last one," he said.

"I was the only one that encountered resistance?"

"Seems so."

"Good work, people," Onegus said in his ear.

Right. As if it had been any challenge at all.

Anandur climbed to the back of the truck and laid down his

cargo next to his buddies. There were twenty of them. Scanning for Grud, at first Anandur didn't recognize him. A trim had changed the way the Doomer looked.

As per Onegus's instructions, Anandur stripped every last stitch of clothing from his Doomer, checked him for any trackers that might have been glued to his body, and then dressed him in the nylon pants and long-sleeved shirt that were designed not to disintegrate during his long rest in the catacombs. All the other Doomers had been given the same treatment.

Jumping down, Anandur stuffed the Doomer's clothing in a trash bag, wiped his hands on his pants, and then reached for the sanitizer he kept in his back pocket.

He tapped his earpiece before rubbing his hands. "What about the other team?"

"They are done as well," Onegus said.

"Any money found?"

"Your brother is working on the safe."

"Let me know. I'm curious."

Onegus chuckled. "Will do."

Magnus pulled down the back door and put a lock on it, then walked over to the front and handed the key to Gregor who had been chosen to drive the Doomer cargo all the way to the keep.

"Don't forget to stop by the warehouse and collect the other two," he told the guy.

"I won't." Gregor turned on the ignition and pulled out into the street.

Casting a look at the upper floors, Anandur was glad to see that no lights were on. Evidently, the humans had slept through the raid with none any the wiser. But then Yamanu had been shrouding the entire area, and they'd been affected as well. Hopefully, the shrouding hadn't compounded the damage to their brains.

Shrouding wasn't as invasive as thralling, but it must've had some effect.

Now the question was how to wake them up and tell them that they were going on a surprise plane trip.

Thralling them again was out of the question.

"The bus is on its way," Onegus said in Anandur's ear.

It was time for phase two of the mission.

Shai had rush ordered T-shirts for all thirty-one humans, the five guardians who were going to accompany them on the bus trip, and extras for the Guardians who were going to assist in herding the humans into the bus. The words *Fabulous Retreat* were printed in thick yellow letters on the blue fabric just below the rays that extended from the illustrated yellow sun.

"So what now?" Magnus asked as the bus pulled into the spot the truck had vacated.

"Now I'm going to look for a T-shirt in my size."

"I mean after that. How are we going to herd the humans out?"

Anandur shrugged. "I'm going to knock on the door, and the moment it's open, I'm going to shout, Surprise! You won an all-expenses-paid vacation in the picturesque Ojai."

Magnus smoothed his hand over his goatee. "What if it doesn't work and they get scared?"

"Then we pick them up, carry them to the bus, and call Yamanu to the rescue. He can sing them a lullaby to calm them down."

Magnus quirked a brow. "A lullaby?"

"Yeah, why not? Or he can just tell them a story. It doesn't matter. All they need in order to calm down is to hear his voice."

49

WONDER

"*R*eady to go?" Kri asked.

Wonder removed her apron and tucked it under the counter. "When are we going to be back?"

"I don't want to be stuck in traffic so we will probably leave there at around two and arrive back here around three."

Since immortals required much less sleep than humans and didn't tire as quickly, their standard workday was longer than that of humans. Wonder's shift at the café was usually eleven hours, from seven in the morning to six in the evening, which meant that she could put in only a total of four hours today.

No complaints, though. She was happy to have something to keep her busy, and Carol was a lot of fun to work with. Besides, the café was a perfect place to meet everyone. Her acclimatization to the village would've never been so fast and so easy otherwise.

"I feel weird about taking more than half a day off. I just started working here."

Carol waved a hand. "Don't worry about it. You need to get out of here once in a while." She gave Wonder a shove. "Go."

"Thanks. I'll be back at four."

"Don't be ridiculous. Take the rest of the day off."

"Are you sure?"

"Yes, go have fun." Carol waved both hands in a shooing motion.

"So, how is life here treating you?" Kri threaded her arm through Wonder's. "I see you in class, but you usually rush out before we have a chance to chat."

That was probably about to change.

After last night's fiasco, she doubted Anandur would be waiting outside Kri's classroom to walk her home. But that was not something she wanted to share with her self-defense instructor.

Already, too many people knew about Anandur and her.

"It has been only a week since I came to the village, but it feels like I've been here for much longer."

Kri pressed the button for the elevator. "It's easy to get used to good things."

That was true. Wonder was never going back to her old life. There was nothing for her there. With or without Anandur, the village was her new home.

The first ten minutes or so of the drive to Ojai passed in awkward silence. Kri wasn't much of a talker, and neither was Wonder. Everyone assumed that the two of them would become friends because supposedly they were both warrior women, but Wonder didn't think of herself as one, and the reality was that she and Kri had little in common.

Out of all the clan females she'd gotten to know, Wonder liked Carol the best. Amanda was still too intimidating, and Syssi was the leader's wife, so in a way, she was intimidating too. There were a few others that had stopped to chat and seemed nice enough, but Wonder didn't really click with any of them.

Maybe she needed to get to know them better.

"I'm totally bummed about being excluded from the raid," Kri said. "Even though I understand why."

"I heard that Kian doesn't allow you to participate in confrontations with Doomers."

"That too. But this time it wasn't about that. Kian said that I lacked the necessary equipment, meaning fangs. They put all of the Doomers in stasis."

Wonder turned to look at her. "You have news from the raid?"

Kri nodded. "Naturally. Even though I don't have a dick or fangs, I am still a Guardian. I have access to all of the communications."

"Is everyone all right?"

Kri smirked. "Of course they are. Onegus, that's our chief, assigned one Guardian for every Doomer. There is no way anyone could've gotten hurt, and that includes the Doomers."

Wonder relaxed in her seat. "But they are practically dead, aren't they?"

"That's not how I see it. I think of stasis as a chance of someday starting a new life. One day, when their leadership finally gets overthrown, we can revive a few and see if we can rewrite their programming."

"Why do you have to wait for their leadership to fall? Can't you rewrite their programming now?"

Kri smiled indulgently. "No, Wonder, we can't. We don't know how, yet. As long as the Brotherhood's main stated goals are the clan's destruction and gaining complete control over humanity, we can't risk it."

Wonder spent the rest of the drive to Ojai pondering the why of it.

Following Vanessa's instructions, she'd done some reading, or rather listening, and what she was learning about the world was not all sunny.

Why would one group of people want to control another?

Why couldn't everyone just mind their own business and take care of their own families? What was the driving force behind wanting to subjugate others and make their lives miserable? What made people murder innocents for no other reason than them believing in something else?

It didn't make any sense to her. There was no logical explanation. The bottom line was that good people didn't want to make others suffer. They didn't want to take away people's rights and dictate to them how to live their lives, brainwashing them to believe that the only way to live was their way.

Maybe she was just a simple girl who didn't know much about the world and its politics, but she thought herself capable of distinguishing between good and evil, between freedom and oppression, between the sanctity of human life and human rights and the disregard of both.

One didn't need to be a genius to figure that out.

The big question that bothered her, though, was what part she could take in fixing wrongs or contributing to the spread of rights.

As an individual, there wasn't much she could do, but according to Anandur, the clan was dedicated to doing just that. Their goals were to correct the wrongs and to spread the kind of freedoms and opportunities the citizens of the western countries enjoyed to everyone on the globe.

In the simplest of terms, helping out the clan meant helping out the world.

Did working in the café count, though?

As a Guardian, she could probably contribute more. But she didn't want to be a soldier. Maybe there were other ways she could contribute?

"What are you thinking about so hard?" Kri chuckled. "The furrow between your eyebrows is as deep as Wonder Woman's."

Touching her finger to the crease, she massaged it away. The actress who played that role had an impressive frown.

"Do you think I should become a Guardian? Is that the best way I can contribute to the clan?"

"No." Kri surprised her. "You have excellent fighting instincts, and you are incredibly strong, but you don't have the heart for it. You're too soft." She cast Wonder a sidelong glance. "I don't mean it as an insult. It's just the way it is. We can't change who we are on the inside." She touched her heart. "I enjoy a good fight. I'm looking forward to it. You, on the other hand, would do anything to avoid one, and not because you're afraid of getting hurt. You're afraid of hurting others."

Wonder let out a puff of breath. "Thank you. You're the first one who gets it."

"You're welcome."

"So what do you think I should do? Is working in the café the best I can do?"

Kri smiled. "Most people would've told you if that is what you enjoy, then why not. But I'm not most people. I think you could and should do more than that."

"Like what?"

"I don't know. You need to expose yourself to more things to find out. You can become a self-defense trainer without becoming a Guardian. I didn't expect it, but teaching those rescued girls how to defend themselves gives me a lot of satisfaction. And you have no idea how good it feels to know that I'm a role model for them."

"That's a possibility."

"Or you can study something. Take Amanda, for instance. She was a spoiled party girl who did nothing with her life. Then one day she decided it was time to grow up and do something beneficial for the clan. She chose to tackle the most important problem we face, which is finding suitable partners we can build a life with. In order to find a way to identify

Dormants, she went to college and became a freaking neuro-science professor."

"That's very impressive. But I don't think I'm as smart as Amanda."

"Pfft." Kri waved a hand. "No one believed she was that smart either, including Amanda herself. Shows that you can never know until you try, right?"

50

ANANDUR

*I*t was time to go home.

The humans had been loaded on the bus, both locations had been put in order, and the car had been returned to the rental company.

Anandur paid the taxi driver, slung the strap of his duffle bag over one shoulder, and the one stuffed with Wonder's things on the other, and together with Magnus headed for the terminal of the private airport the clan used.

"How is Wonder doing?" Magnus asked.

Anandur didn't want to talk about it, but he'd known that the guy was going to ask at some point.

"She's acclimatizing to the village. I got her a job at the café."

"Good move. Sooner or later she's going to meet everyone over there."

"That was the idea."

They climbed the stairs and got into the jet. The four other Guardians who were sharing the plane ride with them were already there, which meant they wouldn't have to wait long for it to take off.

"Is she seeing anyone?" Magnus asked.

"Why? Are you interested?"

Magnus shook his head. "I wish she was my type. An immortal female I'm not related to is quite a catch, but unfortunately she isn't."

Anandur's first response to Magnus's question had been anger, then he'd calmed down when the guy had said he wasn't interested, and then he'd gotten angry once again. Wonder was beautiful, kind, smart, and resourceful. What was there not to love?

"Why the hell not?"

"Everyone has a type. You have yours, and I have mine, and Gregor over there has his."

"Some women are everyone's type. Show me one guy who doesn't think Victoria's Secret models are hot."

"You're wrong." Magnus turned to Gregor. "What's your type, Gregor?"

"I don't have one. I'm a lover of all women."

Anandur waved a hand. "You see? I'm right."

Magnus huffed. "Liar. Who's your favorite actress?"

"Liv Tyler," Gregor answered immediately.

Magnus crossed his arms over his chest. "There you go. That's your type." He looked down his nose at Anandur.

"Okay, let's pretend that I agree with you. Who's your type?"

"Natalie Portman, particularly as Queen Amidala."

"Seriously?" Anandur chuckled. "That tiny, flat-chested thing? That's not a woman, that's a twig with a pretty face."

Magnus glared at him. "I didn't insult your type, don't insult mine. Not everyone is into giant amazon women. I prefer mine delicate and sophisticated. I could also go for Rachel Weisz."

"Now, that's a woman." She was petite, but she had some curves on her. The hair was awesome too. Anandur wasn't particular about the color, but he liked thick, wavy hair.

"I'm glad we agree on something. Now if you don't mind, I would like to catch a nap." Magnus closed his eyes.

Touchy fellow. It was one thing to get offended on behalf of one's love interest, and an entirely different thing to get offended on behalf of an actress he'd never met and wasn't going to.

Love interest. Is that what Wonder was to him?

Was he falling in love with the girl?

Anandur scratched his beard, then his head, and then rubbed his hand over the back of his neck.

It was about time he stopped pretending and manned up to his feelings. The truth was that he'd fallen for her at first sight. He'd never believed in that crap. Even as a romantic at heart, he'd thought that it was nonsense.

A pretty face and a hot body induced desire, not love. To love someone you had to get to know her first. Love was supposed to be about the meeting of the souls, not the bodies.

Well, preferably both.

Maybe what he'd felt at first was only desire, and then when he'd gotten to know her better, that desire had turned into admiration and then into love.

Yeah, that was more reasonable. He'd fallen for her over time.

What the hell was he going to do about it though? If he hadn't been so stubborn and so set in his ways, he would've seduced her by now, and the memory of that other guy would have been just a distant echo.

Not really.

If the kiss had been the catalyst for the memory's return, then it didn't matter when it had happened. In fact, maybe it was better that he hadn't kissed her earlier. The more time they'd spent together, the more feelings Wonder had developed for him.

Yeah, he was glad about waiting. If it had happened earlier, she would have been even more affected by the memory.

Instead of ambivalence, she would've focused on her feelings for that Esag dude.

One thing had become clear to him, though. He wasn't going to give up on her without one hell of a fight.

And if that meant ghost exorcising, so be it.

It was crucial that he found Esag and proved to Wonder that she couldn't possibly love the other guy because she was in love with him.

He had to step up his game and court her properly, take her out on dates and turn on the charm.

But to do that, he needed to have more spare time. Anandur had accumulated plenty of vacation days he hadn't claimed, and there were enough Guardians now so he could take some time off.

Kian would have to manage without him for a few days.

The first thing Anandur was going to do when he returned to the village was to march into Kian's office and ask for time off. The second thing he was going to do was to find Wonder and offer to take her out on a proper date. Not in the café, and not an evening stroll through the village, but a real one in a nice restaurant in town. Maybe he'd even take her to a movie, or to see a musical, or a rock concert.

There were so many possibilities.

He'd never dated anyone before, not in the way of courting. There had been that one time he'd taken Lana to a nightclub. Did it count if it had been part of his mission to get her talking?

Probably not.

Had Wonder dated anyone?

It was highly unlikely. Wonder had been too busy surviving.

He chuckled. As far as dating went, they were on par. A nearly one-thousand-year-old immortal was just as inexperienced as a twenty-year-old.

51

WONDER

*W*onder walked out of the pavilion and headed straight for the café. It was a little after four o'clock. She could still put in a couple of work hours.

But as she neared the place, Carol started shaking her head. "What are you doing here? I told you to take the rest of the day off."

"Aren't you glad to see me?" She rounded the counter and bent to pull out her apron.

Carol gave her a quick hug. "Of course, I am, silly. So how was it? Did you get to talk to Vanessa?"

"For about five minutes." Wonder leaned to whisper in Carol's ear. "Basically she told me to keep kissing Anandur and see if any more memories return."

"I like that advice. Anything else?"

Wonder shrugged. "She said I need to expose myself to more experiences and that reading or listening to books is not enough. According to Vanessa, I need to stimulate the other senses as well."

"I agree. Kisses are just the beginning." Carol waggled her brows. "There is so much more. If you come by my house later,

I can give you pointers." She looked around. "There are too many ears over here."

"Since when has that stopped you?"

"It hasn't, not really." By the twinkle in Carol's eyes, that was the wrong thing to say. If Wonder didn't change the direction the conversation was taking, Carol would give her a sex education lecture in front of all the patrons of the café.

"Are the Guardians back already?" Wonder asked.

That was the main reason for her not going home after Kri had brought her back. The café's central location was perfect for monitoring the comings and goings of clan members. When Anandur returned, he would have to pass by it.

"Yes, but they are in a meeting with Kian. Debriefing and all that. They'll probably hit the sack when that's done. I don't think any of them got much sleep last night."

An immortal whose name Wonder had forgotten, leaned on the counter. "Can I have a cappuccino, ladies?"

"Of course." Carol turned to him with a smile. "Would you like a pastry with that?"

He eyed the display. "That bear-claw looks tasty."

"Would you like me to warm it up for you?"

"Sure."

As Carol stuck the bear-claw in the toaster oven, Wonder started on the cappuccino.

It was weird how Carol knew everything about the Guardians. She worked alongside them in the training center, but she wasn't one of them.

Carol took the cappuccino cup Wonder had made and handed it to the guy together with his bear-claw. "Enjoy."

"I will, thank you." The guy winked at Wonder and walked away to find a table.

"How come you're so well informed about everything the Guardians do?" Wonder asked.

Smirking, Carol tapped her ear. "I have an earpiece.

Brundar gave me one just in case. That was before all the old Guardians returned. Now I'm not really needed, but he never asked me to give it back."

"Just in case what?"

Carol shrugged. "I can be useful. I'm an excellent markswoman. I can also drive an escape vehicle. But you didn't need to wait to ask me. Kri gets all the updates, and she could've told you."

"She was bummed about not being allowed on the raid. I didn't want to upset her with too many questions."

"I bet. It sucks being the only female Guardian." She narrowed her eyes at Wonder.

"Would you stop it? Even Kri doesn't think I have what it takes to be one. She says I'm too soft."

Carol looked doubtful. "Really? She said that?"

"Yep. Do you think I'd lie to you about something like that?"

"No, of course not. I'm just surprised." Carol twirled a lock of hair around her finger, released it, and then twirled it again. "Maybe she doesn't want another girl on the force? It could be that she likes being the only one."

"She's not like that. Kri is cool. You should've seen her with those girls. They worship her."

The trip to Ojai had taught Wonder a valuable lesson. She realized that her opinion of Kri had been based on superficial observation and had done the Guardian a disservice.

There was much more to Kri than met the eye.

The Guardian only appeared tough and uncompromising. On the inside, Kri had a big heart and cared deeply for the rescued girls. She was helping the best way she knew how.

It had been a lesson in humility. She'd been doing to Kri precisely what she hated people doing to her.

Prejudging.

Maybe they could be friends after all, especially since Kri seemed to be the only one who really understood Wonder.

Even Carol, the one person she'd been spending the most time with, didn't get her at all. Otherwise, she would have stopped suggesting that Wonder pursue a career as a Guardian.

Anandur didn't get her either.

Was it too much to hope for a guy to see past her exterior and actually try to understand who she was on the inside?

First of all, she wasn't too young for him. Carol refused to reveal her age, but given her stories, she must've been at least a couple of hundred years old, and yet she acted less mature than Wonder, which proved that actual age was meaningless.

"I'm going to wipe the tables," she told Carol and pulled out a bottle of cleaner and a rag from under the counter.

Cleaning always helped her think.

The thing was, before she blamed Anandur for the sorry state of their relationship, or the lack thereof, she needed to figure out who Esag was and what he meant to her.

As vague as the memory of him was, it evoked a pang of longing that she couldn't deny. But that didn't necessarily mean that she'd been in love with him, did it?

Maybe he'd been her boyfriend, but they'd broken up, and somewhere deep inside her locked memories was sorrow for the breakup?

Or maybe something had happened to him, and the tightness in her heart that his name evoked was grief?

Shit on a stick.

She was running in circles inside her brain. Amanda was right. The smart thing to do was to forget all about the mystery guy and focus on making things right with Anandur.

Then again, she couldn't lie to him and say that the memory meant nothing to her.

More serious cleaning was needed if she were to figure out a solution to this seemingly insoluble problem. Done with the tables, Wonder returned the rag and the bottle of cleaner to their place under the counter and grabbed the broom.

Carol put her hand on Wonder's arm. "Let's wait until closing time to do the sweeping."

"I'd rather do it now if you don't mind. It helps me think, and it calms me down."

With a smirk, Carol let go. "In that case, who am I to interfere in your therapy session with Doctor Broom?"

ANANDUR

*A*s the debriefing ended and the Guardians headed for the exit, Anandur walked up to Kian. "Can I have a moment alone with you?"

Kian arched a brow. "I didn't know you fancied me that way."

Great, suddenly everyone was a comedian. Any other day he would've picked up the thread Kian had thrown his way and continued with the banter until the mighty regent gave up. After centuries of practice, he could go on and on until his verbal opponent conceded defeat. But not today.

Today, Anandur was in no mood for joking around.

Getting no response, Kian's smirk melted into a frown. "What's wrong?"

Anandur cast a glance around to make sure everyone else had left. "I need to take some time off."

Kian let out a puff of breath. "You had me worried for a moment. How long do you need? A day, two?"

"Two weeks."

"That's a long vacation. But I guess we have enough Guardians to pick up the slack."

That wasn't a yes, but Anandur took it as one. "Thanks."

"When do you need it?"

"Starting tomorrow."

Kian raked his fingers through his hair. "Does your sudden need for a vacation have anything to do with Wonder?"

"Yeah, it does."

"What are you planning to do with those two weeks?"

Apparently, Kian loved gossip as much as the next immortal. There was no harm in telling him, though. After all, they'd been friends for a very long time, or as much as a subordinate could be friends with his boss.

Anandur walked over to the door, closed it, then returned and sat down next to Kian at the conference table.

The guy regarded him with curiosity in his eyes. "Is it going to be a long story?"

"Are you in a hurry? Because we can do it some other time."

Kian leaned back in his chair and crossed his arms over his chest. "I'm always in a hurry to return to my mate, but for this, I'm willing to stay for as long as it takes."

Busybody.

Anandur scratched his beard. "You were right. I do have feelings for Wonder."

"I'm always right."

"Yeah, well, you forget who you're talking to. I've been your bodyguard for over nine centuries. I know you better than your own mother, or your sisters, or even your wife. And you've been wrong plenty of times."

Kian shrugged. "Perhaps a handful of times."

"Right. Anyway, I've been fighting my attraction to her because she's so damn young, but when she came on to me, I could no longer resist. I'm not made of stone."

"Good for her. I admire a woman who knows what she wants and is not afraid to go after it. It speaks of strong character." He lifted a fist to demonstrate.

"Wonder is incredibly strong, physically and otherwise. That's one of the many things I find so alluring about her. But she is also inexperienced and a little shy. It took her a while to gather the courage to proposition me. But when my defenses finally crumbled and I kissed her, the kiss triggered a memory of some lost love of hers." He wasn't going to elaborate and tell Kian that she'd called out another man's name while kissing him.

Talk about humiliating.

Kian arched a brow. "So? I don't see a problem with that. This should make you feel better about wooing Wonder because it means she's not as innocent as you thought her to be. She's been in love before."

"The problem is that Wonder thinks she might still be in love with that guy. As long as this phantom hangs between us, I can't have a real relationship with her. I need to get rid of the ghost love interest first."

"Since you're asking for time off, I assume that you have a plan?"

"Very astute of you. Yes, I do."

Kian lifted a brow. "Care to share?"

"Eh, why not?" Anandur waved a hand. "If I told you that much I might as well tell you the rest."

"Do you want some whiskey with your story?"

"As if you need to ask. I'll pour us a drink." Anandur rose to his feet and walked over to the wet bar.

"So you know how Wonder woke up from the coma in Egypt, right?" He pulled out a half-full bottle of Black Label and filled two glasses to the brim.

"Yeah, I do."

"That means that the guy she thinks she loves is there. I want to take her back and see if she remembers any more details. If I can find the dude, I can fight him for her." He handed Kian a glass and took a sip from his.

"Fight him how?"

"When I turn on the charm, no flesh and blood guy can outdo me. A phantom, though, is as perfect as Wonder's imagination makes him out to be."

Kian took a long gulp, then put the nearly empty glass on the table. "Wonder might have reservations about going abroad with you. From what you tell me, I understand that the two of you haven't been romantically involved up until that fateful kiss. Am I right?"

Anandur nodded.

"And you also tell me that she is shy and inexperienced."

"Right."

"Before you suggest a trip to Egypt, you need to cozy up to her and make her feel comfortable with you." The left corner of Kian's lips lifted in a lopsided smirk. "We all know that she has nothing to worry about in regards to you getting handsy with her. The girl proved that she can kick your butt, but she might be concerned about emotional vulnerability."

Anandur shook his head. He was never going to live that down. From now until eternity, everyone would be making fun of him for getting caught by a girl and then tossed aside as if he were some tiny pipsqueak and not a giant of a man who weighed two hundred and eighty pounds. And that was especially true for all of his defeated sparring partners, which included Kian.

He pointed a finger at Kian's smirking face. "If she can kick my butt, and we both know that I can kick yours, it means that she can kick your butt as well. True?"

Kian inclined his head. "Point taken. But what I was trying to say is that you should spend a few days with her as her boyfriend and not just a friend. She needs to internalize that you guys are a couple before you can suggest a trip abroad alone with her."

Anandur emptied his glass and put it down. "I'll play it by

ear. I plan on taking her out to the city tomorrow and spending the entire day with her. If I feel she's ready, I'll ask. If not, I'll wait a day or two."

LOSHAM

*L*osham took another walkabout through the warehouse, searching for any clues he might've missed. Other than the safe, which had been blown open with explosives, there were no signs of struggle.

Which led to only one very unsettling conclusion.

The entire cell had defected, absconding with the drugs and the proceeds from selling them. Gommed, the only one who knew the combination to the safe, had probably resisted, which was why they had blown it open.

The question was whether the men had killed their commander or had taken him prisoner. Not that it really mattered.

What mattered was how Losham was going to hide what had happened from his father. A failure of this magnitude would not go unpunished.

Except, what Navuh didn't know wouldn't hurt Losham.

"I checked the apartment building," Rami said. "It's the same over there as it is here. It looks like everyone just got up and walked away. Our men and the humans. They packed up their things and even emptied the refrigerators and the cupboards. There is nothing left in those apartments."

Losham nodded. "They must've decided they wanted to keep all the profits to themselves."

"Should we summon a hunting team to find them?"

"No, Rami. We need to find a way to keep this from ever getting back to Lord Navuh."

Rami rubbed a hand over the back of his neck. "How are we going to do it?"

"The way I set it up was to make each cell completely independent from the next and operating in a distinct and separate territory. Originally, I did it so they wouldn't find a way to cooperate with each other behind my back, but apparently it was a smart decision all around. There is no contact between the units, so no one other than the two of us knows about this one defecting."

"What about the lost money and drugs?"

"We can hide that as well. If we distribute the losses between all the other cells, they will be hardly noticeable. Especially if I pressure the other cells to increase production and sales. I'll delay reporting until we can cover up what's missing."

Rami still looked unconvinced. "You're right about hiding the losses, but what about the men? We can't hide that forever."

"You're right, we can't. But we can delay it until I find a way to arrange an accident that supposedly killed all of them."

"Like what?"

"Like an airliner exploding with all of them seemingly on board."

Rami smiled for the first time since they'd discovered the defection. "That's brilliant. You're going to charter a private plane and have it blow up?"

Losham shrugged. "Maybe. Or maybe I'll just buy tickets on a commercial flight and have a bunch of patsies take the men's place. All it would take is producing fake IDs for the patsies, or for us to thrall the security people at the different checkpoints."

54

ANANDUR

*A*s Anandur walked out of the war room, he thought about ways to speed up the process of Wonder getting used to the idea of him as her boyfriend.

Funny how one little moan had turned the tables on him.

Two days ago, he'd been concerned about doing as little as possible to encourage Wonder's interest in him, while at the same time still being her friend. Now, when suddenly she might have become unavailable to him, he was concerned with doing as much as possible to make her his.

Served him right.

Taking stock of his arsenal of wooing weapons, Anandur considered his charm and his humor as his best. Other than that he had his rugged good looks, as Wonder had called them, and his position on the Guardian force, particularly as Kian's personal bodyguard.

He also had a substantial amount in his bank account, and his stock portfolio was quite impressive thanks to Kian's advice, but Anandur didn't consider his wealth as a wooing tool.

Then there were Brundar and Callie. As someone who was

all alone in the world, Wonder appreciated family. She might view him more favorably if he made an even greater effort to share his with her.

It was time for another dinner at Callie and Brundar's, and he had no qualms about inviting himself and Wonder over.

Callie wouldn't mind. In fact, he was sure she would be overjoyed.

Pulling out his phone he shot her a quick text. *Are you up to having Wonder and me for dinner tonight?*

Her reply was almost instantaneous. *Yay!!! Be here at eight.*

Smiling, he sent her his thanks and then shot another text to Wonder. *We are invited to Brundar and Callie's for dinner at eight. I'll pick you up ten minutes earlier.*

So what if he was being presumptuous. Phrased like that, it would be hard for Wonder to say no.

He waited for what seemed like a long time before her return message came in.

Okay, was her short answer.

Wonder wasn't one for talking. She preferred listening to his stories.

Damn, he really loved the girl. Not only was she a beauty and a sweetheart, but she laughed at his jokes even when they fell flat.

In short, she was perfect.

It only took him getting hit over the head with the emotional equivalent of a sledgehammer to realize that.

As he got to the house, he was greeted by Magnus's loud snoring. No great surprise since they hadn't gotten much sleep the night before. Interestingly enough, Anandur didn't feel tired at all, even though he'd had even less sleep in the last forty-eight hours than Magnus.

Apparently, the sense of purpose and urgency hiked up his adrenaline production more than last night's mission.

The purpose part was understandable, but why the urgency?

Wonder wasn't going anywhere, and neither was he. And yet, he felt as if at any moment he could lose his window of opportunity with her. He felt a compulsive need to make up for lost time and rush his wooing agenda.

Maybe it had something to do with his voluntary abstinence.

Anandur hadn't gone so many days without sex since he'd hit puberty. That in itself should have been a city-block-sized red flag that Wonder was the one for him. He hadn't wanted anyone else since he'd met her.

Stepping into the shower, Anandur shook his head. He was such a thickheaded idiot.

When he was done scrubbing and shampooing and conditioning, he toweled himself dry and then used the towel to wipe the condensation off the mirror. He could've used a trim, but regrettably there was no time for that. Instead, he splashed himself with his best cologne and went looking for something nice to wear.

His closet didn't have much to offer. Other than stacks of folded jeans and T-shirts, the one garment hanging in his closet was the tuxedo he'd worn to all the recent weddings.

Damn. He had nothing nice to wear.

Magnus, the clothes whore, should have plenty of fancy stuff, except the guy was shorter and slimmer than Anandur. Besides, he was sleeping, and Anandur wasn't going to rummage through the guy's closet without asking permission first.

There were two other guys his size in the village, Yamanu and Dalhu. Yamanu was a closer friend, but his taste in clothes wasn't much better than Anandur's. Neither was Dalhu's, but the dude had Amanda, the queen of fashion, to do the shopping for him.

Amanda owed Anandur more than one favor.

He considered just walking over to their place, but then discarded the idea. What if they had guests? What if they were busy doing other things?

Instead, he chose the least intrusive approach and texted Amanda. *I need a nice shirt. Can I borrow one of Dalhu's?*

Are you going on a date?

Sort of.

With Wonder?

Yes.

I'll be right over.

Hopefully, she wasn't going to take too long. He only had an hour until it was time to pick up Wonder.

He should've known better. The knock on the door came five minutes later.

Holding a travel bag almost as big as herself, Amanda sauntered inside. "Where can I work?"

Work? What is she planning to do?

"Thanks for coming over so quickly." He closed the door behind her. "But what the hell did you bring, and what do you mean by work?"

Striking a pose with one leg forward and a hand on her hip, she pursed her lips and gave him a thorough once-over. "I've been waiting to do this for ages."

"What?"

"Give you a makeover." She waved a hand at his beard. "You need to trim that messy bush you call a beard, and your hair needs some styling too. I brought my shears." She mimicked cutting with her fingers.

He glanced at the bag. "What else do you have in there?"

"Catch." She threw the bag at him.

It was heavier than he'd expected, but it seemed to be filled mostly with clothes.

"It's filled with brand new stuff that Dalhu never wears. I

keep buying him nice things, but since he spends most of his time painting, he never gets to wear them. I think he still uses the hand-me downs you gave him when he first got here."

"Really? I'd forgotten about it."

Amanda walked up to him and kissed his cheek. "But Dalhu never forgot your kindness. You were the only one who treated him like a person and not like a despised enemy."

It hadn't been a big deal. Amanda was making it out to be more than it was. "He's a clean dude. It was one of the first things I noticed about him. That's why I treated him as well as the circumstances allowed. After all, he was a prisoner."

She kissed his cheek again. "Just take the compliment and shut up. Now, where can I get to work on your beard and that thing you call a mustache?"

55

WONDER

*W*onder watched one Guardian after another come out of the pavilion. Some stopped for a bite to eat, and some just waved hello and continued home. She listened to their boisterous voices as they recounted anecdotes from the raid, but she wasn't paying attention to what they were saying.

With a lump of anxiety stuck in her throat, she was waiting for Anandur to emerge from the pavilion.

Would he stop by the café, smile at her, and ask her to take a walk with him later on?

Or would he circle around it to avoid her and continue home?

She should have never pestered him for that stupid kiss. Why did she have to want more than he was willing to offer?

Had she lost not only the opportunity to explore her romantic feelings for him but also his friendship?

Soon it would be closing time, and she would have no excuse to hang around and wait for him to show up. Could it be that he wasn't coming out because he was waiting for her to go home?

Except, Anandur wasn't a coward. If he didn't want to see her anymore, he would tell her that to her face instead of playing evasive games.

She wished he would just come out and tell her already what was on his mind. The anxiety of not knowing was the worst.

Carol nudged her. "Call him or text him. I can't stand seeing you like this."

"What do you mean? Like what?"

"Like you're on the verge of crying."

Shit on a stick. Wonder thought that she had been doing a better job of hiding the emotional storm raging inside her. "I can't. What if he's in a meeting?"

"That's what texting is for. If he's busy, he won't answer, and if he isn't, he will."

Pulling the phone out from her pocket, she stared at it for a moment and then tucked it back in. "I'll wait for him to come out."

Carol shook her head. "As you wish."

If she called or texted, Anandur would feel obliged to respond, but Wonder wanted him to make the first move this time. She was done with pressuring him.

Besides, what could she say to him?

Ask him if he was still willing to be with her despite what had happened? Follow Amanda's advice and try to convince him that it had been nothing worth getting upset about?

When closing time came and went, and Anandur was still a no-show, Wonder hung around for a little longer, wiping the tables until they shone and sweeping the floor once again.

Eventually, though, there was nothing more to do, and she had no choice but to go home.

Struggling to keep her head up and not shuffle her feet like an overtired human, Wonder felt like the walk to her house was much longer than the ten minutes it usually took.

Unlike the anonymity a city like San Francisco provided, there was practically no privacy in a tightly knit community like the village. If she allowed herself to look distressed, someone was bound to stop her and ask what was wrong.

She didn't want to talk to anyone. Especially since immortals wouldn't buy an excuse about a headache or an upset stomach.

As Wonder's phone buzzed in her back pocket, it startled her so that her shoe caught on an uneven paving stone and she stumbled. Somehow managing to regain her balance, she pulled the phone out.

It was a message from Anandur, but the sense of relief that swept over her made her dizzy, blurring the words on the screen.

Feeling faint, Wonder barely made it to the nearest bench. It took a moment for the blur to coalesce into legible words.

The message said, *We are invited to Brundar and Callie's for dinner at eight. I'll pick you up ten minutes earlier.*

The breath she took was the first to fully fill her lungs since she'd woken up that morning.

Okay. Typing with numb fingers, it was the best she could do.

Anandur couldn't be too mad if he was taking her to Callie and Brundar's for dinner, right?

It was going to be okay. He still wanted to see her. After the day she had, Wonder was willing to settle on having Anandur only as a friend. The idea of losing him altogether had felt like a death sentence.

It seemed she'd been pardoned and given a second chance, and this time Wonder wasn't going to blow it over stupid kisses. Having Anandur in her life was more important than her girly desires.

Several calming breaths later, she pushed to her feet and marched home to get ready.

"You look happy," Gertrude said as Wonder got in.

"I'm invited together with Anandur to his brother's for dinner."

"I'm glad. Did you guys have a talk and straighten things out?"

Wonder shook her head. "No, I just got this one text from him inviting me to dinner."

"Well, good luck. You still have to have the talk. This is not something you can sweep under the rug."

"Yeah, I know." Even someone like her, who had no relationship experience, was instinctively aware that if ignored, a thing like that would grow and grow until it blew up in both of their faces. But it didn't have to happen right away. She would take her cues from Anandur and proceed from there.

Caution was the name of the game, and Wonder knew how to play it well. She should've never thrown it to the wind in the first place.

Gertrude smiled. "When is dinner, do you have time for me to do your hair?"

"I'll make time. Thank you."

"No problem. I'm happy to help any way I can."

Her hair had been strangled in a tight braid all day, which meant that it wouldn't look good loose unless she washed it and styled it. But since Wonder didn't know how to go about it and she didn't want to bother Carol, Trudy's offer was much appreciated.

Rushing, she dropped her work clothes on the floor and stepped into the shower. The cleanup part went fast; the choosing of an outfit part, not so much.

Maybe she should wear a dress?

Amanda had given her several, but they were too elegant for Wonder's simple tastes. Besides, as someone who'd never worn a dress or a skirt before, she would feel weird in one.

Wonder remembered longing for a reason to wear a nice

dress, but now that she had it, as well as several nice dresses hanging in her closet, she felt awkward about putting one on.

This dinner was too important for experimental dress-up. She needed to wear something that would make her feel comfortable and confident.

After ten minutes of frantic dressing and undressing, Wonder went back to the first outfit she'd chosen: a pair of stretchy pull-on black pants paired with a long button-down grey silk blouse. It came with a matching camisole that she was going to wear in lieu of a bra. Regrettably, the sports bras she'd bought were too bulky to wear under the blouse's delicate fabric.

She really needed to go shopping, and not on the internet.

After applying a thin line of the black eyeliner Amanda had left for her, she was ready for Gertrude's hairdryer and curling brush.

Perhaps she could ask Trudy for some perfume? That was another item on her growing shopping list.

Apparently, being a woman required a lot of grooming and pampering that Wonder had been aware of but thought she could do without. Like having nice bras and panties, a cosmetics bag that included more than one black eyeliner, and several perfumes because according to Amanda different occasions called for different scents.

She should've taken notes because most of what Amanda had filled her head with had already been forgotten.

"Very nice." Gertrude approved of Wonder's outfit. "Now let's style that gorgeous hair of yours."

ANANDUR

*T*wo whole days had passed since Anandur had last seen Wonder, and he couldn't wait to see her again.

Knocking on the door, he was aware of holding his breath like a kid picking up a girl from her parents' home for the first time. Not that he'd ever done it, but that's how it looked in the movies.

For some reason he expected one of the nurses to open the door, but it was Wonder, looking even more stunningly beautiful than he'd remembered.

Anandur took a step back.

She waved a hand in front of her face. "Too much perfume, right? I had a feeling that I'd overdone it."

He was such a dumbass. Way to make the girl feel self-conscious.

"No, you smell terrific." He took a step forward and leaned to kiss her cheek. It was the first of many he was about to rain on her tonight. "It's just that you're such a knockout that you actually knocked me off my feet."

Wonder smiled. "Thank you for the compliment. You look

awesome yourself. Did you get a haircut?" She followed him down the steps.

"Yes, I did." He stopped at a spot that was well illuminated by the moonlight.

There were no street lamps in the village, and the windows were all covered with blinds, but the moon shone brightly enough tonight.

"Do you like it?"

Personally, he thought that Amanda had gone a little too far with her shears and her hair products. His beard was reduced to a quarter of what it had been before, and his curly mop was wrestled into an orderly, combed-back style. She'd insisted on applying a straightening cream, transforming his tight curls into soft waves. He must've lost an inch or two in perceived height. Not that he needed to make himself look taller, but he didn't want to look like he'd shrunk either.

Giving his jaw a quick glance, Wonder lifted her eyes to the top of his head. "I like the shorter beard, but I'm not sure about the hair. Maybe I just need to get used to it looking so tame."

Anandur ran his hand over the soft waves. "It feels nicer." He dipped his head. "Here, touch it."

As Wonder's hand smoothed over his hair, Anandur closed his eyes. He liked her touching him.

"It feels so soft." Her hand trailed along the waves, starting at the front and going all the way to the back. "You look less wild like this."

Had he imagined it, or had she sounded a little breathless?

Anandur lifted his head back up. "So I'm no longer ruggedly handsome?"

"You're very handsome." She put her hand on his chest. "Nice shirt, by the way. You just look a little less rugged and a little more polished."

"I can live with that." He wrapped his arm around her

shoulders and brought her closer against his body. "Did you miss me?"

It felt so good to go back to his flirtatious persona. That was who he was. He'd been stifling this side of himself for far too long. Acting all righteous and proper wasn't like him. Anandur considered himself a gentleman, but that didn't mean he had to impersonate a dry stick, throttle down his charm, and abstain from flirting.

And sex.

But that was in the future. Right now it was all about the flirting.

Wonder blushed and dipped her head to hide her face. "Yes, I did. Why didn't you call me? Or text me? I thought you didn't want anything to do with me."

Yeah, he'd been an ass, while Wonder had been brave enough to admit her true feelings.

She deserved no less in return, but with a dose of self-deprecating humor. "I did a lot of thinking, which is a strain for a simple guy like me. That's why it took so long."

She slapped his forearm. "You're a smart guy, so stop pretending like you're not. I'm not buying your act."

"Okay, okay. Just don't hit me." He pretended to be hurt.

Wonder rolled her eyes but smiled nonetheless. "So what were you thinking about?"

"I'll tell you after dinner," Anandur said as they climbed the steps to Brundar and Callie's place.

Wonder whispered, "You'll make me wait that long?"

To reassure her that all was well, he hugged her closer to him and kissed the top of her head. "All good things come to those who wait."

"As long as you promise that it's good, I have no problem waiting."

"I promise." He knocked on the door.

RUTH

"*A*ll done." Nick turned off the vacuum cleaner. "The living room is ready for guests."

"Thank you for doing the vacuuming," Ruth called out from the kitchen.

Holding the device, Nick walked in and stored it in the broom closet. "Anything else I can do?"

She handed him the salad bowl. "You can put this on the dining table."

"Yes, ma'am."

Nick was so excited about the dinner get-together she'd organized to celebrate his return from Rio, that it seemed as if he could sense it was about much more than that. Although a more obvious and less mystical explanation could be that he might have picked up on her excitement, or rather apprehension.

A lot depended on the success of tonight's experiment.

Except, it was also possible that he was happy about her inviting Tessa and Jackson and Sylvia and Roni to dinner. Unlike her, Nick loved to socialize even though he wasn't great at it.

So what. With a smile, Ruth repeated Nick's mantra in her head. Everything felt much less stressful when that little two-word sentence was said enough times.

"Can you get the door?" Ruth called when she heard a car pull up into her driveway.

Nick shook his head. "I swear that you have bat ears."

Oops. She'd done it again.

A moment later the doorbell rang.

"I'm coming!" Nick called out, and then winked at her. "Not yet, but later for sure."

Ruth flicked him with a dishrag. "Just go open the door already."

As he rushed to the living room, she pulled the roast out of the oven and started transferring it to a serving platter. It was good that her guests were arriving on time. Heating up the food would have spoiled its taste.

For the best flavor, it needed to be eaten right as it was done.

Walking into the dining room with the platter balanced on her hand, she warned, "Keep clear, this is very hot."

"Hi, Mo…," Sylvia started, stopping herself on time.

Luckily, another knock on the door distracted Nick.

"Careful," Ruth whispered.

"Yeah. Sorry about that."

Roni waited for her to put the tray down before pulling her into a hug. "Hi, Ruth. Thank you so much for inviting us to dinner. I missed your cooking."

She hadn't cooked for him and Sylvia in a long while. Ever since she'd started working at the café, her visits to her daughter had dwindled down to no more than once a week, and then to none at all when she and Nick had gotten closer and were spending most evenings at her home.

"Then I should invite you guys over more often."

"That would be nice. Although it's a schlep getting here

from the village." He leaned closer to whisper in her ear. "Hopefully, you'll be joining us there soon."

"What smells so good?" Jackson walked in and bee-lined straight for the dining table. "Can we eat? I'm starving."

Behind him, Tessa shook her head. "Sometimes he behaves like a caveman."

Jackson turned around. "What did I do this time?"

"You should wait to be invited to the table and not ask if you can start eating."

"That's okay." Ruth patted Tessa's arm. "He is right. Everyone is here and the food is getting cold. Let's eat."

"Yeah." Roni rubbed his hands. He was already seated with a napkin draped over his knees.

Even though everyone other than Nick knew what this was all about, the conversation at the table wasn't strained. In fact it flowed naturally.

"Do you remember that you promised us songs?" Jackson asked Roni.

Forking a second piece of roast, Roni transferred it from the platter to his plate. "I didn't forget. I'm still working on it."

"Do you have anything ready?"

"I have one. But I'm not happy with it. Besides, do you guys play at all since Gordon left?"

"Vlad and I jam from time to time while we are waiting for you to fill the drummer's position. You said you'd have the drums mastered in no time. What happened with that?"

"Life." Roni sighed. "It seems like there is never enough time."

"Are you guys still playing at clubs?" Nick asked.

"Not since Gordon left for college and Vlad started studying while still working part-time at the café." Jackson shook his head. "It's tragic. I feel like my youth is over."

"Do you need a bass guitar player? I'm not great, but I'm decent."

"Sure, but without a drummer there is no band, and Roni is taking his sweet time to get ready."

Roni threw his hands in the air. "Okay, people, enough with the guilt. I'll step up the pace."

Ruth was getting impatient. It seemed to her that Jackson was dragging his feet about the test, and she nudged his foot under the table while lifting her brows at the same time.

Reluctantly, he put his fork and knife down and looked at Nick. "So Nick, what was the last rock concert you saw?"

"A bitching cover band for Pink Floyd. But it was like six months ago. Last November, I believe."

"What's their name?"

"Brit Floyd."

Roni lifted his fork. "Not original, but easy to remember."

"Are they any good?"

By the way he was focusing on Nick's eyes, Ruth could tell Jackson was attempting a thrall.

"As I said, they are bitching. You should go see them the next time they are on tour here. I can check for you if they have anything planned for this year."

"Thanks." Jackson went back to eating.

Five minutes later he put his utensils down, wiped his mouth with a napkin, and turned to Nick. "I forgot. What was the name of that band?"

Nick frowned. "What band?"

"The cover..." Roni started. A kick under the table shut him up quickly.

Jackson smirked. "Never mind."

Rubbing his brows between his thumb and forefinger, Nick grimaced. "I feel a headache coming on. Do you have ibuprofen, Ruthie?"

"No, I'm sorry, but I don't. Would you like an icepack?" She'd seen it in a movie once. Supposedly applying ice to the forehead helped with headaches.

"Do you have Advil?"

She shook her head.

"How come you don't have any pain medication? Did you run out?"

"Ruth believes in natural remedies," Sylvia came to her rescue.

Nick waved a hand. "I prefer a quicker solution."

"Do you still want the icepack?"

"No, I should have some Advil in the car." He pushed to his feet and headed out.

"Well." Jackson puffed out his chest. "It seems your guy is not difficult to thrall at all."

Ruth wasn't sure about that. "Wait a little and then ask him again. I want to make sure the thrall holds."

"Good idea. I will do that."

NICK

*a*s Nick clicked open the driver side door, he tried to figure out what had caused the throbbing headache, which was getting worse by the second.

It came out of nowhere, right after Jackson had asked him about the name of the band he'd supposedly mentioned before.

Nick hardly ever got headaches. The only reason he had Advil in the glove compartment was the wrist he'd twisted during surfing a couple of months ago.

The headache had something to do with Jackson, he was almost sure of that. The guy had been looking into his eyes so intently that if Nick hadn't known better, he would've thought that Jackson had been coming on to him.

What the hell had the guy done? Had he tried to pull some hypnotist crap on him?

And what was that about a band?

That bothered Nick even more than the headache. In fact, he had a feeling it was the reason for it. He was still straining his brain, trying to bring the elusive memory up. But the more he struggled the worse the headache got.

He remembered talking about Jackson's band. But that

couldn't have been what the guy had been asking about. He'd said that band, not my band. And then Roni said 'cover' and stopped as if someone had kicked him under the table.

Were they all playing a prank on him?

A couple of pills in hand, he got back inside and looked at Jackson.

The guy always looked kind of smug, but he definitely looked smugger now.

"Okay, out with it." Nick waved his hand. "What did you do?"

"Who, me?" Jackson pretended innocence, looking at Roni and then Sylvia and finally at Ruth, then back to Nick. "I don't know what you're talking about."

By the guilty looks on everyone's faces, they were all in on it.

Assholes.

He didn't care that the others were playing a prank on him, but it bugged him that Ruth had agreed to take part in it.

He and Ruth were a team, and partners were supposed to watch each other's backs.

"Time for dessert!" Ruth chimed and pushed to her feet.

There was definitely a guilty undertone to her fake excitement.

Sylvia jumped up after her sister. "I'll clear the table."

"Let me help," Jackson said.

Nick sat down, filled a glass with water, popped the pills into his mouth, and washed them down with a long gulp.

The only ones at the table with him were Tessa and Roni. Tessa got busy brushing crumbs into a napkin, and Roni whipped out his phone and was pretending to read something. Or maybe he was really reading, who gave a fuck.

Nick was pissed.

He was disappointed with Ruth and his head felt like it was inflating and deflating with every heartbeat.

What band?

He remembered them talking about Jackson's band and about the song Roni had written but wasn't happy with. He also remembered offering to join their band.

Then Jackson had asked him something, but he couldn't remember what it was. In fact, he didn't remember any of the conversation from that point on until Jackson had asked him about a name of a band.

Ignoring the headache, Nick pushed harder. He had to remember the rest of it. If Jackson had hypnotized him as a prank, he was going to prove to the jerk that Nick was a much tougher nut to crack than Jackson had given him credit for. He was going to break through that barrier and remember what the hell they had been talking about.

Ruth came back with a loaded tray. "I have fruit bowls for the health conscientious, and a chocolate cake for those who are not."

Jackson followed with a coffee carafe, and Sylvia with another tray of mugs.

"Coffee, anyone?" she asked.

"I'll have some," Nick said. "And the fruit bowl and the chocolate cake."

He wasn't hungry or in the mood for sweets, but he was mad and didn't want the bunch of jerks to notice. He was going to play it cool until that memory resurfaced and he would prove to them that he wasn't an easy target.

Play it cool. Play it cool. Something about this sentence tickled his memory.

Play it cool. Band. Cover. All of these were trigger words. *How about changing the order. Play it cool cover band.*

Cool cover band.

It felt like a dam bursting inside his head, with all the missing memories rushing in to fill the void. And just like that the headache was gone.

Nick leaned back in his seat, crossed his arms over his chest, and smirked. "Brit Floyd. That was the name of the cover band I was talking about."

Ruth gasped, Jackson paused with the coffee carafe suspended in midair over Tessa's cup, Roni looked down at his cake, and Sylvia looked sad.

What the hell? Why were they taking this so hard?

So their prank hadn't worked, so what?

"Don't look so glum, people. It's not a big deal that I'm on to you. What was that? An attempt at hypnotism?"

Jackson was the first one to recover. "Yeah, sorry about that. I'm taking an online course and I made a bet with the others. I won and they lost. That's why they look so heartbroken." He smiled at the others. "Pay up, people. You each owe me a dollar."

Nick cast Ruth an accusing glance. "You bet against me?"

She forced a smile. "I just did it to encourage Jackson. He didn't believe he could do it with so little training. Apparently, he was right."

Well, that put everything in a different perspective. Nick was all for helping out a friend. But they should have told him instead of using him like a patsy. He would've volunteered.

"Don't give it up, man. You're pretty good. It took a mighty effort to pierce through the block you put in my head. Next time, though, you should ask first. It's not cool to hypnotize someone without his or her permission. You can get in a lot of trouble doing something like that to some unsuspecting dude, or worse, a dudette. You can get sued."

Jackson nodded. "You're absolutely right. It was stupid of me. Are you up for another round?"

"No way. You've given me one hell of a headache. I'm not up for another go. Maybe next time, or try Roni. Eh?" Nick looked at Sylvia's boyfriend. "How about it, dude? Are you willing to get hypnotized?"

Roni grimaced. "Not really."

"Wuss."

Roni shrugged. "See if I care." He pointed a finger at his head. "This baby is all I have. That's what pays the bills. I'm not jeopardizing it by letting an amateur in there."

He had a point. Nick was in a similar situation, depending on his smarts for his job, and therefore shouldn't allow it either.

Except, he'd already committed himself and couldn't back off. But he could put up conditions.

"Roni is right, Jackson. So until you get your certificate as a licensed hypnotist you're not getting anywhere near my brain, is that clear?"

Jackson grimaced. "Crystal."

WONDER

"*C*an I offer you seconds?" Callie hovered behind Wonder's shoulder.

"Yes, please. I'm stuffed to the brim, but this chicken piccata is so delicious I can't help myself." Wonder was so glad she'd chosen to wear stretchy pants and a loose blouse. With the amount of food she'd stuffed into her belly anything else would have started to feel tight by now.

Other than the other dinners she'd had at Callie's, Wonder had never eaten such tasty stuff. The meals she used to prepare for herself had been simple, and since she'd arrived in the village she mostly ate sandwiches at the café.

"I hear that you're training with Kri. So you don't need to worry about gaining weight. Eat and enjoy."

Careful not to splatter anything on Wonder's silk blouse, Callie put a piece of chicken on her plate and then spooned more of the creamy spaghetti.

Wonder cut a piece of the chicken. "You should open a restaurant."

"I've been thinking about it." Callie put another piece on

Anandur's plate without asking if he wanted more. Apparently it was a given.

"You have?" Brundar asked. "You never said anything about it."

Callie put another serving on Brundar's plate and returned to her seat. "I'm not sure what I want to do. I always wanted to be a teacher, and I like studying the subject, but to actually teach I would have to work in the city because we don't have any school-age kids here. So I was thinking that maybe I should turn my hobby into a business." She winked at Wonder. "Give the café a little competition."

Wonder put her fork down. "On the contrary. The café closes at six, but if we close it a little earlier, you can have the place all to yourself for dinners."

Brundar shook his head. "I don't like the idea at all. If you work evenings in the village, I won't get to see much of you."

Callie frowned. "Oh, so it's okay for me to follow you to the club but not the other way around? You can quit Franco's and come help me with my restaurant."

"You don't have a restaurant."

Wonder felt terrible. If only she'd kept her mouth shut, they wouldn't be arguing now. She glanced at Anandur and mouthed, "What have I done?"

He waved a hand. "Don't worry about it."

"I'll make you a deal," Brundar said. "If you still want to open a restaurant after you get your degree, I'll help you make it happen."

"You will?" Callie's tone softened.

"Of course. Don't you know I'll do anything to make you happy?"

The romantic exchange made Wonder's eyes mist, and she quickly looked away only to see Anandur grinning from ear to ear.

He had such a beautiful smile.

He'd baffled her completely tonight, acting the exact opposite of what she'd expected. Instead of his attitude toward her cooling, he was back to the playful flirting she'd fallen for in the facility.

Heck, it was much more than that.

Anandur was touching her every chance he got. He'd had his arm around her shoulder on their walk over here, then on her knee during dinner, and she'd lost count of how many times he kissed her cheek or lifted her hand to his lips for a kiss.

He was acting like a devoted boyfriend, and she was loving every moment of it. It was like he'd been struck by lightning and his entire predisposition had been rewired.

Go figure that what finally drove him to take her seriously was her moaning another man's name into his mouth. Was it because suddenly there was another challenger for her affections? Did Anandur fear she would become unavailable to him and felt like he had to win her back?

Men's way of thinking was just too strange. It seemed as if nothing followed a straight, logical line. Or perhaps she couldn't figure out the convoluted logic because she was missing some critical component that only other males knew about.

Pushing up to her feet, Callie walked over to Brundar, sat in his lap, and wrapped her arms around his neck. "I love you." She dipped her head and kissed him.

Anandur leaned in and whispered in Wonder's ear. "I think this is our cue to make a quick exit."

Wonder glanced at her second piece of half-eaten chicken piccata. It was such a shame to leave it on the plate.

Anandur must've caught her longing expression. "You can finish your chicken first."

By the time Wonder had finished chewing the last piece of

her chicken, the kiss was over and Callie was resting her cheek on Brundar's chest. "I have the best guy ever."

Anandur got up and started collecting dishes. "Yes, you do."

"Leave it." Callie waved a hand. "Brundar and I can finish cleaning up later."

"Later, you can get busy doing other things. If you want us to come for dinner, you have to leave the cleanup to Wonder and me."

Getting the hint, Wonder rose to her feet and collected the rest.

"Fine. I'm not going to argue with you," Callie said. "The last time I did that, you moved out the next day."

"It wasn't the next day, and it wasn't because of the argument." Anandur put his load in the sink and went back to the dining room to wipe the table clean. "A mated couple needs privacy, and I didn't want to be the third wheel."

Listening to their back and forth from the kitchen, Wonder rinsed out the plates and loaded the dishwasher.

"Yeah, that's what you keep telling me, but I know it was because I insisted on you eating your veggies."

"It wasn't the veggies. It was watching the two of you making kissy faces at each other all day long."

"We weren't home all day to make kissy faces."

And so it went on.

At some point Wonder stopped listening. It was just a little friendly banter. She hadn't detected one disgruntled note in either of their voices.

Anandur got along splendidly with everyone because he was a real sweetheart. If he were hers, she was sure that all of her days would be filled with sunshine and happiness.

Wasn't he worth forgetting any past love she might have felt for the mysterious Esag?

Naturally, she was well aware that endless days of happiness were not realistic, but with Anandur it would be as close as she could get to that fantasy.

"Are you done, Wonder?" Anandur asked.

She looked down at the sink where there were no more dishes. "I guess I am."

"Then let's go." He leaned and kissed her cheek. "The love-birds can't wait for us to leave. Besides, I see some kissing in our very near future as well."

60

ANANDUR

"*P*lease stay for coffee," Callie said. "And I also made dessert."

Anandur was about to bow out gracefully when Wonder beat him to it.

"I'm sorry, but I can't manage another bite. Can you save it for tomorrow?"

That perked Callie up. "I can do that. But it means that you have to promise to come back tomorrow for dinner, and this time leave room for dessert."

"Maybe this time we can come for coffee and dessert only?"

Callie waved a hand. "No way. From now on you're going to be my tasters. If I want to open a restaurant one day, I need to add more items to my repertoire, which means that I need honest opinions about the dishes I make."

"You've got yourself a deal," Anandur said, to put an end to the conversation. "Thank you for having us and goodnight."

When Callie opened her mouth again, Brundar put a hand on her arm and opened the door. "You're welcome."

Grabbing Wonder's elbow, Anandur led her out.

"That was so rude, Brundar," they heard Callie complain as they descended the stairs down to the walkway.

"Your sister-in-law is really nice. I like her."

"They are not married, but yeah. Callie is awesome. Brundar is a new man with her."

"What do you mean?"

"It's a long story. He has some issues that she helps him deal with."

"They are so in love. It's touching to watch."

Wrapping his arm around her waist, Anandur pulled her closer to him. "It's better to do than to watch."

"I bet." Wonder chuckled nervously. "You promised to tell me what you were thinking over the past two days."

"Yes, I did."

He kept leading her toward a secluded corner. There were a few of them along the fence separating the village from the new development. If they were about to do some kissing, he didn't want to get interrupted.

"Well? I'm waiting."

"I think you can guess it by now. I decided not to focus on your age, which none of us can be sure of anyway. Instead, I decided to follow my own advice and listen to my gut."

"And what is your gut telling you?"

"That you're mine."

Wonder's breath caught. She stopped and turned toward him. "That's one hell of a leap from your attitude of only two days ago."

He put his arms around her. "Is it? What is your gut telling you, Wonder?"

She swallowed. "That I want you. Does that mean that you're mine?"

"Do you want me to be yours?"

"I do. But that's not the same as calling you mine, is it?"

He was a little disappointed, but then Wonder was young

and inexperienced and didn't know how to interpret her own emotions. He needed to give her more time.

"Does it scare you when I say you're mine?"

She shook her head. "No, but it worries me. What if I'm not?"

"I have a strong feeling that you are." It was more than a feeling, it was a conviction, but he didn't want to overwhelm her. "What we need is to spend more time together to find out if what we feel is the real deal. That's why I asked Kian for time off so I can take you out of here and show you some good times. How does spending an entire day in the city with me sound?"

"It sounds lovely, but I have to work."

"No, you don't. I asked Carol to give you time off too."

Wonder frowned. "You shouldn't have done that. Not without asking me first."

She was right, but he'd prepared the perfect excuse. "Doctor's orders. Didn't Vanessa tell you that you need more experiences?"

"How do you know about that?"

"Carol told me."

Wonder's frown deepened. "Before or after you asked her to give me time off?"

Damn. The girl was too smart.

"After. But that doesn't change Vanessa's instructions. If you want to get your memories back, you need to expose yourself to more experiences."

She shook her head. "That doesn't change the fact that you should've asked me first. I'll let it slide this time, but please don't do things like that in the future."

"I promise. Am I forgiven?"

This wasn't a good time to tell her that he'd also mentioned to Carol his plan to take Wonder to Egypt. Luckily, he'd been smart enough to ask her to keep quiet about it until he told Wonder.

"Yes." She lowered her head and looked at her feet. "Did she tell you the rest of Vanessa's instructions?"

"Yup." He smacked his lips. "And I'm here to deliver."

She lifted her eyes to his. "Only because Vanessa said I should get more kisses from you?"

He lowered his hands to her butt and pressed her against his hardness. "What do you think?"

"I think you're excited," she whispered.

That was putting it mildly, but he didn't want to scare her off by saying something crass. Instead, he brought his hand to the back of her head and wrapped it around her nape. "Are you excited too?"

It was evident that she was, and not only because of the intoxicating aroma of her arousal. Wonder wasn't wearing a bra, and he would've been blind not to notice the way her nipples had hardened. He could see their exact outline through the thin fabric of her blouse.

"Yes," she breathed.

"Come here." He brought her lips to his.

She tensed in his arms.

If this was about the hard rod he was sporting in his pants, she had one hell of a delayed response. It must've been something else.

Anandur leaned back and looked into those mesmerizing jade eyes of hers. They were glowing, casting a green light on his white shirt. "What's the matter, sweetheart?"

She shook her head. "Just kiss me."

"A moment ago you were all excited and soft in my arms, and now you're stiff as a broom. Tell me what's wrong."

A haunted look extinguishing the glow in her eyes, she hesitated for a moment. "What if I say his name again?"

Aha, that was an understandable reason for worry.

"Then you do, and we keep going. The whole idea is for you to regain your memories. I'd rather find out who that Esag dude is, so I can prove to you that I'm a better choice, than compete with a ghost. Do you get what I mean?"

She nodded. "Are you sure that your feelings won't get hurt?"

He chuckled. "If you haven't noticed, I'm a big boy. I can take one hell of a beating and keep going until I win. That's who I am. That's what I do."

61

WONDER

*W*hy was the reminder that Anandur was a formidable Guardian so hot?

Wonder felt herself go soft all over, and that included her feminine center that suddenly felt awfully empty and needy.

Was it an instinctive female reaction to a powerful male?

But it shouldn't have affected her like that. Gods knew she didn't need a male to defend her and was perfectly capable of taking care of herself.

But the thing was, on some level she liked the feeling of being taken care of, especially by Anandur who was not only the perfect male for the job, but who was also acting as if it was his favorite thing to do.

So yeah, he'd overstepped the boundaries by asking Carol to give her a vacation, but that wasn't really a big deal. Especially since he'd promised not to do it again. Anandur wasn't a controlling bully.

Anandur was a giver and not a taker.

With a sigh, she wrapped her arms around his neck and leaned into his strong body. Pressing her aching nipples to his chest, she no longer cared that the thin fabrics of the blouse and camisole weren't enough to conceal the protruding peaks.

If he wasn't embarrassed about his hard shaft, why should she care about her stiff nipples?

On the contrary, she should let him see and feel that he excited her as much as she excited him.

"Ready for your kiss, love?"

Instead of answering, she stretched up on her toes, lifted her chin, and kissed him.

Anandur's fangs punched out as soon as her tongue darted into his mouth. Gently, she swirled her tongue around one fang and then around the other, eliciting strangled groans from his throat.

His fingers digging into her butt cheeks, he held her in place as his hips gyrated, rubbing his hardness against her soft mound.

Wonder was so turned on that if at that moment Anandur were to lower her to the ground and pull her clothes off, she would have let him do whatever he pleased with her.

Heck, she would've spurred him on.

They were all alone in the dark, with the nearest house over a hundred feet away, and they wanted each other, so why not?

"Touch me," she whispered. "I'm aching all over."

Never before had she felt so needy, so hungry for his touch. It was as if with every caress the craving intensified.

"Oh, lass," he groaned and lifted her up as if she were a dainty little thing and not a hefty female.

"Where are you taking me?"

"Just over to that bench. Don't worry, I'm not taking you to my place to do all kinds of wicked things to you."

How disappointing. She was all for him taking her home and doing those wicked things to her. "Why not?"

"Because you're a virgin and this is only your second kiss. You shouldn't run before you learn to walk."

Gods, he was going to tease her to destruction.

As he sat on the bench with her in his lap, his eyes glowing and his fangs elongated, Anandur should have looked scary to her, but he didn't.

Instead, she only desired him more.

This was what a male of her species looked like when aroused. She knew now that his fangs were meant for delivering pleasure, not harm. Well, to a female. Other males were a different story.

"Are you going to bite me?"

Anandur looked up to the sky as if praying for strength. "You have no idea how much I want to do that. But if I do, I'm going to come in my pants, and it will get very messy."

"Then do it. Who cares about a little mess?" She was craving his bite just as much as he was craving sinking his fangs into her neck.

Looking at her neck longingly, he started to shake his head, but Wonder was done waiting around for what she needed.

She'd promised herself to follow Anandur's cues and not push him, but it was obvious that this was what he wanted too. The tether holding him back was nearly unraveled, and he was hanging by the last thread. One little tug and he would succumb.

Pulling her hair to one side, she turned her head to elongate her neck in an unmistakable gesture of offering.

Her only warning was a loud hiss. Wonder closed her eyes, more in anticipation of pleasure than fear of pain.

As his fangs pierced her skin, his large hand closed around one breast, diverting her focus from the burning pain of the twin incision points to the incredible pleasure of being touched intimately for the first time.

Seconds later the pain dissipated, and all she felt was unimaginable bliss. That too didn't last for more than a few short moments.

As a wave of intense lust washed over her, bringing about a powerful climax that shook her body from top to bottom, the sound that left her throat wasn't human, and the name she called out wasn't Esag's, it was Anandur's.

To be continued...

Dear reader,

Thank you for reading the ***Children of the Gods series.***

If you enjoyed the story, I would be grateful if you could leave a **short review** for *Dark Survivor Echoes of* Love on Amazon. (With a few words, you'll make me very happy. :-))

COMING UP NEXT
DARK SURVIVOR REUNITED

FOR EXCLUSIVE PEEKS AT UPCOMING RELEASES

Join my *VIP Club* and gain access to the VIP portal at

ITLUCAS.COM

CLICK HERE TO JOIN

(or go to: http://eepurl.com/blMTpD)

If you're already a subscriber and forgot the password to the VIP portal, you can find it at the bottom of each of my emails. Or click HERE to retrieve it.

You can also email me at isabell@itlucas.com

EXCERPT: DARK SURVIVOR
REUNITED

"What are you doing?' Anandur asked as Wonder pulled out her phone and aimed the camera at the appetizers the waitress had just delivered to their table.

"It's for Callie." Taking a quick glance, she checked that no one was looking, then snapped several pictures in quick succession.

The restaurant was a bit fancy but not too much so. The tables were covered with white tablecloths, but there were no candles, and most of the diners were dressed casually. Even if someone caught her in the act, she doubted anyone would mind.

Like little pieces of art, the appetizers were a feast for the senses, and not just the sense of taste or smell. She loved their colors, and the way they were arranged on the platter, with the sauce poured in a meandering pattern around them and several mint leaves scattered around like little trees on a riverbank.

"They look delicious." She opened up the menu and took a picture of the ingredients. "Callie should add them to her recipe collection."

"I don't think it's okay." Anandur regarded her with amusement dancing in his eyes. "What if recipes are copyrighted? Besides, Callie still has two years of studying to do before she makes up her mind whether she wants to be a teacher or a chef. Until then, she might change her mind about the restaurant business and come up with another idea, or just teach. It would be a waste to spend four years studying a subject and then not use what she learned."

Wonder saw nothing wrong with that. Learning new skills and gaining new knowledge was rewarding in itself, and having several options was always better than having none or just one. "I have a feeling she's not going to wait until she's done, and I also think that learning new things should be a goal in itself. It's not just about getting ready for a job."

Wonder put the phone away and lifted her utensils. "I don't think she is going to change her mind. Callie is excited about it. And as for copying recipes, no one is going to find out what she serves in the village. She can also change them around and make them her own."

Hands hovering over the platter, she hesitated. "It's almost a shame to destroy the display." With a sigh, she scooped a piece onto her plate, cut it in two, and lifted one of the halves into her mouth.

As the flavors hit her taste buds, she groaned with pleasure.

Eyes glued to her lips, Anandur cleared his throat. "How is it?"

Swallowing, Wonder rolled her eyes. "Amazing. It tastes even better than it looks."

"That's one of Kian's favorites. The dude is vegan, so there is no meat in it, which means I would've never ordered it for myself. But once I gave it a try, I was sold." He forked a whole piece and winked. "You can tell Callie I'm eating my veggies."

Anandur was so easy to be with.

After last night, Wonder had expected things to be a little

awkward between them, but he was acting as if nothing had happened, or as if it wasn't a big deal.

Maybe for him it wasn't, but it sure was for her.

In one evening, Anandur had officially become her boyfriend and had given her first venom bite as well as her first explosive climax.

Remembering her powerful reaction, a shiver of desire rocked Wonder's body. A girl could get addicted to that, and according to Anandur it was bound to happen if they kept at it.

Though he wasn't sure if the process would start with the bite alone.

Not that Wonder planned on waiting much longer for the rest.

As usual, Anandur had his weird opinions about when and how that should happen. Perhaps he was right about that, but she wasn't going to take his word for it. When they returned to the village, she was going to talk to Carol, who'd made several offers to expand Wonder's education on the subject.

But at least he was showing her a lot of affection, touching and kissing her at every opportunity. Except, to do that without getting all fired up, the man must've been made from solid rock and determination. Every kiss, even to the back of her hand, sent electrical currents throughout her body, flipping the switch on her arousal.

Was Anandur just as affected and only better at hiding his responses?

Wonder had tried to sniff for it, but she was either a lousy sniffer, or the constant touching was not making him as hot and bothered as it was her.

It probably had something to do with experience. She suspected that after nearly a millennium of existence, and gods only knew how many partners, Anandur wasn't as easily excitable. Carol had said something about men getting bored with the mundane and seeking new thrills with the exotic and unusual, naturally regarding herself as the latter.

Last night, though, Wonder hadn't been the only one erupting in an explosive climax. Even though it must've been embarrassing for a male his age, Anandur had been such a gentleman for choosing to ejaculate in his pants and not take advantage of her euphoric state. He could've easily taken her right then and there on the bench, and Wonder would not have minded if he had.

No, actually that wasn't true.

She would've regretted it later. Not because she didn't want Anandur, and not even because she wanted to wait, but because she wanted their first time together to be magical and not a quick romp on a public bench.

Anandur waved a hand in front of her eyes. "If you keep on daydreaming, I'm going to finish both appetizers."

She glanced at the platters, expecting to see only a few pieces left, but she should've known better. Like the true gentleman he was, Anandur had left more than half of each for her.

"You can eat the rest. I want to save room for the main course."

He arched a brow. "Are you sure?"

"Yes."

Eying the platters, he still hesitated. "We can order another serving."

"No need. Please, eat the rest." Wonder put her hand over his.

Eyes flashing with inner light, Anandur sucked in a breath.

That was interesting. How come the small touch elicited such a strong reaction from him? Was it because she had touched him and not the other way around?

Wonder frowned.

When Anandur touched her, she got all excited while he

seemed in control. But when she touched him, the effect was reversed.

Evidently, getting touched was more stimulating than touching.

Gods, she was such a novice. This was yet another question for Carol.

"Are you done with the appetizers?" The waitress reached for one of the platters.

"No, not yet," Wonder said.

The woman smiled. "No problem, take your time."

Glancing down, Wonder realized she was still holding on to Anandur's hand and that he needed it to eat. Except, as soon as she tried to pull hers away, he caught it and brought it up to his mouth for a kiss.

Her reaction was instantaneous. His hot breath fanning over her skin followed by the soft brush of his lips sent a bolt of lightning straight to her center.

Wow, she'd actually guessed it right. Being touched was hotter than touching.

Was it like that with all couples? Or was it just them?

Yet another question she needed to ask Carol. At this rate, by the end of their all day long date in the city, she would have an entire list of them.

"I want to ask you something," Anandur said.

"Yes?"

"I know it's a little early for this, but I'm impatient." He rubbed a hand over the back of his neck.

Wonder's breath caught in her throat. In the movies, the guy usually said something like that to the girl before asking her to marry him.

Was Anandur about to propose?

He couldn't be. This outing was their first official date.

He squeezed her hand. "I want to take you to Egypt."

"What? Why?"

"Maybe it will help bring your memories back. Vanessa said that you need to have more experiences. I thought that going back to where it all began might be beneficial."

What the heck? He wanted her to remember Esag?

Up until that moment, Wonder hadn't internalized how terrified she was of regaining her memories. Without making a conscious decision to do so, she wanted to forget the past and concentrate on a future with Anandur.

She didn't want to remember loving someone else who might have abandoned her to die, or who'd left her. And if Esag had died and his death had been the cause of her trauma, she certainly didn't want to remember that and go through the grief of losing a man she loved twice.

It was a cowardly approach, but she had started building a new life with the clan, and it was a good one. She didn't want to lose it.

She didn't want to lose Anandur.

Wonder shook her head. "I don't understand. Why would you want me to get my memories back? What if I remember loving Esag? Don't you want to give us a chance?"

"Oh, lass, that's exactly why I want you to remember. I want to find him and prove to you that I'm the better man. Otherwise, his shadow will always hover between us."

He leaned forward. "I don't want you to live with what ifs and what could've beens. Hell, I don't want to live with that. I want you to choose me, knowing that I'm the one for you and never second-guess it."

Wonder swallowed. "Maybe I'm a coward, but I'm afraid of what the past holds. Perhaps losing my memory was a good thing. It allowed me to start a new life."

"You'll not be doing it alone. I will be with you every step of the way. And just so we're clear, I'm not giving up on you no matter what. Your past isn't going to scare me away. I'm going to fight for you."

Despite his earnest promises, Wonder wasn't sure Anandur would stay by her side if she remembered still loving someone else. No one was that selfless.

On the other hand, there was a good chance that the trip would not bring her memories back. She could have a great time with Anandur and try her best not to remember anything.

Yeah, that seemed like a good plan. It could be like a honeymoon, only before the wedding.

Way to get carried away, Wonder Girl.

Still, the trip could be an excellent opportunity for Anandur and her to get closer. He wouldn't get them separate hotel rooms, right?

Suddenly, Wonder was very excited about going to Egypt.

Except, there was the issue of her job at the café that she didn't want to lose. Also, she didn't have a passport or know how to go about getting one, and plane tickets were probably costly. She had some money saved up, but would it be enough?

"So what do you say, lass, are you in for an adventure?"

"I can't take a vacation. I just started working. It's not fair to Carol."

"Carol managed just fine without you before. She can manage for two more weeks."

"Two weeks is a lot. And I don't have a passport."

"Not a problem. I can have one made for you by tomorrow."

Wonder pulled her hand out of Anandur's and crossed her arms over her chest. "On one condition. I pay for my own plane ticket."

Anandur shook his head. "Not going to happen, so don't even think about arguing. This trip is my idea, and I'm paying for it."

"I have money saved up, and I no longer need it for renting an apartment. I can pay for my own ticket." Crossing her fingers under the table, she wished for what she had to be enough to cover the cost of the ticket. After all her bluster, it would be so embarrassing to ask Anandur to pay for it.

"I'll make you a deal."

The smirk on his face promised that she wasn't going to like the deal he was about to offer.

Wonder narrowed her eyes at him. "What is it?"

"After we are done with lunch, I'll take you shopping, and you can use that money you've saved up to buy yourself some nice things for the trip. I wanted to pamper you and pay for it, but I'm willing to compromise."

No wonder he looked so smug. His version of a compromise wasn't a compromise at all. "That's…"

He put a finger on her lips. "That's the best deal you're going to get. So I suggest you take it."

THE CHILDREN OF THE GODS SERIES

THE CHILDREN OF THE GODS ORIGINS

1: GODDESS'S CHOICE

When gods and immortals still ruled the ancient world, one young goddess risked everything for love.

2: GODDESS'S HOPE

Hungry for power and infatuated with the beautiful Areana, Navuh plots his father's demise. After all, by getting rid of the insane god he would be doing the world a favor. Except, when gods and immortals conspire against each other, humanity pays the price.

But things are not what they seem, and prophecies should not to be trusted...

THE CHILDREN OF THE GODS

1: DARK STRANGER THE DREAM

Syssi's paranormal foresight lands her a job at Dr. Amanda Dokani's neuroscience lab, but it fails to predict the thrilling yet terrifying turn her life will take. Syssi has no clue that her boss is an immortal who'll drag her into a secret, millennia-old battle over humanity's future. Nor does she realize that the professor's imposing brother is the mysterious stranger who's been starring in her dreams.

Since the dawn of human civilization, two warring factions of immortals—the descendants of the gods of old—have been secretly shaping its destiny. Leading the clandestine battle from his luxurious Los Angeles high-rise, Kian is surrounded by his clan, yet alone. Descending from a single goddess, clan members are forbidden to each other. And as the only other immortals are their hated enemies, Kian and his kin have been long resigned to a lonely existence of fleeting trysts with human partners. That is, until his sister makes a game-changing discovery—a mortal seeress who she believes is a dormant carrier of their genes. Ever the realist, Kian is skeptical and refuses Amanda's plea to attempt Syssi's activation. But when his enemies learn of the Dormant's existence, he's forced to rush her to the safety of his keep. Inexorably drawn to Syssi, Kian wrestles with his conscience as he is tempted to explore her budding interest in the darker shades of sensuality.

2: Dark Stranger Revealed

While sheltered in the clan's stronghold, Syssi is unaware that Kian and Amanda are not human, and neither are the supposedly religious fanatics that are after her. She feels a powerful connection to Kian, and as he introduces her to a world of pleasure she never dared imagine, his dominant sexuality is a revelation. Considering that she's completely out of her element, Syssi feels comfortable and safe letting go with him. That is, until she begins to suspect that all is not as it seems. Piecing the puzzle together, she draws a scary, yet wrong conclusion...

3: Dark Stranger Immortal

When Kian confesses his true nature, Syssi is not as much shocked by the revelation as she is wounded by what she perceives as his callous plans for her.

If she doesn't turn, he'll be forced to erase her memories and let her go. His family's safety demands secrecy – no one in the mortal world is allowed to know that immortals exist.

Resigned to the cruel reality that even if she stays on to never again leave the keep, she'll get old while Kian won't, Syssi is determined to enjoy what little time she has with him, one day at a time.

Can Kian let go of the mortal woman he loves? Will Syssi turn? And if she does, will she survive the dangerous transition?

4: Dark Enemy Taken

Dalhu can't believe his luck when he stumbles upon the beautiful immortal professor. Presented with a once in a lifetime opportunity to grab an immortal female for himself, he kidnaps her and runs. If he ever gets caught, either by her people or his, his life is forfeit. But for a chance of a loving mate and a family of his own, Dalhu is prepared to do everything in his power to win Amanda's heart, and that includes leaving the Doom brotherhood and his old life behind.

Amanda soon discovers that there is more to the handsome Doomer than his dark past and a hulking, sexy body. But succumbing to her enemy's seduction, or worse, developing feelings for a ruthless killer is out of the question. No man is worth life on the run, not even the one and only immortal male she could claim as her own...

Her clan and her research must come first...

5: Dark Enemy Captive

When the rescue team returns with Amanda and the chained Dalhu to the keep, Amanda is not as thrilled to be back as she thought she'd be. Between Kian's contempt for her and Dalhu's imprisonment, Amanda's budding relationship with Dalhu seems doomed. Things start to look up when Annani offers her help, and together with Syssi they resolve to find a way for Amanda to be with Dalhu. But will she still want him when she realizes that he is responsible for her nephew's murder? Could she? Will she take the easy way out and choose Andrew instead?

6: Dark Enemy Redeemed

Amanda suspects that something fishy is going on onboard the Anna. But when her investigation of the peculiar all-female Russian crew fails to uncover anything other than more speculation, she decides it's time to stop playing detective and face her real problem—a man she shouldn't want but can't live without.

6.5: My Dark Amazon

When Michael and Kri fight off a gang of humans, Michael gets stabbed. The injury to his immortal body recovers fast, but the one to his ego takes longer, putting a strain on his relationship with Kri.

7: Dark Warrior Mine

When Andrew is forced to retire from active duty, he believes that all he has to look forward to is a boring desk job. His glory days in special ops are over. But as it turns out, his thrill ride has just begun. Andrew discovers not only that immortals exist and have been manipulating global affairs since antiquity, but that he and his sister are rare possessors of the immortal genes.

Problem is, Andrew might be too old to attempt the activation process. His sister, who is fourteen years his junior, barely made it through the transition, so the odds of him coming out of it alive, let alone immortal, are slim.

But fate may force his hand.

Helping a friend find his long-lost daughter, Andrew finds a woman who's worth taking the risk for. Nathalie might be a Dormant, but the only way to find out for sure requires fangs and venom.

8: Dark Warrior's Promise

Andrew and Nathalie's love flourishes, but the secrets they keep from each other taint their relationship with doubts and suspicions. In the meantime, Sebastian and his men are getting bolder, and the storm that's brewing will shift the balance of power in the millennia-old conflict between Annani's clan and its enemies.

9: Dark Warrior's Destiny

The new ghost in Nathalie's head remembers who he was in life, providing Andrew and her with indisputable proof that he is real and not a figment of her imagination.

Convinced that she is a Dormant, Andrew decides to go forward with his transition immediately after the rescue mission at the Doomers' HQ.

Fearing for his life, Nathalie pleads with him to reconsider. She'd rather spend the rest of her mortal days with Andrew than risk what they have for the fickle promise of immortality.

While the clan gets ready for battle, Carol gets help from an unlikely ally. Sebastian's second-in-command can no longer ignore the torment she suffers at the hands of his commander and offers to help her, but only if she agrees to his terms.

10: Dark Warrior's Legacy

Andrew's acclimation to his post-transition body isn't easy. His senses are sharper, he's bigger, stronger, and hungrier. Nathalie fears that the changes in the man she loves are more than physical. Measuring up to this new version of him is going to be a challenge.

Carol and Robert are disillusioned with each other. They are not destined mates, and love is not on the horizon. When Robert's three months are up, he might be left with nothing to show for his sacrifice.

Lana contacts Anandur with disturbing news; the yacht and its human cargo are in Mexico. Kian must find a way to apprehend Alex and rescue the women on board without causing an international incident.

11: Dark Guardian Found

What would you do if you stopped aging?

Eva runs. The ex-DEA agent doesn't know what caused her strange mutation, only that if discovered, she'll be dissected like a lab rat. What Eva doesn't know, though, is that she's a descendant of the gods, and that she is not alone. The man who rocked her world in one life-changing encounter over thirty years ago is an immortal as well.

To keep his people's existence secret, Bhathian was forced to turn his back on the only woman who ever captured his heart, but he's never forgotten and never stopped looking for her.

12: Dark Guardian Craved

Cautious after a lifetime of disappointments, Eva is mistrustful of Bhathian's professed feelings of love. She accepts him as a lover and a confidant but not as a life partner.

Jackson suspects that Tessa is his true love mate, but unless she overcomes her fears, he might never find out.

Carol gets an offer she can't refuse—a chance to prove that there is more to her than meets the eye. Robert believes she's about to commit a deadly mistake, but when he tries to dissuade her, she tells him to leave.

13: Dark Guardian's Mate

Prepare for the heart-warming culmination of Eva and Bhathian's story!

14: Dark Angel's Obsession

The cold and stoic warrior is an enigma even to those closest to him. His secrets are about to unravel...

15: Dark Angel's Seduction

Brundar is fighting a losing battle. Calypso is slowly chipping away his icy armor from the outside, while his need for her is melting it from the inside.

He can't allow it to happen. Calypso is a human with none of the Dormant indicators. There is no way he can keep her for more than a few weeks.

16: Dark Angel's Surrender

Get ready for the heart pounding conclusion to Brundar and Calypso's story.

Callie still couldn't wrap her head around it, nor could she summon even a smidgen of sorrow or regret. After all, she had some memories with him that weren't horrible. She should've felt something. But there was nothing, not even shock. Not even horror at what had transpired over the last couple of hours.

Maybe it was a typical response for survivors--feeling euphoric for the simple reason that they were alive. Especially when that survival was nothing short of miraculous.

Brundar's cold hand closed around hers, reminding her that they weren't out of the woods yet. Her injuries were superficial, and the most she had to worry about was some scarring. But, despite his and Anandur's reassurances, Brundar might never walk again.

If he ended up crippled because of her, she would never forgive herself for getting him involved in her crap.

"Are you okay, sweetling? Are you in pain?" Brundar asked.

Her injuries were nothing compared to his, and yet he was concerned about her. God, she loved this man. The thing was, if she told him that, he would run off, or crawl away as was the case.

Hey, maybe this was the perfect opportunity to spring it on him.

17: Dark Operative: A Shadow of Death

As a brilliant strategist and the only human entrusted with the secret of immortals' existence, Turner is both an asset and a liability to the clan. His request to attempt transition into immortality as an alternative to cancer treatments cannot be denied without risking the clan's exposure. On the other hand, approving it means risking his premature death. In both scenarios, the clan will lose a valuable ally.

When the decision is left to the clan's physician, Turner makes plans to manipulate her by taking advantage of her interest in him.

Will Bridget fall for the cold, calculated operative? Or will Turner fall into his own trap?

18: Dark Operative: A Glimmer of Hope

As Turner and Bridget's relationship deepens, living together seems like the right move, but to make it work both need to make concessions.

Bridget is realistic and keeps her expectations low. Turner could never be the truelove mate she yearns for, but he is as good as she's going to get. Other than his emotional limitations, he's perfect in every way.

Turner's hard shell is starting to show cracks. He wants immortality, he wants to be part of the clan, and he wants Bridget, but he doesn't want to cause her pain.

His options are either abandon his quest for immortality and give Bridget his few remaining decades, or abandon Bridget by going for the transition and most likely dying. His rational mind dictates that he chooses the former, but his gut pulls him toward the latter. Which one is he going to trust?

19: Dark Operative: The Dawn of Love

Get ready for the exciting finale of Bridget and Turner's story!

20: Dark Survivor Awakened

This was a strange new world she had awakened to.

Her memory loss must have been catastrophic because almost nothing was familiar. The language was foreign to her, with only a few words bearing some similarity to the language she thought in. Still, a full moon cycle had passed since her awakening, and little by little she was gaining basic understanding of it--only a few words and phrases, but she was learning more each day.

A week or so ago, a little girl on the street had tugged on her mother's sleeve and pointed at her. "Look, Mama, Wonder Woman!"

The mother smiled apologetically, saying something in the language these people spoke, then scurried away with the child looking behind her shoulder and grinning.

When it happened again with another child on the same day, it was settled.

Wonder Woman must have been the name of someone important in this strange world she had awoken to, and since both times it had been said with a smile it must have been a good one.

Wonder had a nice ring to it.

She just wished she knew what it meant.

21: Dark Survivor Echoes of Love

Wonder's journey continues in *Dark Survivor Echoes of Love.*

22: Dark Survivor Reunited

The exciting finale of Wonder and Anandur's story.

23: Dark Widow's Secret

Vivian and her daughter share a powerful telepathic connection, so when Ella can't be reached by conventional or psychic means, her mother fears the worst.

Help arrives from an unexpected source when Vivian gets a call from the young doctor she met at a psychic convention. Turns out Julian belongs to a private organization specializing in retrieving missing girls.

As Julian's clan mobilizes its considerable resources to rescue the daughter, Magnus is charged with keeping the gorgeous young mother safe.

Worry for Ella and the secrets Vivian and Magnus keep from each other should be enough to prevent the sparks of attraction from kindling a blaze of desire. Except, these pesky sparks have a mind of their own.

24: Dark Widow's Curse

A simple rescue operation turns into mission impossible when the Russian mafia gets involved. Bad things are supposed to come in threes, but in Vivian's case, it seems like there is no limit to bad luck. Her family and everyone who gets close to her is affected by her curse.

Will Magnus and his people prove her wrong?

25: Dark Widow's Blessing

The thrilling finale of the Dark Widow trilogy!

26: Dark Dream's Temptation

Julian has known Ella is the one for him from the moment he saw her picture, but when he finally frees her from captivity, she seems indifferent to him. Could he have been mistaken?

Ella's rescue should've ended that chapter in her life, but it seems like the road back to normalcy has just begun and it's full of obstacles. Between the pitying looks she gets and her mother's attempts to get her into therapy, Ella feels like she's typecast as a victim, when nothing could be further from the truth. She's a tough survivor, and she's going to prove it.

Strangely, the only one who seems to understand is Logan, who keeps popping up in her dreams. But then, he's a figment of her imagination —or is he?

27: Dark Dream's Unraveling

While trying to figure out a way around Logan's silencing compulsion, Ella concocts an ambitious plan. What if instead of trying to keep him out of her dreams, she could pretend to like him and lure him into a trap?

Catching Navuh's son would be a major boon for the clan, as well as for Ella. She will have her revenge, turning the tables on another scumbag out to get her.

28: Dark Dream's Trap

The trap is set, but who is the hunter and who is the prey? Find out in this heart-pounding conclusion to the *Dark Dream* trilogy.

29: Dark Prince's Enigma

As the son of the most dangerous male on the planet, Lokan lives by three rules:

Don't trust a soul.

Don't show emotions.

And don't get attached.

Will one extraordinary woman make him break all three?

30: Dark Prince's Dilemma

Will Kian decide that the benefits of trusting Lokan outweigh the risks?

Will Lokan betray his father and brothers for the greater good of his people?

Are Carol and Lokan true-love mates, or is one of them playing the other?

So many questions, the path ahead is anything but clear.

31: Dark Prince's Agenda

While Turner and Kian work out the details of Areana's rescue plan, Carol and Lokan's tumultuous relationship hits another snag. Is it a sign of things to come?

32 : Dark Queen's Quest

A former beauty queen, a retired undercover agent, and a successful model, Mey is not the typical damsel in distress. But when her sister drops off the radar and then someone starts following her around, she panics.

Following a vague clue that Kalugal might be in New York, Kian sends a team headed by Yamanu to search for him.

As Mey and Yamanu's paths cross, he offers her his help and protection, but will that be all?

33: Dark Queen's Knight

As the only member of his clan with a godlike power over human minds, Yamanu has been shielding his people for centuries, but that power comes at a steep price. When Mey enters his life, he's faced with the most difficult choice.

The safety of his clan or a future with his fated mate.

34: Dark Queen's Army

As Mey anxiously waits for her transition to begin and for Yamanu to test whether his godlike powers are gone, the clan sets out to solve two mysteries:

Where is Jin, and is she there voluntarily?

Where is Kalugal, and what is he up to?

35: Dark Spy Conscripted

Jin possesses a unique paranormal ability. Just by touching someone, she can insert a mental hook into their psyche and tie a string of her consciousness to it, creating a tether. That doesn't make her a spy, though, not unless her talent is discovered by those seeking to exploit it.

36: Dark Spy's Mission

Jin's first spying mission is supposed to be easy. Walk into the club, touch Kalugal to tether her consciousness to him, and walk out.

Except, they should have known better.

37: Dark Spy's Resolution

The best-laid plans often go awry...

38: Dark Overlord New Horizon

Jacki has two talents that set her apart from the rest of the human race.

She has unpredictable glimpses of other people's futures, and she is immune to mind manipulation.

Unfortunately, both talents are pretty useless for finding a job other than the one she had in the government's paranormal division.

It seemed like a sweet deal, until she found out that the director planned on producing super babies by compelling the recruits into pairing up. When an opportunity to escape the program presented itself, she took it, only to find out that humans are not at the top of the food chain.

Immortals are real, and at the very top of the hierarchy is Kalugal, the most powerful, arrogant, and sexiest male she has ever met.

With one look, he sets her blood on fire, but Jacki is not a fool. A man like him will never think of her as anything more than a tasty snack, while she will never settle for anything less than his heart.

39: Dark Overlord's Wife

Jacki is still clinging to her all-or-nothing policy, but Kalugal is chipping away at her resistance. Perhaps it's time to ease up on her convictions. A little less than all is still much better than nothing, and a couple of decades with a demigod is probably worth more than a lifetime with a mere mortal.

40: Dark Overlord's Clan

As Jacki and Kalugal prepare to celebrate their union, Kian takes every precaution to safeguard his people. Except, Kalugal and his men are not his only potential adversaries, and compulsion is not the only power he should fear.

41: Dark Choices The Quandary

When Rufsur and Edna meet, the attraction is as unexpected as it is undeniable. Except, she's the clan's judge and councilwoman, and he's Kalugal's second-in-command. Will loyalty and duty to their people keep them apart?

42: Dark Choices Paradigm Shift

Edna and Rufsur are miserable without each other, and their two-week separation seems like an eternity. Long-distance relationships are difficult, but for immortal couples they are impossible. Unless one of them is willing to leave everything behind for the other, things are just going to get worse. Except, the cost of compromise is far greater than giving up their comfortable lives and hard-earned positions. The future of their people is on the line.

43: Dark Choices The Accord

The winds of change blowing over the village demand hard choices. For better or worse, Kian's decisions will alter the trajectory of the clan's future, and he is not ready to take the plunge. But as Edna and Rufsur's plight gains widespread support, his resistance slowly begins to erode.

44: Dark Secrets Resurgence

On a sabbatical from his Stanford teaching position, Professor David Levinson finally has time to write the sci-fi novel he's been thinking about for years.

The phenomena of past life memories and near-death experiences are too controversial to include in his formal psychiatric research, while fiction is the perfect outlet for his esoteric ideas.

Hoping that a change of pace will provide the inspiration he needs, David accepts a friend's invitation to an old Scottish castle.

45: Dark Secrets Unveiled

When Professor David Levinson accepts a friend's invitation to an old Scottish castle, what he finds there is more fantastical than his most outlandish theories. The castle is home to a clan of immortals, their leader is a stunning demigoddess, and even more shockingly, it might be precisely where he belongs.

Except, the clan founder is hiding a secret that might cast a dark shadow on David's relationship with her daughter.

Nevertheless, when offered a chance at immortality, he agrees to undergo the dangerous induction process.

Will David survive his transition into immortality? And if he does, will his relationship with Sari survive the unveiling of her mother's secret?

46: Dark Secrets Absolved

Absolution.

David had given and received it.

The few short hours since he'd emerged from the coma had felt incredible. He'd finally been free of the guilt and pain, and for the first time since Jonah's death, he had felt truly happy and optimistic about the future.

He'd survived the transition into immortality, had been accepted into the clan, and was about to marry the best woman on the face of the planet, his true love mate, his salvation, his everything.

What could have possibly gone wrong?

Just about everything.

47: Dark haven Illusion

Welcome to Safe Haven, where not everything is what it seems.

On a quest to process personal pain, Anastasia joins the Safe Haven Spiritual Retreat.

Through meditation, self-reflection, and hard work, she hopes to make peace with the voices in her head.

This is where she belongs.

Except, membership comes with a hefty price, doubts are sacrilege, and leaving is not as easy as walking out the front gate.

Is living in utopia worth the sacrifice?

Anastasia believes so until the arrival of a new acolyte changes everything.

Apparently, the gods of old were not a myth, their immortal descendants share the planet with humans, and she might be a carrier of their genes.

48: Dark Haven Unmasked

As Anastasia leaves Safe Haven for a week-long romantic vacation with Leon, she hopes to explore her newly discovered passionate side, their budding relationship, and perhaps also solve the mystery of the voices in her head. What she discovers exceeds her wildest expectations.

In the meantime, Eleanor and Peter hope to solve another mystery. Who is Emmett Haderech, and what is he up to?

———————————

THE PERFECT MATCH SERIES

Perfect Match 1: Vampire's Consort

When Gabriel's company is ready to start beta testing, he invites his old crush to inspect its medical safety protocol.

Curious about the revolutionary technology of the *Perfect Match Virtual Fantasy-Fulfillment studios*, Brenna agrees.

Neither expects to end up partnering for its first fully immersive test run.

Perfect Match 2: King's Chosen

When Lisa's nutty friends get her a gift certificate to *Perfect Match Virtual Fantasy Studios*, she has no intentions of using it. But since the only way to get a refund is if no partner can be found for her, she makes sure to request a fantasy so girly and over the top that no sane guy will pick it up.

Except, someone does.

Warning: This fantasy contains a hot, domineering crown prince, sweet insta-love, steamy love scenes painted with light shades of gray, a wedding, and a HEA in both the virtual and real worlds.

Intended for mature audience.

Perfect Match 3: Captain's Conquest

Working as a Starbucks barista, Alicia fends off flirting all day long, but none of the guys are as charming and sexy as Gregg. His frequent visits are the highlight of her day, but since he's never asked her out, she assumes he's taken. Besides, between a day job and a budding music career, she has no time to start a new relationship.

That is until Gregg makes her an offer she can't refuse—a gift certificate to the virtual fantasy fulfillment service everyone is talking about. As a huge Star Trek fan, Alicia has a perfect match in mind—the captain of the Starship Enterprise.

FOR EXCLUSIVE PEEKS AT UPCOMING RELEASES & A FREE COMPANION BOOK

Join my *VIP Club* and gain access to the VIP portal at
ITLUCAS.COM

CLICK HERE TO JOIN
(or go to: http://eepurl.com/blMTpD)

Included in your free membership:

- **FREE** Children of the Gods companion book **1**
- **FREE** narration of Goddess's Choice—Book **1** in The Children of the Gods Origins series.
- Preview chapters of upcoming releases.
- And other exclusive content offered only to my **VIPs**.

Also by I. T. Lucas

THE CHILDREN OF THE GODS ORIGINS

45: Dark Secrets Unveiled
46: Dark Secrets Absolved
Dark Haven
47: Dark haven Illusion
48: Dark Haven Unmasked

PERFECT MATCH

Perfect Match 1: Vampire's Consort
Perfect Match 2: King's Chosen
Perfect Match 3: Captain's Conquest

The Children of the Gods Series Sets

Books 1-3: Dark Stranger trilogy—Includes a bonus short story: **The Fates take a Vacation**
Books 4-6: Dark Enemy Trilogy —Includes a bonus short story—**The Fates' Post-Wedding Celebration**
Books 7-10: Dark Warrior Tetralogy
Books 11-13: Dark Guardian Trilogy
Books 14-16: Dark Angel Trilogy
Books 17-19: Dark Operative Trilogy
Books 20-22: Dark Survivor Trilogy
Books 23-25: Dark Widow Trilogy
Books 26-28: Dark Dream Trilogy
Books 29-31: Dark Prince Trilogy
Books 32-34: Dark Queen Trilogy
Books 35-37: Dark Spy Trilogy
Books 38-40: Dark Overlord Trilogy
Books 41-43: Dark Choices Trilogy

Printed in Great Britain
by Amazon

56661555R00190